'History is brought convincingly and absorbingly to life'
– Nicolette Jones, *Sunday Times*

'Underlying the fast-paced action of this vivid mini-epic
set during the Irish potato famine is a thoughtful
look at the challenge of emigration . . . Sandi Toksvig
leaves an impression of courage in the face of adversity'
– *Guardian*, 'The Best Children's Books of 2015'

'Sandi Toksvig's mini-epic is a roller-coaster of a
read that races headlong through an important slice of
history bringing it vividly to life as it does so . . .
Sandi Toksvig brings alive important-to-know radical
history by dressing it up in a fine coat of adventure'
– Julia Eccleshare, *Lovereading4kids.co.uk*

'Slim is an engaging character who makes friends
with all kinds of people along the journey, facing up to
danger and grief with great courage. There are important
themes running through the book, including the power of
storytelling, literacy, freedom of speech, and equality . . . It's also
a good, pacey story written with humour and understanding'
– Lynne Taylor, *booksforkeeps.co.uk*

'A thumping great historical read, thick with complexity'
– Kitty Em

www.sanditoksvig.com
@sanditoksvig

A Slice
OF THE
Moon

SANDI TOKSVIG

CORGI BOOKS

CORGI BOOKS

UK | USA | Canada | Ireland | Australia
India | New Zealand | South Africa

Corgi Books is part of the Penguin Random House group of companies
whose addresses can be found at global.penguinrandomhouse.com.

www.penguin.co.uk
www.puffin.co.uk
www.ladybird.co.uk

First published 2015
This edition published 2016

3

Typeset in Sabon by Falcon Oast Graphic Art Ltd
Printed in Great Britain by Clays Ltd, St Ives plc

A CIP catalogue record for this book is available from the British Library

ISBN: 978–0–552–56659–9

All correspondence to:
Corgi Books
Penguin Random House Children's
80 Strand, London WC2R 0RL

Penguin Random House is committed to a
sustainable future for our business, our readers
and our planet. This book is made from
Forest Stewardship Council® certified paper.

To Deej

CHAPTER ONE

It's a funny thing about the potato. It came to Ireland from the Americas in the first place, and yet it's also the very thing that made us leave home and head to the New World. You wouldn't think something so ordinary as a potato, something I used to eat every day of my life, could have had such an effect – but, well, it did. The potato once grew in the ground right by our front door, but because of it, me and my family left home and travelled six thousand miles to find a new life. This is the story of that journey – and I've quite a tale to tell, so you'd better make yourself comfortable. Some of it is unbelievable, but it's the truth, sure as my name is Slim Hannigan.

Ah, well, I should stop right there. Everyone calls

me 'Slim' but my real name is Rosalind. Rosalind? I ask you. What kind of a name is that for a girl who can ride a horse and fire a gun? For a girl who once wrestled an Indian boy with a feather in his hair and won? For a girl who started her own newspaper and sold it on the streets of New York aged twelve? But I'm getting ahead of myself. My father chose Rosalind from some play called *As You Like It*. Well, I *don't* like it, so 'Slim' I'll be, thank you very much.

I was always making my own mind up about things and I don't think I was an easy child. The story my family always told was about my hair. I was about ten. It was Christmas and we were going to have a small party. Ma had told me a hundred times, 'You tidy your hair, Rosalind Hannigan, or I will cut it off with your father's knife.'

Da's knife always lay ready to use by the fire. It says something about me that I didn't like to have tidy hair – I didn't like having long hair at all. I just found it annoying. I wasn't anything like my big sister, Beatrice, who loved nothing better than to try different styles. I just thought long hair got in the way. Refusing to brush, I simply took Da's knife and cut it off myself to save Ma the time. When she saw me with my new haircut she nearly dropped the pail of milk she was carrying. She stood completely still and I thought she was going to be cross.

'It was you who suggested it,' I said, quietly waiting for her anger to burst out, but instead she was silent before she suddenly began to laugh.

'Oh, Slim, whatever shall we do with you?' she wondered through peals of laughter. I loved her laugh. It brightened our little house every day.

Anyway, Da – that's my father, Patrick Hannigan – always said that a story has to start some place, so I need to take you for a little while to the great green fields of Ireland. We're not stopping for long as I don't live there any more. Despite that, and everything I've been through, there's still something about even the thought of Ireland that makes my heart pound. The symbol of Ireland is a little tiny green clover with three leaves called the shamrock. I can't even picture the shamrock growing by the lane alongside my old home without a tear coming to my eye. I don't approve of being too soppy, but my big brother, Henry, says it's all right, it just proves I'm still Irish in my heart.

Henry. He's the one who started a lot of the trouble. Not that I blame him. If I had been a bit older I might have caused some trouble too.

I was born in 1834 in a small place called Ballysmaragaid, which I'm sure you won't have heard of. It's about two days' walk from Dublin, which is the biggest city in Ireland and which I suppose you might know. *Ballysmaragaid*. What a lot of letters! It means 'Place of Emerald', and sure enough it was so green that St Patrick himself was once said to have been struck almost blind with the beauty of it. I don't know why a saint would have come to our village at all.

The last time I remember when everything was

completely normal was a day off from school. Maybe it was a Sunday, I don't know. Ballysmaragaid was so small, we didn't even have a church so we didn't go. I think Ma believed in God but she didn't make a fuss about it. That day I was wandering through the woods. I used to spend hours amongst the trees by myself but I never got lost.

'Look for the moss,' Da taught me. 'It's a natural navigator. Find a bit of tree not too near the ground. If there is moss growing, it will be on the north side of the trunk. Moss needs moisture and it will grow there because that is in the shade in the middle part of the day when the sun is doing most of its drying.'

It was 3 July 1845. The day before my birthday. I was ten, nearly eleven, when my story begins. I was probably wearing a pair of my brother's old trousers, and certainly no shoes. In fact I never had a pair of shoes at all until much later. We were poor but it didn't feel like it. With my short hair and trousers I must have looked like a boy.

I was happy in the woods. The woodland went on for miles – great oak trees made a canopy of green but there were also crab apple trees, wild privet, and little Irish whitebeams covered in a fine mist of white flowers in the spring and small red berries in the autumn. I loved the place. Ma was good with nature too. She taught me about the delicious mushrooms you could eat for free and how to look carefully at everything that was growing.

'Look closely and you will see great wonders. See this?' She picked up a green plant with rounded leaves and little pink flowers. 'They call it Enchanter's Nightshade. Isn't that a beautiful name? Now, most people will tell you it's a sort of weed but even if it is, I think it's lovely. If you look carefully you can see it has delicate little downy hairs all over the stems.'

I looked at the fine soft covering on its stem.

'Look for beauty, Slim, and you will find it,' she advised.

No matter what the season, the woods seemed to

be alive with colour – the richness of the early purple orchid, the tiny shaft of sun from the yellow pimpernel and the red of the wild strawberry.

'Who needs great museums and galleries of art when we have this?' Da would say as he picked bluebells to take home for Ma.

Anyway, this last normal day I was in one of Da's old shirts with the sleeves rolled up. I had been fishing in the stream. I wasn't supposed to. Beatrice said it wasn't right for a girl of my age to still enjoy 'such nonsense'. She wanted me home, in the house but I could never settle to sewing or cooking like my big sister, Beatrice. I liked outdoor things. I had caught a little brown trout and was feeling very pleased with myself. Ma might well be cross about me going fishing but she would appreciate the fish. We never had a great deal to eat and a trout would be welcome. I walked along carrying my fish on the end of the long stick I had been using as my fishing pole and no doubt whistling, which I was not supposed to do either. I had played in these woods all my life so

I think I was surprised to come across a turning through the trees that I didn't recall taking before.

I had only walked for a few moments when the woodland seemed to give up and I came out into a clearing. I looked up and saw the grandest house you could ever imagine. It was a great grey square place, the size of a castle. It stood on a small hill with lawns the size of fields rolling up in waves towards it. The late-afternoon sun was shining on the windows. I had never seen so much glass. We didn't have any windows at all in our little stone house. To my young eyes this magnificent place seemed to have hundreds. The light glinted back at me, bouncing off the shiny surfaces as if the place were on fire. It was beautiful. Three long sets of stone stairs swept up towards the front door, with fancy marble columns set on either side. I had never walked this far before, but I knew what it was.

This was Cardswell Manor, a grand house that belonged to a lord so English that he didn't even stay there. Ma said they had linen on the beds and a fireplace with a chimney in every room. A child living in such a place had a room all to herself just for sleeping and was never cold in the winter. There was even a library of books which the people in the house could read whenever they liked. How Da would love such a thing!

I was mesmerized by the house and stepped forward onto the lawn. I could see roses growing over a small wooden house to my right. They were red and yellow, pink and white. I had never seen such lovely flowers, so I headed towards them, thinking I could perhaps take just one for Ma. As I got closer the scent was enough to knock you over. It was wonderful. I couldn't resist putting my head down to a particularly large flower and had just plunged my nose into the soft petals when I heard a gentle voice say, 'Well, hello there.'

I looked up into the face of a woman. She was beautiful – about the same age as Ma but dressed completely differently. She had a long silk gown in an emerald green with white lace at the shoulders.

Her hair was dark, with lovely curls that peeked out from a matching green bonnet, also trimmed with lace. I had never seen a woman like her. She smiled at me and I thought she seemed nice.

I was about to say something when I heard a man behind me shout angrily, 'You, boy, what do you think you're doing?'

I spun round, and in my haste my fish swung out from the stick on my shoulder and slapped straight into the woman. She gave a gasp of surprise and I turned back in horror. The trout had fallen from the line onto her chest, and she stood there for a second with the fish hanging from her gown. I didn't know what to do.

'I'm so sorry,' I began.

'You little beggar!' yelled the man, moving towards me. He was old but he looked quite fit, so I'm afraid I ran. I wanted my fish, but didn't feel this was the moment to try and get it back. Instead I ran as fast as I could across the lawn. I thought for a moment that someone was calling my name but I didn't stop. I carried on racing through the woods and all the way back home. I ran past the stream, past the giant oak where Ma liked to picnic, and on past Uncle Aedan's small blacksmith's shop. I could tell he was there because smoke rose from the chimney where he worked the forge. As I sped past the open door I could see him raining blow after blow, down with a giant hammer on to hot metal as easy as I might lift a spoon to my mouth. He was the strongest man I'd ever seen. Under his buckskin apron the muscles on his arms and legs bulged like something that might hold up a small bridge . . . But I didn't stop. I ran past the other little *teachs* or houses that made up our small *clachan* or village. There was no proper road, just a dirt path worn down by our feet, but I knew every step. Our two chickens, Rosencrantz and Guildenstern, nearly tripped me up as they flapped about at my arrival. I sprinted towards our small house; it was built of such rough stone that from a distance it almost looked like part of the ground. I dashed inside and slammed the door behind me. It was just one room, with no windows to let the light in. The only light came from the fire. It was dark and smoky, and I thought it would be easy to hide.

Once inside, I raced up the ladder which rose up to a platform where we kept the potatoes. Sometimes I slept up there and it was the place where I felt safest. My chest was heaving as I lay on the wooden boards looking at the door. I tried to calm myself. I looked at the great wooden beam above the door where Da, long before any of us children had come along, had once carved his name with Ma's. *Pat & Peg*, it said, with the shape of a heart neatly marked around it to keep them together. Peg was Ma's nickname. I liked looking at that. When I saw their two names joined together, it made me feel safe and happy; as though everything was all right. Slowly I started to get my breath back.

The first person back was my little brother, Toby, and our pig, Hamlet. I could hear Toby coming before the door even opened.

'We won! Me and Hamlet won!' he was shouting. You always knew where Toby was for he had the loudest voice you ever heard in your life. As soon as he could talk, out came this booming sound, like a grown man in a tiny boy. It was hilarious and used to make us all laugh. He was eight then and he had the roundest, happiest face. Toby loved nothing better in the world than eating and laughing – usually at the same time. He was slightly out of breath but still managing to chew on a piece of bread while Hamlet grunted behind him, hoping for a scrap. Da had named him for some other Shakespeare play, even though Ma said he 'shouldn't be giving a name to a poor creature we would some day have to sell at market'. We weren't supposed to be fond of Hamlet, but he was a funny little fellow, more like a dog than a pig. He was the palest pink you ever saw, with small, slightly darker pink nose and ears. His eyes seemed huge in his head and his hair lay smooth across his body. He loved to play with a ball and he followed my little brother around like a small shadow.

Toby must have been racing the rest of the family home as they were a way behind him. My big sister Beatrice was next in. She was sixteen and a miniature of Ma, with the same curly red hair. She was carrying great bricks of peat bog and looked hot and bothered. She dumped the lumps of soil down by the fire. I realized with a sinking feeling that I would be in trouble; that I should have been with the family digging out the peat instead of fishing and wandering in the woods. The land was soft in the summer and it was easy to dig, so we gathered in enough to last the winter. Usually we worked together, digging and collecting the 'bricks' which Ma and Da would then leave to dry. Once it was all dried it would burn better than wood on the fire. We used it to cook with and to keep us warm. It was important work and I should have been helping.

I watched Beatrice push her hair back from her hot face and try to smooth out her dress. Even though she was my sister I could see that she was a beauty. We were so different. She always worried about her appearance in a way that never crossed my mind.

My father was not far behind. Da, with his scruffy beard and dark hair sticking out at all angles from under his old round hat with the battered brim. He had heavy boots and trousers to the knee. He was carrying a great load of peat, but I knew he would rather be reading the books that stuck out from both pockets of his jacket.

'Where the devil is our Slim?' he asked, looking around as he dropped the peat onto the pile Beatrice had started.

I moved to hide further back on the platform, but Toby looked up and saw me. 'She's up there.' He pointed with a grin, giving me away with pleasure.

I sat up, expecting the worst, but just then Ma came in, and as usual everything became calm. She was the most beautiful woman I ever saw, with curly hair that was so bright it was almost like the pretend hair I once saw on a doll. She wore it pulled up in a bun with a single white clasp that Da said had been made from the tusk of an elephant. Imagine such a thing! She had so many freckles on her face that she never seemed anything except full of colour, but even so there was something so elegant about Ma. She didn't speak like the rest of us, all in a hurry and a jumble, but chose each word with care.

'Where have you been, Slim?' she asked gently. Her accent was soft and she sounded nothing like Da. As she spoke she carried on working, taking down the wooden bucket we used to fetch water which hung on a nail on the wall.

I swung my legs round to the top rung of the ladder. 'I went fishing.'

'Where's the fish?' asked Da.

'I . . .'

Ma shook her head and raised her right eyebrow at Da the way she did when a subject was not to be discussed any further. Ma always found something good in everything.

'Well, I'm glad you didn't come with us, Slim,' she said brightly. 'That'll mean you're not too tired to help me sort the supper.'

I nodded and slowly climbed down the ladder just as my older brother, Henry, brought in the last of the peat. He was carrying too much but wouldn't let Da help him. Henry was fourteen but he was a big lad. It wouldn't be long before he was as tall as Da, but right now he was somewhere between a boy and a man. He banged into me, and I'm sure it was on purpose.

'You're in the way, Slim,' he muttered, but he saw Da shoot him a warning look and moved away from me. Henry was strong and he liked to solve things with his fists. How he made Da sigh. I hoped no one would mention the fishing – I didn't want my brother to think I had been too stupid to catch anything. I would never hear the end of it. I hated it when he teased me but I didn't want to tell anyone the truth. Henry had no time for me. He thought girls ought to stay home.

Ma went about making supper and giving me jobs to do. I got our only chair to climb on so I could reach up to the single shelf by the fire and take down the only two tin plates we owned. As we worked I watched my mother in her long skirt, worn thin with many patches, and her woollen shawl pulled and holed in so many places. It was nothing like the dress I had seen earlier up at the big house but I thought Ma looked the perfect lady.

Later that evening Toby and Hamlet lay curled up on the floor like brothers.

Ma sat in the chair darning a pair of socks. She shook her head at Toby. 'No good will come of it, Patrick,' she sighed. 'There shouldn't be a pig in the house. The boy treats the creature like a dog.'

Hamlet gave a little snore, confident he was not going anywhere. Da wasn't really listening for he was lost in a book. He sat on the floor, frowning as he tried to read by the light of the fire. He was always frowning, which was odd because in all of Ireland there was never a man with a laugh closer to his lips. When I look back now I think maybe he frowned because he needed glasses to see properly but we couldn't afford them. Most people's fathers in Ballysmaragaid did something practical to make a living. They built things or planted things. My da told stories, which I thought was best of all. They were all different, his stories, but they all started the same. 'Shall I tell you a tale?' he would begin, and soon you would be lost in his imagining.

I looked around the familiar room. There was nothing in it really. A wooden table against the wall, Ma's chair, the two tin plates and the water bucket. On a nail banged in by the door hung Da's great-coat. We didn't have anything else but I don't remember anyone thinking it wasn't enough.

Beatrice was drawing on a scrap of paper, as usual. She could draw like an angel and she would sit for hours dreaming about a different life. I had no idea how she could sit so still for hours and not fidget. Bea could even sew, a job which made me frown as much as Da.

'Let's see, Beatrice,' urged Ma.

Beatrice blushed and then shyly held up a drawing of a fancy dress.

Henry laughed when he saw it. 'That's so fancy no one would be able to walk in it.'

'And what do you know about dresses, Henry Hannigan?' Beatrice demanded.

'I think lace would be nice,' I offered. 'On the shoulders.'

Ma looked at me and smiled. 'Do you now, Slim? And what would you know of such things?'

'Nothing,' I muttered, not wanting to explain about the woman I had seen.

Beatrice gave a great dreamy sigh. 'Lace! One day I will dress as fine as I like,' she said. 'I'll go to balls and theatres and have lovely suppers and wine, and I shall have a big bed where I'll lie all day just as long as I please, combing my hair.'

I gave a little laugh because it seemed ridiculous, but Da wasn't having it.

'And why not?' he agreed, looking up from his reading. 'You're a beautiful lass, Beatrice.' He smiled at Ma and she smiled back. 'That reminds me,' he continued with a grin. 'I saw the McClusky boy, Colin, hanging about again. Not waiting for you, was he?'

Beatrice's face went bright red. I knew she liked him. Colin was a little older than Henry and had grown a beard, which Beatrice thought was a marvellous thing. She would draw men with beards over and over when she wasn't sketching fancy clothes.

'He wants to take me walking,' she said shyly.

'Does he now?' said Ma.

Beatrice looked embarrassed.

'You're too young,' declared Da.

'She's the age I was when we began walking together, Mr Hannigan,' Ma reminded him.

Da changed the subject. 'Time for a tale,' he announced, clapping his hands. 'Have I told you the story of the great *Comedy of Errors*? It's a marvellous tale of travel and misunderstanding by our old friend Mr Shakespeare.'

And we sat by the fire as Da spun stories and travelled the world with us in our minds.

'Where do stories come from, Da?' I asked.

He thought for a moment. 'Well, now, they're sort of magic. They're all around but most people don't take the time to let them in. If you open your mind you'll be amazed at the wonder which can appear. It's like reaching out and grabbing a slice of the moon for yourself.'

That night Ma kissed me goodnight. She stroked my head with her right hand and I held onto it. I liked to look at her ring. It was the only jewellery she owned. A Claddagh ring – a band of silver with a pair of hands holding a heart and a crown. She looked at the ring on her worn-down hands and said, 'The heart is for love, the hands for friendship and the crown for loyalty. It's all you need, my lovely Slim.'

She was just perfect. To me she even smelled perfect. I, on the other hand, was not perfect and I wish I had been a better daughter.

CHAPTER TWO

The next day it was my birthday. Uncle Aedan had made me a new fishing pole and even tied a beautiful hook with tiny bits of feather from a pheasant. Ma smiled at how pleased I was even though I knew she didn't really approve. Da had made me a small wooden box for 'precious things', and Henry, Beatrice and Toby fetched my favourite mushrooms from the woods for breakfast. Ma even managed to get a little flour for a cake.

'I have one more surprise for you,' said Da, patting his pocket, 'but you'll have to wait till this evening.'

That night everyone from the whole *clachan* danced in front of the house. The men had been drinking poteen, a strong drink made from potatoes which Ma only allowed on special occasions, for it made the grown-ups silly and red in the face. Beatrice was having a wonderful time. Ma had found her some ribbon and done her hair up. My sister stood there like a lady at a ball, pretending not to notice that Colin McClusky was standing stroking his beard and trying to summon up the courage to ask her to dance. I thought waiting about for boys was silly. Instead I followed Henry round the back of the house. I was surprised to see him with a boy called Kyle who he'd never liked all that much. Kyle's mother was a strange woman who didn't seem right in the head. She had no other family and had let Kyle, as Ma said, 'run wild'. He was as big as Henry but there had been an accident when he was little. His mother had let him crawl too close to the fire and he had burns over the side of his face and on his right hand. It made him frightening to look at. Maybe because of it he had a terrible temper and was always in trouble. You might think he'd want nothing to do with fire, but he had been caught setting things ablaze plenty of times. Over the years he and Henry had had so many fights that Da stopped them seeing each other. Now they were together and I could see Kyle had sneaked a glass of poteen.

He was handing it to Henry when he saw me. 'Go away, Slim. You're not wanted,' he called.

I stood my ground. 'I'll go if you give me a taste,' I replied.

Henry knew he would be in trouble if I told on him, so reluctantly he handed me the glass. I sipped and thought I was going to retch. It was disgusting. Henry laughed at me and then pretended to like it by taking a great swig. Kyle moved towards me and I felt scared.

'You shouldn't be here,' I managed – before turning to run back to the party.

Uncle Aedan must have liked poteen a lot because his face was nearly purple – but he played the fiddle anyway, his huge fingers getting faster and faster. Da and Uncle Aedan hardly looked like brothers.

They were as different as me and Beatrice. Where Da was slight and mad for a bit of reading, Uncle Aedan was built like a bull. He was a practical man but he could play the fiddle better than anyone. His wife, my Aunt Eimear, stood beside him smiling. She was a tiny, thin woman who looked even smaller next to her giant of a husband.

Toby tried to make his feet go as fast as the music. His round belly was wobbling. Then Henry reappeared looking flushed. Ma looked at him frowning but before she could say anything Henry called out, 'Toby, I think your belly can dance on its own.'

So Toby tried to make his stomach move to the music, and tears of laughter fell down our faces. Hamlet started squealing and running about as if he were dancing too. Toby picked him up and danced with him as though they were a fine lady and gentleman, and we all joined in.

Da put his arm around his brother and smiled. 'Ah, Aedan, how I wish our Niall could be with us now.' He pulled me over towards him too. 'As we've stopped the music for a moment it's time for my gorgeous daughter Slim's final present. Knowing how much you love doing your hair, we've bought you a comb.'

I think I must have looked terribly disappointed because everyone laughed. I felt quite giddy from the drink and had to sit down.

'I'm joking.' Da smiled, ruffling my hair. 'We've done no such thing.' He reached into his pocket and pulled out an envelope which he waved in the air and announced, 'I've a letter! From America! From Uncle Niall!'

Da knew I liked nothing better than hearing from Uncle Niall. He was the third and oldest Hannigan brother but I had never met him. He had left Ireland before I was born to go to America, to a place called Oregon. Hardly anyone went because it was a very long way away and the journey was full of terrible dangers – but oh, how I loved to hear about it.

Da had laid a fire outside in a circle of rocks and everyone gathered round it to hear him read. The women made themselves comfortable on the ground while the men stood with arms folded, still clutching on to a final glass of poteen. Of all the people in the world Niall was the one I most wanted to meet. When he wrote '*Come to America, step through a golden door to a place of plenty*,' all I wanted to do was leave straight away. How marvellous it sounded! What an incredible thing to see the Pacific Ocean, where my uncle said the waves were higher than a man. How I longed to see the great redwood trees and maybe meet an Indian man with his face all painted in bright colours.

'*The soil is rich, the climate mild and the scenery beautiful*,' read Da. '*All it lacks is my family of brothers and their loved ones. I dream each day that you might come and be with me. Your ever loving Niall.*'

Da beamed and went on, 'And that's not all!' He produced another piece of paper from the envelope which he carefully unfolded. The crowd muttered with excitement. Hardly anyone ever got a letter at all and certainly not from America.

'There's a drawing!' Da held it up. 'This is the American flag. They call it the stars and stripes on account of it having thirteen red and white stripes for the original thirteen colonies and twenty-eight stars in the blue corner, one for each of the states they have now.'

'Stars and stripes,' I repeated.

'Twenty-eight!' said someone else. 'Must be a grand place. Big.'

'And there's a map!' Da showed the second drawing to everyone. It was hand drawn and showed the whole town where my uncle lived. Everyone moved closer to see as he pointed to it.

'This is Niall's town. Now, it *was* called *Stumptown* when he first arrived, which is a terrible name, but they have renamed it *Portland*, and I shouldn't be at all surprised to find that Niall had a hand in that. *Portland!* Doesn't that sound grand? What a place to live! And here are the streets near his house, and this is a great body of water called

29

the Columbia River, which apparently is a roaring thing.'

There was silence as everyone tried to picture such a place.

'Sounds like paradise,' I said.

Ma looked around and said quietly, 'I don't know, Slim. I can't believe it's better than what we have right here. We're happy. We have each other. We have enough.'

'True, true, Peggy,' Da agreed, 'but did you know a woman can earn six shillings for making one dress in Oregon?'

The women at the party gasped at this. It was a great sum for a single piece of sewing.

'Do you think we would like it?' asked Toby, cuddled up to Hamlet at Da's feet. 'Oregon?'

Da smiled. 'Well, now, I've never been but they say that out there the pigs are running around under the great acorn trees, round and fat and already cooked, with knives and forks sticking in them so that you can cut off a slice whenever you are hungry.'

Toby did not like the sound of this and took Hamlet off to see if there was any cake left.

Da folded the letter carefully and then handed it to me. 'You keep that and have a very happy birthday, my lovely girl,' he said as he kissed me on the top of the head.

I held the letter tight, thinking I would never own anything more precious. I sat in front of the fire with the world spinning round me, my head fuzzy from the strong drink. When at last Ma made me get up to go inside, I put the letter in the box Da had made me. The box was for precious things and it was the only thing in it.

That night I dreamed of cutting off a slice from a pig as it ran past. I imagined seeing the American flag waving over the town as I walked Uncle Niall's map in my mind, along the streets and up the lane to knock on the door of his house . . .

Outside in the fields the potatoes grew. We had potatoes in the loft. There were potatoes in our bellies. We had buttermilk for a treat and we were well.

I'm sure you've had a potato, but what you may not know is how they grow. They're like a sort of wonderful secret. Da always called them 'Sir Walter's great gift'. They grow down underground, in the dark, in the rich brown soil where no one can see them. The only way that you know it's happening is because above the ground luscious green leaves begin to sprout, and soon white flowers wave in the breeze. By September that year Ma and Da were ready to bring the potatoes home to the loft so that they might lie waiting, plump with goodness, to keep us fed all through the winter.

Before the harvest Da and I would often sit by our field. It was a special time just for the two of us. In most families it was the oldest boy who was supposed to take an interest in farming but Henry didn't care about it. He was always off out. Beatrice didn't like the dirt and Toby was too little. I was glad. It left me alone with Da and I loved it.

I think I believed then that I would one day grow up to be a farmer and work the land with my father. The fact that I was a girl was not going to stop me. We would sit on the ground and look out at row after row of the bushy plants which the whole family had helped to lay in the earth. Da would put a finger to his smile and say, 'Now, Slim, shall we sit quiet and see if we can hear the little beauties growing?'

And we'd tip our heads to the ground to listen. Then he would laugh and tell a story.

'So there was a man called Sir Walter Raleigh who, like any sensible man, lived in Ireland. He lived in a place called Youghal.'

'Have you been?' I asked.

Da shook his head. 'No, but I hear it is by the sea and very beautiful.'

'I should like to see the sea,' I declared, even though I had no idea what that might look like.

'You, my lovely Slim, want to see everything, and that is a wonderful thing, but I agree' – he smiled – 'to see the sea would be a particular marvel. Sir

Walter saw the sea many times for he was what you call an "explorer".' Da said the word as if it were about the best thing a person could be.

'*Explorer*,' he repeated, just for the sound of it. 'A man who travelled the world, to places no one else had ever seen, and brought back wonders. Well, wonder of wonders, Sir Walter brought back the potato from America. No one in all the land had ever seen one before. So what was he going to do with this marvel?'

'Eat it?' I suggested.

'Of course, but first he took it to show the Queen of England. I mean, I've never met a queen, but I imagine they should like the sight of a potato, and if you've the chance to show her such a new thing, well, why wouldn't you? Well, the Queen, who was called Elizabeth, thought it was a marvel. What a thing was the potato. "What do you do with it?" she asked Sir Walter. "You eat it," he replied, so she called for all her cook—'

'Did she have many?'

'Hundreds, I would imagine – and told them to prepare this incredible new food, but the cooks had never seen a potato before so they looked at it for a long time and then, do you know what fool thing they did?'

I shook my head.

'They threw away the actual potato.'

I gasped.

Da held up his hands in horror. 'I know . . . they got rid of what they thought was just a brown lumpy bit covered in soil and they boiled the leaves instead. Then they served these to Her Majesty and all the fine lords and ladies she asked in for dinner. Well, the leaves of the great potato are poisonous and, it doesn't matter how grand you are, will make you sick. All of those fancy people in their fancy clothes fell down sick, even the Queen, and as she lay there, pale and, I suspect, a tiny bit annoyed' – Da fell backwards coughing and pretending to be the sick Queen – 'she banned the potato from the court!'

He laughed and sat up again. 'We, on the other

hand, Slim, are more sensible and eat the brown lumpy bit. We may have no jewels but we've a heap of common sense, my lovely girl, to keep us warm.'

Ma laughed as she came up behind us. 'If I had a penny for every time you've shown common sense, Patrick Hannigan, I'd be a very poor woman indeed.'

Da stood up laughing too. He grabbed Ma round the waist and kissed her soundly. 'And that is the God's honest truth, my beautiful wife. I'm little use to you but you have my heart.'

'And that will do me,' replied Ma with a smile.

Harvest time was when the potatoes in the ground were ready. Then everything in the village stopped while we all gathered them in. I don't know what you have for your meals so it may be hard to imagine, but the potato was everything to us. I can't think of a meal we had that didn't have a potato in it. We loved them and they kept us going. On the big day that we were to dig them Da organized a Parade for the Potato. Uncle Aedan led the way playing his fiddle while Da joined in on a wooden flute. We all marched behind them singing and carrying on. Everywhere in the village you could see people smiling. Uncle Aedan's wife, Eimear, made special biscuits for the children, and even though there was work to do, the day felt like a holiday. There were no shops to buy food where we lived. We only had the potatoes, a little flour and milk, but soon we would have enough food to see us through the winter.

Da was singing as he carefully put down his flute and Ma handed him a small trowel. He smiled at us all, then got down on his knees to dig the first shovelful of soil out of the way. We all held our breath, waiting to see the first potato, as Da sang his heart out. It took me a moment to realize what was happening. First the song died on Da's lips and then Uncle Aedan stopped playing. He stood with the fiddle hanging down by his side. I had dropped down onto my hands and knees, getting ready to dig, but I remember stopping there and then, for I knew that something was wrong. Ma gave a little cry and put her hand to her face as Da pulled a potato from the ground. This was not the brown, fat food we were waiting for. The thing Da held in his hand was black and rotten.

'Oh dear God, Peggy, look at them,' he whispered, hardly able to speak.

A strange disease had come to our field, to our potatoes. Instead of coming out of the ground hard, these potatoes were soggy and they stank. I knew we couldn't eat them.

Ma reached out and put her hand on Da's shoulder, which had begun to shake. 'It'll be all right,' she soothed. 'We'll manage. You mustn't worry.'

But as she spoke, all around us the women wept, the men cursed and even the youngest among us knew it was a disaster.

CHAPTER THREE

Ma tried to save some of the rotten potatoes. She boiled them and then squeezed the finished mess in a cloth to make a kind of *boxty* or potato cake, but they gave us belly ache. Even Toby, who could eat anything, did not want a blighted *boxty*.

Enough potatoes had survived to see us through the harsh months, but not enough to ever feel full all winter. There were stories of fields across Ireland which had failed just the same as ours. It was all anyone talked about. Anyone except Da. He refused to spend his time worrying about food. He would say, 'There's a whole world of beauty out there and we need to keep looking for it.'

Because there was no money in stories, Da also

ran the local *scoileanna scairte*. That probably sounds odd to you as it's Irish, but I think the English for it sounds just as strange. It means 'hedge school'. Every child in Ireland was supposed to be able to go to school, but our village of Ballysmaragaid had no building. Most of us in the village were Catholic, but there were a few Protestants as well. I'm not sure what the difference is. I think it's just that everyone believes in God but with different hymns. I know that the landlord up at the big house didn't think it was right, Protestants and Catholics learning together, so he had made sure no school was built.

Da just shrugged and welcomed any child to our house who wanted to learn. 'I'm teaching, not preaching,' he would mutter whenever anyone complained about his work.

Mostly everyone about the place was grateful. The children who worked in the fields during the day, or helped their parents with woodcutting and peat gathering, would come as the sun set to sit with Da and learn their sums and their reading. Sometimes

Da got money for it, but mostly it was eggs or milk, some peat bog or whatever people could manage. Occasionally there was nothing – but he taught everyone anyway. He was wonderful at making learning exciting and he always seemed sure that every child had a bit of genius in them. I remember when he taught us about science and Henry teased me for trying to learn.

'Science isn't for girls,' he scoffed.

Da was reading and he snapped his book shut with a bang. 'Henry Hannigan, learning is for everyone. Your sister has as good a brain as any. Possibly better than yours at the moment. You mark my words, in her lifetime we shall see great women scientists. Why, I shouldn't be at all surprised if one day there isn't even a lady doctor.'

Henry made a sort of harrumphing noise as if he didn't believe it.

'You mind your sister, Henry. Do you know why we call her Slim?'

I wasn't sure myself, there were so many stories.

'Because she's too skinny?' suggested my big brother.

'No,' replied Da. 'That's too easy. It's because she's clever.'

'What's being slim got to do with being clever, Da?' I asked.

'Odd, isn't it?' he agreed. 'When you were born, my darling,' he said to me, 'you were not at all well and the doctor came and said you had a "slim chance of surviving", but I knew you'd make it. You were a fighter even then. I liked the sound of "slim", so I looked it up. It comes from the Dutch for clever, and that you are.' He smiled, and it was nice to feel that he was proud of me. 'That you are,' he repeated. 'Words matter, Henry, so pay attention to them.'

Da loved nothing better than reading. I think Ma liked it too but she didn't really have time. She was too busy doing what she could with the food we had and finding anything else we could eat growing in the woods around us. She would take me into the forest, all the time teaching me things I would remember all my life.

'Some things look as though they might harm you, but if you are patient, even those things which appear harmful can help you.'

She pointed to a pretty plant whose spear-shaped leaves grew almost as if they had teeth. I reached down to pick one but Ma stopped me.

'No, it will sting!' She took the cloth of her apron and protected her hand to pluck some of the plants. They were nettles, and I remembered that, of course, I had been stung by them when I was younger. I had avoided them for years but now we gathered as many as we could find.

Ma boiled a great kettle of water. 'First you need to blanch them to take the sting out of them. Then we shall make soup. Fetch me some wild garlic from the loft.'

I knew that food was scarce and there was very little garlic left. 'Should we not save it?' I asked.

Ma smiled. 'Probably, but we shall want the soup

to taste nice.' She stopped what she was doing and pulled me into a hug. As she kissed the top of my head she whispered, 'We are poor, Slim, but we are not dead yet.'

She was wonderful, but even the food in the woods did not last. Soon the snow came and there weren't even nettles left for us to eat. We were all hungry, and there was an ache in our stomachs that never really went away that winter. We did our best to make what little food we had last, but with each passing day it became more difficult. Both Ma and Da tried to keep everything normal. She always had a cheerful word and he still told his tales.

I remember one night we were sitting by the fire, and you could hear our stomachs rumbling. Da was teaching me to play chess while Beatrice drew pictures of a grand kind of carriage which she wanted to ride in one day. Ma sat repairing a pair of Da's trousers. Henry had only just come in and had gone straight up to sit at the top of the potato-loft ladder. He sat there kicking the top rung, in some kind of temper which everyone pretended not to notice. In just a few short months Henry had changed, but I probably hadn't noticed until then. He had grown his first whisker and he sat stroking it as if surprised that it had appeared at all. As usual, Toby and Hamlet were playing on the floor, this time a kind of tug-of-war with an old bit of cloth. Suddenly Toby stopped and held his stomach. 'I'm hungry,' he groaned.

Ma moved to get up. 'I'll fetch you a nice cup of hot water,' she said brightly. 'It'll fill you right up.'

Toby looked serious. 'I don't think so,' he replied and silently began to cry.

Da got up and pulled my little brother towards him. He sat down on the chair and put Toby on his knee. 'What is it, lad?' he asked gently.

Toby began to sob. 'If I don't eat I won't grow. I'll always be small and the other boys will tease me.'

Da nodded and hugged him close. 'Well, now,' he began, and we all knew that a story was on the way. 'The real question is, what is wrong with being small? Why, staying small might be the very thing. Have I ever told you about Lord Minimus?'

Toby shook his head as great fat tears trickled down his cheeks.

Ma stood beside them and wiped them dry with her apron. 'Tell us, Patrick,' she encouraged.

Da smiled and began.

'There was once a man called Jeffrey Hudson and he was a dwarf, but a famous one, for he was the Queen's Dwarf, which if you are going to be small is probably the thing to be. He lived at the palace of Queen Henrietta Maria. She was French but became Queen of England, which seems odd but what do I know of such things? Anyway, Jeffrey's parents and his brothers and sister were a perfectly usual size but he was marvellous in how tiny he was. Everything looked perfect but he was no higher than my knee. The Duke and Duchess of Buckingham heard about him and wanted to meet him. As soon as they did they loved him. One night they thought they'd have a party for the King and Queen Henrietta Maria. It was such a banquet as no one had ever seen, and the climax was a giant pie placed in front of the Queen, out of which popped Jeffrey. Oh, the Queen loved it! She ate the pie and kept the dwarf. She called him Lord Minimus. So one day, my boy, if you don't grow, we shall have a grand party with lords and ladies. There'll be a whole roasted lamb, mountains of potatoes, and your mother will bake a pie which we can pop you in and—'

We were all laughing at the thought when Henry suddenly jumped down from the ladder with a thud. 'Stop it!' he shouted at Da. 'Stop it!'

'Henry! Do not shout at your father like that!' scolded Ma.

He was shaking with rage. 'What is wrong with you?' he yelled. 'We're all starving and all you can do is tell tales! We want food, not some bloody slice of the moon.'

Henry reached into his jacket pocket and pulled

out a ragged newspaper. 'Have you seen this? Have you heard what the bloody Prime Minister says?' he bellowed.

Ma looked upset. 'Language, Henry, language,' she scolded.

Henry held up the paper to the light from the fire and read out the words of the man in charge in London. 'The Prime Minister – *the Prime Minister*! – has the nerve to say that everyone in Ireland is exaggerating the trouble with the potato.' He threw the paper down. 'Exaggeration! If he smelled just one rotten potato, he'd change his tune.'

'We'll manage, Henry,' soothed Ma. 'Besides, the next crop will be well again. You wait and see.'

Da put Toby down and put his hand out for the newspaper. 'Where did you get that?' he asked.

Henry handed it over and mumbled, 'A travelling man. Passing through.'

Da squatted down by the fire and looked at the paper.

'We need to find out what's going on, Da,' Henry

continued. I could tell he was trying to be calm but not managing it very well. 'We've no information, but you need to know that there are those who are talking of a famine. Can you imagine such a thing in our own land and time? A famine! That's a thing from history, in far-off countries.'

It was the first time I'd ever heard the word.

'What does that mean, Da? A famine?' I asked.

Ma spoke more sharply than I had ever heard before. 'Don't you go frightening the children now, Patrick.'

Da looked away into the fire. 'A famine is a terrible thing,' he explained quietly. 'It's when there is so little food that people begin to die.'

'Is that going to happen to us?' I asked, but Da wouldn't look at me.

'Patrick!' warned Ma.

Da turned his head to me. 'No, of course not.'

I thought that was the end of it, but Henry didn't want to let it go. He stood by the fire. Ma had given him one of Da's old jackets. It was brown, with patches on the elbows in blue. It was a little big, but Henry wouldn't wear anything else. I think he thought it made him a man. He put his hands deep in the pockets, still trying to hold back his anger.

'Exaggeration! That's what he said. Words matter, Da, so pay attention. But how can you expect the Prime Minister to understand? He's English. None of the English have any idea because they don't come here,' he said through gritted teeth.

'Not all the English are bad,' said Ma quietly but firmly, 'just as all the Irish are not always good.'

There was a long silence from all of us. We had never heard Henry speak like this. At last he said, 'I know that, Ma, but it's not right. Our own lord up at the big house doesn't even bother with us,' he continued.

Ma had sat down again to her sewing but now she stopped and looked at Da. He looked away. The uncomfortable silence continued.

'I'm sure Lord Cardswell has a reason for his decisions,' Da finally said.

Henry banged his fist against the stone wall. 'It shouldn't be up to the English to decide anything,' he almost shouted. 'Why do you allow it, Da?' His eyes blazed. I had never seen him stand up to Da like that.

'Allow?' Da asked quietly. 'I didn't realize I was "allowing" it. What should I do?'

Henry lifted his chin and looked at him. 'Fight,' he said.

Da shook his head, which seemed to enrage Henry. Suddenly he moved over to where Da was squatting and grabbed him by his shirt front.

'Da! We can't just sit here!' He pulled Da close. He had grown again and could now speak straight into Da's face. 'Do you know what one of those men in London has said? Do you, Da?'

Ma got up from her chair. 'Henry!' she shouted, but he wasn't listening.

'He said that rotten potatoes mixed with grass

51

make a very wholesome and nutritious food and that everyone knows Irishmen can live upon anything.'

Da put his hands gently on Henry's arms and pushed them away. Henry seemed to be having trouble breathing. He stood looking at us all for a second and then waved his arms towards the fields outside. 'That's what the English think. There's plenty of grass so we'll be fine even without the potatoes.'

Da turned away and led Ma back to her chair. He stood quietly in front of her, holding her hands in both of his. 'Where do you hear that?' he asked.

Henry looked away. 'There's talk,' he mumbled. He looked at Da, and for one moment I thought he was going to cry. 'We need to fight, Da, or we'll die.'

Everyone, even Beatrice, was listening now.

Da let go of Ma and turned back to Henry. 'Just to be clear, lad,' he said calmly, 'we Hannigans will fight, but we will do so with words and not our fists.'

'What words, Da? Stories about dwarfs and pies?' asked Henry evenly. He stood his ground, but a few moments later he turned and slammed out of the house.

It was the end of the discussion but Henry was different after that. Perhaps we all were.

That night I heard Ma and Da talking.

'The boy's right,' whispered Da. 'We can't just sit here. People need to be told what is going on.'

'You are not to get into trouble,' replied Ma. 'Let me go up to the manor house.'

'No, Peggy. Please. Trust me to find a way.'

There was a long silence. Then I heard Da say, 'They named a place in America after her.'

'Who?' asked Ma.

'Queen Henrietta Maria. Maryland. It's a state. Must be odd to be that rich – to have somewhere named after you even though you never went there.'

There was another long silence.

'A slice of the moon . . .' Da said quietly.

I didn't really understand any of it, but I knew I didn't want Ma to go up to the manor. I thought if she did I would get into trouble because of the fish. I also felt confused. Why would the people in that grand house, with their many windows and fine clothes, help us?

As the weather worsened, so too did our hunger. One day Ma sent me to see if I could find some elderflowers growing in the woods. As I searched I suddenly realized what a foolish errand it was. It was the wrong time of year for the flowers. I thought Ma must have forgotten so I ran back home to remind her. As I opened the door I saw Da standing by the table holding Hamlet in his arms. His big knife lay on the table, looking sharp and ready to use.

Ma was standing beside him. 'You can do this, Patrick,' she was saying.

Da picked up the knife. As he did so Hamlet turned in his arms and seemed to look him straight in the face. He made a little grunt noise, as if he thought it was a game. Da turned and looked at me with a terribly guilty face. He started to speak, but no words came out. I wanted to be sick, but I hadn't eaten for a day or two and there was nothing there. I knew I had been sent to the woods so that Da could kill Hamlet while I was gone. I couldn't bear it. The pig had been part of the family, and just as Ma had predicted, no good was going to come of it. To make matters worse, just then Toby came running in; he had been sent off to play over at Uncle Aedan's forge. He was excited about something, but he stopped the minute he saw Da standing there with the pig in his arms.

'What are you doing with Hamlet?' he asked, his eyes wide with fear.

Da looked at Toby and then at me. 'It's no use, Peg' he said to Ma.

Ma gave a deep sigh. 'We have no food. There is nothing.' She moved to put her arm around Toby as she explained quietly, 'We can't manage on the few eggs we get from Rosencrantz and Guildenstern. I am so sorry, Toby, but we have to eat Ham— The pig.'

Toby gave a terrible scream, and when Toby screamed it was so loud that it was enough to stop the whole village. He tried to pull Hamlet from Da's arms. Da was much bigger and stronger and he held Hamlet high above his head, out of Toby's reach. The little pig must have thought it was a new game because he squealed with delight, adding to the chaos. He wriggled so much that Da had to let go, and Hamlet ran towards me. I scooped him up and held him tight.

'You can't kill Hamlet, you can't,' sobbed Toby, in a terrible state. Ma put her arms around him and held him close.

She and Da looked at each other for a long time before Da slowly lowered his knife and put it on the table. 'No, I can't,' he agreed.

Hamlet looked at me, and I felt he could almost speak. I put him down, and he ran off squealing as if he knew he'd had a lucky escape.

Da got down on his knees and put his hands on Toby's shoulders. 'He can't stay with us any more, Toby. There isn't enough food. You wouldn't want him to starve, now, would you? I need you to be kind to him and let him go.'

Tears ran down Toby's face and he shook his head.

'I know you have a big heart – you can do this,' continued Da as he stood up and looked at Ma.

'I shall take Hamlet to a new home,' he said calmly.

'Patrick—' Ma tried to interrupt, but Da held up his hand.

'It's all right. The pig will have a great adventure. You'd like that for him, wouldn't you, Toby?' Toby was not at all sure but he nodded anyway. 'I shall have to take him in the morning so you will need to say goodbye. It's a kind thing, lad, to let him go. We can't look after him.'

It was one of the saddest things I had ever seen, Toby saying goodbye to his pet pig. He lay on the floor cuddling him goodbye, and the next morning Da set off with Hamlet for his great adventure.

He was gone for a couple of days. I think the rest of us knew that Da had taken the pig to market, but Toby was happy believing that Hamlet was doing something exciting.

When Da came back he was looking especially pleased with himself. He carried a large wooden box which he put on the table, calling for all of us to come and look.

'What is it, Patrick?' asked Ma, her face hot from trying to griddle a little flour and water over the fire. 'What did you get?'

Da smiled. 'I had a date with destiny,' he said mysteriously. He winked at me and then slowly opened the wide lid of the box.

CHAPTER FOUR

I thought for a minute we were rich. Inside the box there was a jumble of silver pieces that looked a bit like very small coins.

'Look!' exclaimed Da, holding up one of them. 'H! For Hannigan!'

I looked more closely and saw that each of the silver pieces was a letter of the alphabet. Hundreds of them, in different sizes and shapes.

Da continued his excited explanation. 'It was like the hand of fate. I was meant to buy them. Look what we shall do with these. Why, we could change the world!'

He explained that he had walked all the way to Dublin with Hamlet and he was about to . . . He

looked at Toby. 'I was about to send the pig . . .
Hamlet to—'

'His great adventure!' Toby shouted gleefully.

Da nodded and looked a little awkward. 'Indeed,
on his great adventure, when—'

'Will I see him again?' Toby interrupted.

'Who?'

'Hamlet,' persisted my little brother. 'When he's
finished his great adventure.'

Da looked at Ma, and she raised an eyebrow the
way she did when she was warning him to be careful,
so he replied, 'Well, the thing about life is that you
never know how it is going to turn out.' He looked
at me and I knew not to say a word.

'Anyway,' he continued, 'I was on my way when
I passed an office where they printed books. Well,
you know, since the potatoes had failed a lot of
people have no money and certainly no money
for books. Like lots of businesses the printing
shop was in trouble and closing down. The
man in charge let me have this great box of letters

for almost no money. Isn't that grand?' He beamed.

'But what shall we do with them? All these letters?' asked Ma.

Da gave a little laugh as if she should have guessed.

'Why, change the world.' He patted the wooden box with huge pleasure. 'All we need is the machine to set the letters in . . . and . . . I've a drawing of one of those,' he said, producing a piece of newspaper from his pocket. He spread it out on the table for us to see. A drawing of a large machine with the name *The Albion* was carefully sketched out on the paper.

Just then Beatrice came in. She was out a lot 'walking' with Colin McClusky now. She had taken to wearing her hair up in a bun and talking as though she were a grown-up and I was an idiot. She hardly bothered with me any more as I was too young to be of interest, but when she did speak it was as though her words came from a great height. Not that she spoke much to anyone. Mostly she just sat dreaming by the fire. Ma said it was perfectly normal for her age but I found it annoying.

Da smiled as she entered. 'The very person I need,' he said. 'Beatrice, look at this.'

She had been out all morning and hadn't heard about the letters or the machine. She looked at the drawing of *The Albion* and frowned. 'I don't understand,' she said. 'What is it?'

Da smiled. 'This, my lovely girl, is the answer to our troubles. You know how we love to read? Well, this machine is what you call a printing press. It can take whatever writing a man or' – he looked down at me – 'a girl might want and turn it into a book or newspaper. Just think – you come up with a story or you hear a piece of news, you write it down and then you can print it yourself. Why, the next thing you know you could be holding whatever was in your head in your hand instead, and then you can sell it to someone else. You can work the whole machine with just one man. I expect even Slim, little thing that she is, could do it.'

I looked at the drawing. I had never heard of such a thing. I don't think I had ever even thought how a book might be made. But I was fascinated.

Da picked up some of the metal pieces from the box. 'Each of these is a separate letter. There are hundreds of them in this box. You put them in the order you want, get ink and paper, and then you print. You need letters and you need a printing press like the one in the drawing.'

I looked at it. 'Are we to buy such a thing – to go with your letters?' I asked.

Da shook his head. 'We've no money for such a grand thing, so your Uncle Aedan is going to make one. He doesn't know it yet, but he is, and I need you, Beatrice, to look at this picture and make some bigger drawings so Aedan can see exactly how it works.'

'And will you write your stories down?' asked Toby.

'One day I might, but first we need to tell people

the truth about what is happening here – like Henry said.'

I still could not see what we would do with the box of letters. 'What do you mean?' I asked.

Da smiled. 'The Hannigans, Slim, are going to fight. We're going to start a newspaper.'

It was a shocking moment for all of us because Ma, who had been so strong for so long, suddenly began to cry. 'Oh, Patrick,' she sobbed. 'We've the rent to pay and no food. How could you have done such a thing?'

I'd never heard Ma and Da have cross words before but now she was very angry that he had spent money on such a 'box of nonsense'.

We did need food. The hurting in our stomachs from being hungry was getting worse. It made all of us tired, and some days we were so cold we thought we'd never get warm but I had heard enough about what was happening from Henry to know that Da was right. People needed to be told about it – and how wonderful if our family could help with that.

Maybe Henry would be in less of a temper if he felt we were trying to help.

Life carried on, with Da teaching and Ma doing her best in the house. Beatrice took the drawing of the machine and made larger-scale versions of it which were easier to look at.

One night the local children had gathered for school as usual. Da was trying to get us all to act out *Romeo and Juliet*, and we were laughing as we pretended to be Italian. It was fun – I loved those evenings of learning with laughter. In the past Henry had always joined in – he liked to play kings – but now he was being a sulk in the corner. Suddenly he got to his feet.

'What is the point of this, Da, when people are starving?' he demanded.

There were about five other children of different ages in the room, who were not part of the family. They stopped their play-acting and stood still. The tension was terrible and everyone seemed to hold their breath.

Da had been holding his ancient copy of the play, but now he put it down and said calmly, 'The point of learning about great writing is to help you to know people. Shakespeare has it all – love, hate, envy, joy, decision-making, suffering, laughter, life and death – all those things that are part of who we are.' He picked up his copy again. 'This great writer knows people from all walks of life. From the very poor to the very rich and all those in between, and from him you can learn how to conduct yourself.'

Henry snorted his disagreement. 'Yes, well, you read your plays, and the rest of us can all starve to death. I'm going out.'

He left – and never came back to the school again.

After that he was off out even more than before. I knew he was up to something but I wasn't sure what. I'd seen him a few times with Kyle, but he never brought him back to the house as Ma didn't like him. Once I followed them both to the woods to see if I could find out what they were up to and hid in a tree; I could see that they were not alone. A half-dozen or so other lads turned up and sat around on logs having some sort of meeting. I tried to inch closer to hear what they were saying, but the branch I had chosen was rotten and I fell right into the middle of their meeting.

Henry leaped up and grabbed me by the collar, shaking me like a naughty puppy. 'Stay away, Slim, do you hear? This is not for girls.'

It seemed to me that most things – most *interesting* things – were 'not for girls'. How I grumbled if I had to stay in the house, cooking and sewing. Ma knew it was not for me, and sometimes she would invent a little something to let me get outdoors.

'There you are, Slim,' she said as I snuck back into the house that day. She had been trying to keep the fire going but now she stopped and wiped her hands on her apron. She looked so tired and thin. I hugged her and stood close as she stroked my back. Then she sighed and went back to poking the fire.

'I've a job for you,' she said. 'I hear Mrs O'Connor

has a little milk she will trade for an egg. Guildenstern was kind enough to provide us with one this morning so I want you to take it and get as much milk as she can let us have.'

The egg sat in a little coil of cloth on the table. Eggs had become quite a rare thing. Even the chickens seemed depressed about how little food there was and they were laying fewer and fewer.

'Be careful now!' warned Ma as I picked it up. It was a valuable thing and I cradled it in both hands as I set off to Mrs O'Connor's. 'And don't be long!' she called after me.

On the way I had to pass Uncle Aedan's *cérdcha* or workshop, and as I did so I heard chatter coming from inside. It was frosty and cold and the usual fire inside the forge seemed like a welcoming idea. Plus sometimes Aunt Eimear, who had no children of her own to feed, left a tiny bit of food about the place. I crept towards the door and could see Da inside helping, which was unusual. I knew they must be making the marvellous new printing machine. I was desperate to have a look but didn't want to get into trouble for not getting the milk quickly for Ma.

Da was standing by a makeshift table, frowning over some large pieces of paper on which he had been sketching with a pencil. Uncle Aedan, standing like a great oak tree in the middle of the room, was listening with an empty pipe in his mouth while he stroked his old rough-haired dog, Clancy. I could see lots of the drawings Beatrice had done pinned up around the workshop. Da had that look of excitement in his eye he often had when he was just getting to the best bit of a story. I wanted to know why. Carefully holding the egg in my right hand, I crouched low and tried to slink along the shadows by the wall. Clancy moved away to lap water from the *umar* or trough.

Da scratched his beard. 'The trouble is, this doesn't tell you what size it ought to be, but we should work it out from these.'

'Are you sure about this, Patrick?' asked Uncle Aedan.

'We have to do something,' said Da.

Just then Clancy came over to me, sniffing at the egg in my hand. I tried to push him away, but as I stood up in a hurry, ready to slip away outside, I banged my arm against a large piece of metal. The egg slipped out of my hand and, before I could catch it, broke instantly over the dirt floor.

'Slim? Is that you?' called Da.

I didn't dare move. The bright yellow of the egg stared up at me from the pieces of broken shell and I don't think I am exaggerating when I say I wanted to die. My curiosity had killed any chance of getting milk. In that moment I felt like the worst daughter anyone had ever produced. Clancy ran over wagging his tail and was soon licking up this unexpected treat.

Da walked towards me and looked down. 'Lucky dog,' he said quietly. 'Your ma won't be pleased will she, Slim? Mind you, I'm already in trouble myself.'

'Are you making the machine? The one for printing?' I asked.

Da nodded.

That night Ma was very cross with me. I knew I had done a bad thing, but I had never heard her be so angry.

She stood with her hands on her hips asking, 'Have I not been clear about how little food we have? Did I not tell you to be careful?'

I always tried not to cry, but Ma's being angry was more than I could bear. Tears flooded down my face. I had nothing to say to defend myself. Even Beatrice, who paid me very little attention, got up and fetched a small cloth to wipe my tears. As she did so, Ma tried to calm her voice.

'Why must you always make life difficult, Slim?' she asked. Now all I could hear was her disappointment in me, which was even worse than her anger.

She sent me to bed in the potato loft. I lay there weeping and listening to my stomach rumbling. I tried to distract myself by dreaming of food, any sort of food, but all I could think about was how badly I had behaved. Down below, Toby and Beatrice were asleep on a pile of rags by the fire. I could hear my brother lightly snoring as once more Ma and Da were disagreeing.

'But, Peggy, this *is* important work,' said Da urgently. 'Think what we could do with our own newspaper. People are told that the government has ordered Indian corn from America to help us now the potatoes have failed, but it's not true. There's none on the way. It's just a rumour to keep everyone calm. We have to make sure everyone knows it's just talk. That the government doesn't and won't care for us.'

'Patrick, you went to market with the pig to pay the rent, not start a newspaper. What will we do when the agent comes to collect? No one has money for a paper.'

'I couldn't let Hamlet die for nothing. I just couldn't.'

'I told you—' Ma began, but Da interrupted.

'Peggy, this is about something bigger. It's not just about our life; it's about liberty for everyone.

It's the future – to say what we want, to shout it from the leaves of a book or a newspaper which we made ourselves. Imagine such a thing where we can unite everyone. Just think if I could find the words to help everyone work together for our homeland, ruled by Irishmen, whatever their religion.'

It was a wonderful speech but Ma sounded desperate. 'Most of our neighbours can't even read,' she said.

'Which is why I'm a teacher,' replied Da.

'Which is splendid, but we still have to pay the rent.'

'Well, if you wanted money you shouldn't have married the school teacher. You had your chance.'

Just when it seemed the row was going to grow, Ma's voice softened. 'No, I did not have a chance, Patrick Hannigan, for the moment you appeared on my doorstep my heart was lost.'

I must have fallen asleep, but later that night I could hear Ma pacing up and down. The door opened and Da came in. The wind blew into the house and he had trouble closing it. He looked chilled to the bone; he must have been out for some time.

'Anything?' asked Ma, getting up from her chair.

Da shook his head and hugged her. Toby was still asleep but Beatrice was up. She fetched the large iron kettle and hung it over the fire. 'I'll boil some water,' she said.

I knew something even more important than my breaking an egg had happened so I dared to climb down the ladder. 'What is it?' I asked.

Ma and Da didn't speak so Beatrice answered.

'Henry,' she said. 'He hasn't come home.'

I could hear heavy rain starting. It pounded down on the roof. Ma held Da's hand and they both looked pale and anxious.

'Where did he go?' I asked, my bare feet cold on the stone floor. I shivered as I spoke. Beatrice fetched her shawl and put it around me. It was not like her and I smiled, but no one else did. Everyone looked so serious.

Henry was gone for two days without a word. Ma could hardly speak. I had never seen her so worried. When he finally came in through the door, my big brother had a sprig of oak in his hat and a green ribbon slipped through the buttonhole of his coat.

Ma went to hug him, but when she saw the ribbon she stopped. She put her hand to her mouth and quietly whispered, 'Oh no, Henry!'

I didn't know what it meant but I could tell we were in terrible trouble, and more was about to arrive.

CHAPTER FIVE

Henry had become what they called a 'Ribbonman'. I didn't understand all of it except that they were Catholic men angry with the Protestants and the English landlords. They would fight anyone trying to collect money from the poor. He and Da had a lot of angry words about it, but Henry was set on his own way and wouldn't listen. After I'd broken Ma's egg I was too busy trying to be good to pay as much attention as I should have. I spent all my free time foraging in the woods, and became almost as good as Ma at sorting the edible food that grew wild from the plants that were dangerous to eat. Toby missed Hamlet terribly and he took to following me about.

'You need to be a hundred per cent certain of

your mushroom,' I explained to him as we poked about under a log looking for what might be available. 'If you have any doubt about it being all right to eat, then just leave it.'

It was what Ma had taught me and I passed it on to my little helper. I'd never really had a lot of time for Toby, but actually I started to enjoy our outings to look for food. He liked nothing better than grubbing about in the soil, getting as filthy as possible, and I was happy to let him.

Most of the mushrooms grew only in the autumn but even in the winter you could find a few called Wood Blewit, which you knew by the pale purple edge of their caps. You had to cook them well, but they were delicious in a stew with onions. Cow parsley was fine too, but we would spend hours making sure that the leaves we gathered weren't hemlock or rough chervil, both of which were poisonous. You had to look for the U-shaped groove down the leaf stalk to make sure you had the right thing.

'Hemlock has purple blotches on its stems,' Ma told us, and Da's eyes lit up.

'This is the very stuff, Peggy, which we could print in a newspaper!' he exclaimed excitedly. 'Helping people to find food by giving them the right information.'

'I thought we were going to have stories,' said Toby.

'That too!' said Da. 'You can have both, you know. Information *and* a story. I mean, those purple patches on the plant are said to be the bloodstains of poor Abel, who was killed by his brother, Cain. Cain did his terrible deed and then wiped the blood from his hands with the hemlock stalks. Imagine such a thing! No wonder we don't want to eat them.'

The thought made Toby shiver. Mind you, it was cold that winter. We shivered a lot. We were used to being barefoot, but there were snowy days when even our tough feet felt as though they might fall off with the cold. Our breath hovered in the air as we searched for food one late afternoon. I had just stopped at a fallen tree when Toby grabbed my arm.

'Ssh,' he whispered. 'Listen!'

Through the woods we could hear the sound of banging like drums in the distance. I pulled Toby down behind the tree and we crouched there, peeking over the top. In a few moments a great gang of men and boys appeared, marching through the woods. They had cut big sticks and most of them appeared to have two, which they banged together as they walked. They were chanting, '*Death to the Orangemen, death to the Orangemen.*'

I had no idea what that meant. We were trying to be quiet, but Toby gave a sharp intake of breath and pointed. In the midst of the crowd, was Henry who marched along beside Kyle. They were both banging their sticks and following behind Beatrice's Colin, who seemed to be in charge. All the men had green ribbons on their chest. I didn't know where they were going but I knew it wasn't good.

That night we munched on a few stewed mushrooms. Da came in late from what had become his usual evening search for Henry.

'Did you find him?' asked Ma as she chopped cow parsley leaves into vinegar to keep them fresh.

'No,' Da said.

Toby looked at me and I shook my head. I didn't want to get Henry into trouble.

'They say the tavern at Abbeyfarm has been attacked,' Da added quietly.

Beatrice had been helping Ma, but she stopped and could hardly bear to ask, 'Anyone hurt?'

Da tried to smile but he was too worried. 'I don't know, my love,' he replied.

When Henry at last came home no one said anything. Da didn't seem to have the energy to be cross. We were all hungry and getting more tired every day. No one asked him where he had been or what he had been doing. It was as though everyone knew.

*

And so the winter passed. Toby and I looked for food, Ma cooked what she could, Henry was gone and Beatrice mooned about the place when she wasn't out walking with Colin. Meanwhile Uncle Aedan and Da spent any spare moment working in the forge, building their machine.

When at last spring came, everyone in Ballysmaragaid planted more potatoes. It was wonderful to feel the air getting warmer and to feel the soft soil under our hands as we laid the new crop in their beds.

'It won't come again – the disease?' asked Toby as he wiped more dirt onto his face than seemed possible.

Da shook his head. 'I don't think so.' He stood up and put his arm round Ma. 'It's been bad, but we made it through.'

Once more we could imagine the great plates of food growing quietly underground. The worst, everyone agreed, must surely be over. We could almost taste the glorious potatoes with butter dripping all over them.

After the planting everyone seemed a little more cheerful, and one night when we were all at home Da announced, 'Tomorrow I would like you all to come up to Uncle Aedan's. You too, Henry.'

'But I—' began Henry.

'Please, son,' pleaded Da, and Henry grumpily nodded that he would.

We had none of us been allowed into the forge while the work was underway, but now we all trooped up to have a look. Aunt Eimear had managed to make some biscuits and Uncle Aedan got his fiddle down for the first time in months. The machine was covered in a cloth, and Da said a few words before he got Ma to pull the cloth off and reveal the finished piece.

'What gunpowder did for war the printing press has done for the mind,' he said. 'This – this is the way forward.' Da smiled at Ma and said formally, 'I now call upon my wonderful wife, Mrs Margaret Hannigan, to reveal our triumph.'

Ma pulled off the cloth in a great sweep as Uncle

Aedan struck up a tune and we all clapped like mad. Only Henry stood to one side, uncertain how to react.

The machine was a thing of wonder – black and even more beautiful than the original drawing. Uncle Aedan and Da couldn't stop grinning. What a thing they had made! Everyone was smiling – Bea, Toby, me and even Ma, who'd been so cross about it – we all went over to stroke and admire the thing.

It was Henry who spoke first.

'How does it work?' he asked.

'Ah, well,' began Da – and then he was off, explaining each piece, how the letters fitted into special frames, where the paper went, and then pretending to make all manner of printing. It was very exciting, but after that and for weeks afterwards nothing happened.

The newspaper that was supposed to change everything was never made. Da had the letters, he had his press, but there was no money for paper and ink.

Henry scoffed at the whole affair. 'You wasted

your time, Da, building that thing. What is the point if we can't print anything?'

Da hung his head and couldn't look at us. 'I didn't think it through,' he muttered.

The new potato crop was not ready yet and there was no money at all. Uncle Aedan put a cloth back over the wonderful machine, and there it stayed. Da told fewer stories. He blamed himself for 'being foolish', 'a dreamer', and he spent his days telling Ma what an 'idiot' he had been and how he could never forgive himself. Ma stroked his cheek and we all waited for the potatoes to grow.

Not everyone in the village was poor. There was a man known as 'the agent'. He collected all the rents from everyone, including us, and he had money. The agent came to our house one early morning before everybody was up. Even Ma, who was always so optimistic, had stopped getting up with the sun. She didn't rest well when Henry stayed out, and by the time she fell asleep she was exhausted. That morning

Henry came in at first light. He looked tired too, and even the green ribbon on his jacket seemed to be fading. Da was trying to get the fire going but we were low on peat and it was a battle. He looked up as Henry came in. The morning light shone through the door and lit up Da's face, and for the first time I noticed how thin he had become.

He moved to hug Henry, but my brother brushed him aside and went to lean against the table.

'Henry,' Da began, but almost immediately seemed to run out of energy. He went back to squatting by the fire. Just then there was a knock at the door. We never really had visitors so I couldn't think who it might be. Henry was closest so he answered.

In the doorway stood a tall man. The minute we saw him we knew that he was not like us. Everything about him looked fat with food and all his clothes shone like new money. His black boots sparkled with polish and he wore a shiny black top hat that showed the strokes of someone's thorough brush.

His long black cloak had a velvet collar, which fastened at the neck with a great silver clasp. He was a careful man. Neatly buttoned and arranged. His long dark whiskers curled around his mouth and up towards the trim lines of beard which ran either side of his face. The whiskers were exactly even and held at the ends with the tiniest bit of wax. In the dawn light two things shone forth – the brilliant scarlet lining of his cloak, which flashed at us each time he raised his arm, and the glow of the large cigar he held in his mouth. This was the agent of our landlord, Lord Cardswell, come to get his money from us.

'Ah, young man,' he declared with a puff of smoke into the air, 'my name is—' He stopped for a minute and his eyes flicked over the green ribbon on Henry's jacket. I thought he was going to say something, but instead he continued, 'my name is Parker Crossingham.'

The sound of the knocking had woken Ma, and now the mention of this name caused her to give a little gasp. She jumped up and pulled Toby, who was just rising, to her. Parker Crossingham saw all this and smiled before carrying on as if nothing had happened.

'I am Lord Cardswell's new agent. It seems so awfully unpleasant, but kindly inform your parents that regrettably' – he puffed on his cigar once more and smiled – 'I am here for the rent.'

He was new to collecting the rents in Ballysmaragaid but he did not seem new to Ma. She was up and at the door before you could blink. I had never seen her move so fast. She tried to stop Mr Crossingham from coming in, but his sparkly boots were already clicking their way towards the fire.

'Parker, you may not—' she began, but he interrupted her.

'Why, good morning, Margaret. How divine you look in that . . .' He paused to look at her in her old skirt and shawl. 'Well, I don't really know what to call it.' Although he was wearing leather gloves, Crossingham rubbed his hands together. 'Chilly in here, isn't it?' he said. 'Still, it would be much worse to have no house at all, now wouldn't it?'

Da stood up from where he had been tending the fire. He put his arm round Ma, and looked at the intruder.

'You are not welcome here, Parker,' said Ma.

Crossingham smiled. 'Oh, but I am, Margaret. Lord Cardswell – you remember him, don't you? Such a nice man. A *family* man.'

Da held Ma tight and seemed about to say something, but Ma raised her eyebrow warning him to be quiet. The agent kept smiling as he puffed on his cigar and looked at us all. 'Well, Lord Cardswell has made me his agent for this entire area. It's exhausting, of course, but he personally asked me to collect your money, which is – well, how can I put this delicately? Overdue.'

Just then Beatrice appeared from the potato loft, where she had been sleeping. She put her feet on the top rung of the ladder and her skirt caught on a board so that her bare legs could be seen by us all.

The movement caught the agent's eye. 'Oh, I say . . .' He smiled yet it didn't seem quite nice. He blew cigar smoke towards my sister and licked his lips. 'Aren't you lovely? What's your name?'

Bea looked a little afraid. She continued to climb down until she stood on the ground and replied softly, 'Beatrice.'

Mr Crossingham looked at Ma. 'Just like you, isn't she, Margaret? How many years is it now? My dear . . .' He moved closer to look at Beatrice. 'You don't know me but I know your ma – I know her very well. We were going to get married, weren't we, Margaret?'

What was he talking about? This horrible man marry Ma? How ridiculous, I thought. Crossingham turned to indicate Da. 'Then this peasant turned up and spoiled everything. It was really rather embarrassing.'

'I would never have married you, Parker,' exploded Ma.

Crossingham gave an odd little laugh and began to put a hand out towards Bea's hair. Ma and Da both seemed paralysed, but Henry quickly stepped between the agent and Beatrice.

'Don't you touch her,' he demanded in a low voice.

Mr Crossingham looked at him for a long moment, then used his riding crop to flick the end of the ribbon Henry wore. His eyes narrowed and he lowered his voice so it seemed much more menacing. 'Careful, lad,' he said. 'Be very careful.'

Henry was not someone who was ever careful, and I thought he was going to hit the agent but Da reached out to pull him away. Toby had no idea what was happening, but he could feel the tension and began to cry. I didn't know what to do so I grabbed him and pushed him behind me.

Crossingham shrugged and appeared uninterested in the effect he was having on us, suddenly discovering a piece of invisible dust to shake off his sleeve. 'Beatrice, Beatrice,' he repeated, and then smiled at Ma. 'Pretty thing. I never did marry, but do you know, I think I fancy a wife. Now, there's a thought.' He looked up and smiled. 'Perhaps we could come to some . . . arrangement? The rent? Your daughter? I do feel you owe me, Margaret.'

Henry pulled back his arm as if to hit the man, but Da held onto him and Crossingham laughed.

'We'll get your money,' said Ma. 'Now go. You are not welcome here.'

The agent stood and looked at her. I thought he was going to say something else, but instead he twisted his neck as if his collar suddenly felt too tight. 'You will consider my offer,' he said, almost spitting out the words. 'I promise you will,' and with that he left.

Henry was beside himself with fury. 'You should have let me hit him, Da.'

Da tried to hug him, saying, 'You're just a boy,' but my brother moved away, furious.

'Well, why didn't *you* hit him, then, Da?' exploded Henry.

Da put both his hands up in despair. 'That's not the answer. I won't be violent. We have to find another way. If I could just get paper and ink, I'm telling you . . .'

He carried on telling us how a newspaper could change the world, but even *he* didn't sound like he believed it. Ma put her arm round Bea and held her tight.

'What did he mean, Ma,' I asked, 'about marrying you?'

Da began to speak but Ma shook her head.

'There are lots of things, Slim, that you don't know,' she said, 'and it is better that way.' It was clear that she would not talk about it any more. All she would say was, 'The potatoes will come soon. Then we can sell some and eat and even pay that dreadful man.'

The day before we were due to harvest the new crop of potatoes the whole village was alive with excitement. You have to understand how hungry we had been all winter long. There had been days when I had even thought of trying to eat the grass in the fields like the man in London had suggested. I knew it was poisonous but my stomach hurt so much with the lack of food. Now, everywhere you looked, there were potato stalks thick with white flowers and a sense of promise. I remember how warm it was. It was nearly my birthday again and the summer months brought more for us to eat in the wild. I had been out looking for food in the woods and had found some mushrooms which I thought could be eaten. I had found them down by the stream, and as I bent to pick them I caught sight of myself reflected in the water. I did not recognize what I saw. We had been starving all through the cold months. Instead of looking six months older I looked younger and thinner. My skin was tight around my face as if it didn't fit. I looked unwell.

I turned away and, picking up the mushrooms, started to run home but my legs were too tired to run. Instead I walked slowly, as if in a dream. As I got closer to the house, the strangest thing occurred. It was summer, it was mid-afternoon yet a thick white fog seemed to be creeping across the fields. I felt a chill in me that could not be warmed. I should have known then that something bad was going to happen.

The next morning we woke to a terrible smell. Overnight the leaves on the potato plants had gone black. Where just the day before they had stood fresh and upright, now they hung loose upon their stems. The stalks were still green but it was no use. The flowers had been a lie. We knew without even digging that the whole crop was ruined; 'blighted', the grown-ups said. Even with your eyes shut you'd have known you were near the fields. The smell was so terrible, it tore at the back of your nose. It was the work of a single night. Everyone in the village was rushing to dig in case they might save something – anything, even food for a pig or a cow – but it was no use. Everything was spoiled. Not a potato could be eaten. There was no food and no plan from anyone, least of all the men in London, to get us some.

We got back to the house filthy from our frantic digging. We were too tired to cry. We sat in a great heap on the floor. Toby laid his head on Beatrice's lap and Henry lay against Ma as if he were a little boy again. Da had no stories and I had no strength even to boil water for us.

Then the rain came and we could not get the peat that we needed for the fire. Coal was out of the question and soon we were not just hungry but cold as well. Uncle Aedan gave us *cual crainn*, the charcoal he used in the forge, but he could not spare much, for without it he could not work if an order should come in. At night we slept in a great huddle by the tiniest of fires. All of us except Henry, who was mostly never there any more. I knew he was out with the Ribbonmen, causing trouble. Every now and then you would hear tell of something that had happened – a fight, a fire, trouble at some Protestant place or other – and we all knew that Henry was involved.

Once he came in with a black eye and blood streaming from a cut to his head. Da patched him up, and as he did so he tried to talk about his newspaper, about the power of words instead of fists.

'The pen is mightier than the sword,' he would say. 'Words have the power to light fires in men's souls. I know you want to fight. I understand that you are angry, but this is not the way. If we could just get some paper . . .'

Beatrice was watching Da tend to him. I think she knew that Henry had something to say.

'Colin is dead,' he announced quietly.

I thought Beatrice was going to faint.

'There was a fight,' Henry continued, 'and I . . . I tried to help him.'

Tears began to fall down my sister's face. Soon they developed into sobs and the sound filled the whole room. Ma sat on her chair. Instead of getting up to be with Bea she too began to cry and that set Toby off. The whole family began quietly weeping and then sobbing. I think we were all sad about

Colin but mostly it was all just too much to bear.

'I'm so sorry,' Henry stuttered.

'You shouldn't be doing this, Henry,' Da began, but Ma stopped him.

'Come here, son,' she said, and put her arms around him just as she had done when he was a little boy.

Henry had been a Ribbonman for some time and no good seemed to come of it. I believed Da when he said that the newspaper was a better answer. I began to dream about getting what he needed so that we could print fine words and change the world.

CHAPTER SIX

The next morning the light from the sun shone under the door but no one wanted to move. There was nothing to get up for. That night Henry did not come home, and we didn't see him again for a long time.

Da heard news that the government would provide work for men if they would help build a road nearby. All the men of the village went – Da and even Uncle Aedan – to try and earn the few pence a day that they were promised. I never saw what they were doing but Da would come home exhausted each evening. He said they broke stones all day and moved them from one side of the ditch to the other, but it turned out it was a road to nowhere. No one needed a road. Someone in the government was just making work for work's sake for people who were starving.

I know Da would have been no good at such work. He was magic, my da, but he was better with stories than with stones. Every night Ma tried to soothe his hands with a medicine she made from a plant she and Bea gathered in the woods. I think it was called Irish Lace, but it's a long time ago and there's bits that I don't remember. I know well enough that Da's hands swelled up and hurt so he couldn't sleep. There were nights when we would all lie awake, so hungry that sleep was impossible. We would torture ourselves with talk of food while Ma wrapped Da's hands in a wet cloth.

The whole of Ballysmaragaid was starving, but we were not the only ones. They said there were places where people were living on nothing but seaweed. I didn't even know what that was but Da said it was not nice. I think I began to forget what it was like to have food when you wanted it. Every day the prices of everything we needed went up and up. We began to see beggars passing through on the road to Dublin, and death came to the village.

The husband of Mrs O'Connor, who never got that egg, clutched his chest one morning and fell down dead, broken by the road work. As soon as she heard, Ma went to help wash and shave Mr O'Connor, which seemed strange to me as he wasn't really going anywhere. Then he was laid on the table with candles lighting the room. At first Mrs O'Connor made a lot of wailing noises, which you could hear all the way to our house.

'What's that?' I asked Bea when it started.

'That'll be Mrs O'Connor keening for her husband,' she explained with a slight sob in her own voice. We never talked about Colin but I knew she tought about him.

The sound of the keening was awful, but by the time I arrived at her house the poor woman had settled onto a chair in silence. Da took Toby with him to order the coffin and Beatrice was sent to find snuff and poteen from anyone who might have some.

'Where will I find them?' she asked Ma. 'Surely no one has anything.'

'This is Ballysmaragaid,' she replied. 'Knock on any door and people will try to help.'

And they did. Hardly anyone had anything but what they had they shared.

'Poor Mrs O'Connor,' they declared, handing over a 'little something' for the wake. Bea and I laid out the small bits of food and drink on the mantelpiece and then sat quietly with Ma, the dead man and his wife. I couldn't stop looking at Mr O'Connor and wondering where he'd gone.

Suddenly a small clock on their mantelpiece chimed. 'I'm so sorry,' exclaimed Ma, although I couldn't think how a clock chiming was her fault. She jumped up, opened the clock case and put a piece of cloth inside to stop it ticking.

I had never seen a dead person before. It seemed so odd seeing him laid out where he had once had his meals. His face was pale and all his clothes were too big on his shrunken frame. I wondered if his spirit had flown away, and if it had, where to?

After that we had a 'wake' for him. I don't think it's just an Irish thing. It's a sort of, well, party . . . Maybe not a party exactly, but a gathering you have for the person who's died. The small bits of food were handed round as all the neighbours arrived. Every now and then someone new would arrive to 'pay their respects'. They all made their way to the side of the corpse, knelt down and silently bowed their head in prayer. After that they got up and went to Mrs O'Connor, saying, 'I'm sorry for your trouble. He was a good man,' or, 'I'm sorry for your trouble. I always liked him.' That sort of thing.

Da told a funny story about him and Mr O'Connor dealing with a difficult donkey years ago, and everyone laughed quietly before falling silent again.

'Thank you, Patrick,' Mrs O'Connor mouthed to Da.

After the story the men all went outside and started drinking. At midnight someone said the rosary. I know because Ma woke me and Toby to hear it and then sent us home.

We didn't have any more wakes because after that death came too often. It seemed to be everywhere, and soon there was no one with the energy even to say goodbye. Mrs McClusky died not long after her boy, Colin. Some said it was from grief, but she was also very thin like the rest of us. We heard that in one town there were so many deaths, they were making coffins with hinged bottoms to carry the corpses to the graves. They would open these over the grave and then take the coffin right back for the next body. You never knew who might be next. Aunt Eimear developed a cough and took to her bed, and Uncle Aedan would not leave her side.

And all the while Henry was missing. More and more men were joining the Ribbonmen and wearing the green ribbon for Ireland. People said they were attacking the men in charge, the men who still had money, and Ma was frantic with worry. Those who were caught by the police were sent straight to a place called Australia as convicts, and never came back. If Henry were caught, we would never see him again.

I couldn't stop thinking about the newspaper. I felt it was important, but I didn't know where you could buy ink and paper even if you had the money. Now that Uncle Aedan was looking after his wife the forge was always empty. When I couldn't sleep I used to sneak up there and stand by the printing press, imagining what words might fly from it. I don't think I have ever been so taken with anything in my life. One night as I arrived I heard an owl hoot, and then I thought I heard a noise of someone in the forge.

'Uncle Aedan?' I called out, but there was no reply.

The cloth that had covered the grand machine since it had been built was lying on the floor. I moved towards the press and saw the strangest thing. A piece of paper lay on the floor beside it and when I touched the ink plate for the first time ever, it was wet. Someone had been using it. I heard something scuttle behind me, and as I turned someone ran from the shadows out into the night. I couldn't be sure – it was dark – but I thought it was Henry.

All the while the agent, Parker Crossingham, kept circling around our Beatrice like a lion around a lamb.

Even though she had not been engaged to Colin I knew she had dreamed of it. She had drawn pictures of wedding dresses and fine images of herself standing beside a man with a beard. She became restless and took to walking the same paths that she and Colin had enjoyed together. Sometimes I went with her, and it was not unusual for us to see Mr Crossingham out and about.

Every time I saw him he was eating something – an apple, a delicious piece of cheese or a great slice of bread. One afternoon we had been to fetch water when he rode up on his great horse. He had a chicken leg which he was eating slowly. He stopped the horse so that it nudged Beatrice a little. She was carrying the heavy bucket and a little of the water splashed out onto her skirt. Crossingham smiled and carefully put the last of the chicken into his mouth, licking his lips as he looked at my sister.

'That looks awfully heavy, my dear,' he smirked. 'I do wish you would allow me to help.'

We turned away, but we soon saw him again. Like almost everyone else in the village we still had not paid the rent, and he came to the house more and more often, making demands. Sometimes he offered Ma food but I don't know what he wanted in exchange. Whatever it was, Ma always turned him down.

'I will have what I want in the end,' he would say as she closed the door on him time after time.

One night there was a knock at that self-same door. We thought it must be Crossingham but it was the constabulary. They had come on horseback wearing pointed helmets and looking all official. They carried guns with something called a bayonet which was like a sharp knife strapped to the end.

'We've an order to arrest Henry Hannigan,' they declared.

CHAPTER SEVEN

Ma put her hand out to the table to hold herself up. Her cheeks were bright with freckles as always but somehow she looked as pale as moonlight.

I could see Da trying to be steady.

There were three men on horseback.

'Daniel Graham,' Da said in his best teaching voice, 'where are your manners?'

He was talking to the slightest of the men, who hesitated for a second and then got off his horse to come to the door. He wore the same outfit as the others, but it wasn't until he took his hat off that I realized he was a fellow from our village. He was a little older than Beatrice and I remembered him from the many nights he had come to be taught at Da's school. We knew him well – but not like this. Not in police uniform.

'Daniel,' said Da to him as if they had just met out walking.

'Mr Hannigan,' he replied and put out his hand to shake Da's. He seemed embarrassed. 'Look, I'm sorry about this . . .'

Da put up his hand to stop him as if he understood. 'What is it that you accuse my boy of?' he asked.

'Hurry it up!' urged one of the men still sitting on his horse.

'All right!' replied Daniel over his shoulder as he reached into his pocket and pulled out a piece of paper. It was neatly printed and headed LORD CARDSWELL, THIEF AND MURDERER! Underneath it were listed all the crimes the writer thought Lord Cardswell was guilty of. It also threatened his lordship and his family with terrible things if he didn't help the poor people who lived on his land.

'This was pinned to the door of the manor house.

A likeness of Lord Cardswell was burned upon the lawn,' explained Daniel.

'It is clear that whoever wrote this means his lordship harm,' barked one of the other constables.

'And why might you think our Henry was involved?' asked Da.

The man who had shouted pulled a jacket from his saddle bag. It was brown with blue elbow patches. We all knew it was Henry's.

'One of the other officers . . .' explained Daniel. 'They caught him but he got away.'

Behind him the other constables were growing irritated. 'Just find the young bastard and let's go,' one of them exploded.

Da moved towards the man in a fury. 'Don't you call my son—'

He got as far as the horse when the officer raised his gun to push Da back and caught him with the sharp end. A cut sliced across Da's cheek.

Ma rushed forward to pull him back. 'Enough, Patrick!' she said.

'Mr Hannigan, I'm so sorry,' said Daniel, who did seem appalled by what was happening. I had never seen Da hurt like that before and felt as though the whole world was turning upside down. No one had ever wanted to hurt my wonderful father. I was desperate to do something but couldn't think what.

Bea ran and got a piece of cloth and tried to stop the blood flowing down Da's cheek – though he didn't even seem to notice he had been injured. He folded the piece of paper Daniel had given him, and as he returned it he said, 'You know, Daniel, that you can only read this because I taught you.'

For a moment Daniel and Da both had their hands on the leaflet and were almost touching. Daniel paused, and it was a while before he nodded and replied, 'I know. I'm sorry.'

Ma stepped forward and took charge. 'We haven't seen our son for weeks,' she said calmly. 'You are welcome to search for him if you wish.'

I felt terrified. I thought I had seen Henry in the forge, and not that long ago. I hadn't said anything to anyone because there was a bit of me that was proud of him. There was a bit of me that wished I could be out in the woods, at least doing something to try and make things better. I was also afraid of what Kyle might do to me if I said anything. Now I shrunk back into a dark corner of the house. I was shaking with fear that the policeman might ask me something and I wouldn't be able to lie.

For what seemed like ages I thought they might come in and I would have to speak, but in the end they nodded and the stern constable said, 'If we find you have been hiding him, there will be no mercy for the entire family,' and with that they rode away.

We all stood outside the house and watched them go. As they galloped off, the piece of paper that had caused them to look for Henry in the first place fluttered from Daniel Graham's pocket and landed on the ground. I was curious about what it said so I ran to pick it up. Behind me I could hear Da getting upset.

'Oh, Peggy, I've been such a fool with my ideas.

I should have just paid the rent with the money from the pig and now . . . now they say they won't pay us for the road work after all and I didn't know how to tell you. Our boy, our Henry – he was right. I should have been fighting, not telling stories. What good is a slice of the bloody moon? That's all I'm good for. Your father knew that. He warned you. You should have listened.'

Her father? I had never heard anyone speak of Ma's father. Who was he? What was going on and what had he warned Ma about?

I grabbed the piece of paper and turned back. Ma was reaching her hand out to Da when we heard the sound of horses returning, but this time it was not the constabulary. It was Parker Crossingham on a great black horse, his face red with strong drink. He pulled up so fast that the horse almost skidded.

'Patrick Hannigan. Patrick Hannigan,' he repeated. He thwacked his riding crop across the palm of his hand and I thought for a minute he was going to hit Da with it. The blood from the cut on

Da's face continued to run down onto his shirt. Crossingham pulled a large ham from a bag slung from his saddle. He sat and looked at us before taking a knife, cutting himself a large slice and then resting the ham on his saddle.

'Do you know, I've had enough of you,' he slurred as he stuffed his mouth with the delicious-looking meat. 'Always in my way, aren't you? You snivelling little bookworm. I'm sure we all thought you'd give in one day, but you just keep going, don't you? Well, here's what we shall do. What *I* shall do. I am a civilized man. I am offering to marry your daughter.' Mr Crossingham looked at Ma. 'You'd love that, wouldn't you, Margaret? Peg? The man you despise marrying your daughter. What fun – and as a wedding present I will waive the small matter of the rent – or . . .'

He waved his riding crop in the air as if everyone were having a party; then suddenly his face changed and he leaned down to sneer at Da.

'Or I will see you out of here. This house will be

torn down. You have until morning.' With that he stuffed the ham back in his saddle bag, cracked his whip across the flank of his horse and was gone.

Toby had been asleep, but now he appeared in the doorway looking bewildered by what was happening.

Beatrice pulled her shawl tight and spoke in a low voice, thinking he and I might not hear. 'Let me go to Mr Crossingham. He will save us if I go to him. He will give us food. Look how much he has.'

'No,' declared Ma in a voice so loud and determined that for a moment she sounded like someone else. She took a deep breath and reached out to stroke Beatrice's cheek. 'That is not the answer. We will starve before I let that happen.'

I still had the paper in my hand. Da suddenly snatched it from me. 'Oh my word!' he exclaimed. He looked paler than I had ever seen him.

'What is it?' asked Ma.

Da held the writing close to his face. 'I'm not sure, but I think this was made on our printing press.'

'How can you know that?' I asked, amazed.

'It's the particular type of letters. They're very recognizable. I mean, it would be a strange coincidence for someone near here to have the same ones. No one has a printing press for miles around. It's not exactly common.'

Ma shook her head. 'But we've no paper or ink, so how could . . . ?' She stopped speaking. She and Da must've had the same thought, for without another word they both began to run towards the forge. Bea looked at me, and soon the whole family were all running towards Uncle Aedan's workshop.

When we arrived the place was empty. I knew that Aunt Eimear was worse and Uncle Aedan spent all his time with her. Even when she had been well he hardly ever got any orders, so mostly now the fire wasn't lit. The press still stood in the centre of the room covered in a cloth. Da pulled a corner of it and revealed the machine. He put his hand on the plate where the ink should go and held up his fingers.

They were stained black. As I had realized not long ago someone had been using the printing press.

'Oh dear God,' he whispered, and looked at all of us. 'We have to move the press,' he said urgently.

I still didn't understand what was happening. 'Why?' I asked.

Ma was beginning to clear a path from the forge, moving things out of the way. 'Because if they find this, then the whole family will be in trouble. Uncle Aedan too.'

'But we didn't print anything,' I protested.

'No one will care about that. They will think we did it and use this piece of paper to prove it,' said Da. 'Right, all of you, grab hold of the press and lift.'

Da and Ma stood on either side, with Bea and me on a corner each. Bless him, even Toby tried to lend a hand, but it was no use. The thing was too heavy for us to move.

Ma looked around. 'The handcart!' she shouted.

Da let go of the press and raced to get the hand-cart which my uncle used to move sacks of charcoal. It was a wooden, two-wheeled thing, strong and sturdy. It was not easy to manoeuvre and it took Da a few moments to wheel it near the press.

'Toby, go and make sure no one is coming,' urged Ma as she helped Da.

Toby ran to the door while the rest of us tried once more to shift the press and this time slide it onto the cart. Try as we might we could not move it at all. It was too heavy.

'Slim, run and fetch your uncle,' ordered Da.

I raced off, with my heart beating with fear. My uncle's house was right nearby, and in a moment I was banging on the door with both fists. I could hear him moving about inside.

'Uncle Aedan, Uncle Aedan!' I called.

After what seemed an age he finally opened the door. I was shocked. I had not seen him for a while. He had been so busy with Aunt Eimear that he had not been to visit. He had changed and now looked so thin, not at all the bull of a man I was used to.

'Uncle Aedan, Uncle Aedan, someone has been using the printing press to print bad things about the lord up at the manor. Da is worried the police will think it's us so we have to move the machine. We have to hide it!'

Uncle Aedan shook his head as if it were all too much to take in.

I could hear Aunt Eimear call out, 'Aedan?' in a weak voice.

I thought Uncle Aedan wasn't going to leave her and was relieved when he shouted, 'I'll be right back.' He reached for his boots and was still pulling them on as we ran towards the forge.

Toby was at his post by the door. As we ran towards him he jumped forward with both arms and legs spread out as if to stop us. 'You can't go in there!' he yelled. I was impressed. He was tiny but he was brave.

'It's us, you fool,' I shouted as we raced past him and went inside.

My uncle stopped in his tracks when he saw Da. 'Patrick! What happened to you?' he exclaimed.

It was then that I noticed the great gash on Da's cheek was bleeding once more. He put his hand to the wound and felt the blood. 'There isn't time,' he said. 'Help me!'

My uncle saw what we had been trying to do, and once more all of us grabbed a piece of the press. This time we managed to get it onto the cart, but the wooden sides were soon smeared with Da's blood. Everyone was out of breath and exhausted.

'Now what?' asked Bea.

'We'll have to take it into the woods,' urged Uncle Aedan. 'Maybe the thick part down by the old oak. There's a lot of bushes there.'

'Toby, Slim,' ordered Ma, 'you lead the way. Make sure no one is coming.'

'And keep quiet,' urged Da.

The woods were dark, and even though I knew them well I felt frightened. I had never been out in them at this time of night. Clouds covered the moon so there was hardly any light, and we stumbled over tree roots on the way. Toby reached for my hand and I was glad to take his. Behind us the cart creaked with its heavy load as Ma, Da, Bea and Uncle Aedan silently guided the press along.

At last we reached the old oak and found the bushes that might conceal the machine.

'I have to go back to Eimear,' whispered my uncle. 'Be careful, Patrick.'

Da looked at Uncle Aedan as if he might never see him again. They hugged and I thought Da was going to weep.

'Thank you, Aedan,' whispered Ma, stroking his back.

Aedan nodded, looking all around him, then left without another word.

Bea's voice was shaking with fear. 'Now what?' she asked.

Just then the clouds parted and the moon seemed to shine straight down onto the press. Even though it was black, it almost glinted.

'We have to hide it better,' said Ma.

'We need my big knife from the house so I can cut some branches to put on top. Toby . . .' Da turned to my little brother, but we could all see how frightened he was.

'I'll do it,' I said. I don't know where my courage came from but I knew I was quick and that Toby was too little.

'Be careful, Slim,' said Ma, but I was already on my way.

I ran as fast as I could, but as I turned the corner to our place I saw a terrible sight. Mr Crossingham was there with a great gang of men and they were tearing down our house! The strong drink seemed to have made him forget that he had promised to wait till morning. They must have started almost straight away, for the men had already pulled the roof to the ground and now they were setting fire to the table to burn the inside. They had thrown all our things – not that we had much – out onto the patch of dirt by the door and I could see Da's knife and greatcoat lying there. The two chickens, Rosencrantz and Guildenstern, had been let loose and were running about in a fright. My box for precious things lay open on the ground and Uncle Niall's letter from America was blowing in the breeze.

I was a brave girl but fear swept through me. My heart was pounding so hard I could almost feel it in my ears. What was I to do? Da wanted his knife. It was up to me, so I took a quick, deep breath, and before I could think any more about it, I suddenly sprinted forward. I picked up both Da's things in my arms and started to run off. I was nearly away when something made me turn back to pick up Uncle Niall's letter and map inside. I grabbed it and was off again, but Crossingham was quick. He caught me by the shoulder, and I did a terrible thing. I turned my face and bit him hard on the thumb. He screamed and as he let go it was almost as though the chickens were on my side because he tripped over the pair of them. Before he could get to his feet

I was off, running away carrying the coat, the knife and the letter. As I ran, the drawing of the American flag slipped from my hand and fluttered to the ground. I had no choice but to leave it behind.

I didn't dare run towards the place where my family were hiding in case I was followed, so I raced the opposite way, as fast I could manage. I was just running past the old stream where I had caught sight of my own shrinking face when a hand reached out and tripped me up. I was winded but I had Da's knife: I got to my feet, holding it out in front of me. I have no idea what I thought I might do with it as I looked up into a face I hardly recognized.

'Slim! It's me.'

It was my brother Henry! I dropped the knife and fell into his arms. 'Oh, Henry, I didn't know it was you. I thought you were going to kill me.'

'It's all right, it's all right,' he soothed.

I tried to calm my breathing and look at my brother. I hadn't seen him for some weeks and what I saw was a shock. There was nothing of him but bones, and there seemed to be dried blood in his hair.

His voice was weak. 'Slim!'

We hugged, even though that was not something Henry usually thought was a good idea with his irritating little sister. He winced as I squeezed him.

'You're hurt!' I exclaimed. It was then that I noticed a great gash in Henry's shirt and blood weeping from his side. His face looked funny: his right eye was completely closed, swollen shut with purple bruising, and there was blood coming from his ear.

'I know, but I can't come to the house. The constables are after me. They'll take everyone. They don't care.'

I explained about Crossingham and the house, and Henry grimaced and then nodded. 'It's happening everywhere. The English own the land. We only rent it and now they want us off it, swept from the soil.'

I didn't really understand. All I knew was that I needed to get Henry and myself to the rest of the family. I made sure no one was about, and then picked up the knife, coat and box, and began to lead him back to where the others were hiding. Henry could hardly walk so it was a slow business. He leaned on me and we had to stop every few moments for him to get his breath.

'You saw me in the forge, didn't you, Slim?' he asked as we hobbled forward.

'Yes,' I said.

'Did you tell anyone?'

I shook my head.

'Thank you.' Henry squeezed my shoulder and I felt as though I had done something good. Even in all my fear I managed a tiny smile.

By the time we got to the old oak Ma had become frantic about how long I'd been gone.

'Slim! Slim!' she called in a low voice, running towards me. It was then that she saw Henry. He had been managing quite well, but the sight of Ma was too much for him. He collapsed on the ground.

'He's hurt,' I explained. 'His side, I think. And his face.'

Da and Bea both raced over and began to tend to his wounds.

'The constables?' asked Da.

Henry nodded.

'The house!' I suddenly remembered. 'They're tearing it down.'

'Oh no,' cried Bea, but there was no time to sit and weep.

'Did you get my knife, Slim?' asked Da urgently as he tried gently to pull Henry's shirt away from the injury.

I gave Da the knife and he began to cut away at the shirt.

'Bea,' ordered Ma, 'go look for some Lady's Mantle. It's early in the season but there might be some. Little green flowers without petals, velvety leaves which look pleated. Slim, some dock leaves. You'll find them anywhere there are nettles. Toby – water.'

We all moved quickly about our tasks. I found the dock leaves quickly and Ma used them to stem the flow of blood from Henry's head. Toby was surprisingly resourceful. He used Da's hat to fetch water from the stream. As he bent over Henry I noticed for the first time that my little brother no longer had a belly. His trousers hung down from his waist.

When at last Henry was patched up and lay against a tree root, we all stopped to think what might be next. Da still had the piece of paper from the constables.

'Henry, did you print this?'

Henry nodded. 'I was trying to do what you said, Da. After Colin died I didn't want any more to do with the Ribbonmen. It was so shocking.'

Bea gave a choked cry and Henry tried to reach for her hand. 'I'm sorry, Bea, and I'm sorry, Da, that I didn't listen to you. I was angry. I wanted to do something.'

'I know,' soothed Da.

'Then I thought I could do what you said – fight with words – but Kyle had to mess things up by setting fire to that image of Lord Cardswell.'

Da seemed to swallow a great lump in his throat. He ruffled Henry's hair and couldn't speak.

'Where did you get the ink and the paper?' asked Ma.

'I walked to Dublin, to the offices of *The Nation* newspaper. The men there wanted to help. They couldn't believe a place as small as Ballysmaragaid might have a newspaper and said what a fine thing it was.'

Da smiled but there was not time to stay pleased.

'Things are bad, Da,' Henry went on. 'I'd heard talk but then I saw it for myself. Ships are leaving Ireland on every tide carrying enough food for everyone. While we are starving, the best food in the world, all grown and made in Ireland – flour, wheat, beef, the best bacon and butter – is all going to England day after day. I saw enough corn for thousands of starving Irish but it's all being sold abroad. People are starving when there is plenty of food.'

Ma and Da looked at each other and both shook their heads.

'I'm sorry, Da, for the trouble, but the people need to know the truth,' Henry mumbled.

'Indeed they do, son, indeed they do,' agreed Da softly, but I saw that Henry was asleep.

An owl hooted and the moon shone down on us. We had no house to go to and no food to eat. Ma reached for Da's hand. The cut on his face was deep, and for the first time I thought they both looked as frightened as I felt.

CHAPTER EIGHT

It was dark in the woods but no one dared move.

'What shall we do?' whispered Bea.

I looked at my sister, my two brothers and my wonderful da and ma. I still had Uncle Niall's letter in my pocket. I pulled it out.

'I think we should all go to Oregon in America,' I said, suddenly very sure of what we needed to do. 'To be with Uncle Niall . . . and those pigs that run around. I've got the map.'

Da looked exhausted but he smiled. 'Wouldn't that be grand . . .'

'Do we have to stay here?' asked Toby, his unusually loud voice echoing in the woods.

'Ssh!' hissed Bea, looking around, frightened.

Ma clutched her shawl around her shoulders and turned to leave.

'Where are you going?' Da asked.

'Up to the manor,' she said quietly.

'They'll not be there,' he replied. 'Besides, we promised each other that we'd never ask for help.'

'I know, but this is bigger than us, Patrick. The blight is not your fault. There was nothing you could do. Maybe I can get a message to my father. We can't stay here. The police will take us, and Aedan and Eimear too.'

I was confused and I was not the only one.

'Your father?' queried Bea. 'What do you mean, your father? I didn't know you had a father.'

'Don't be stupid, Bea. Everyone has a father sometime,' snorted Toby.

'I know that,' she snapped, irritated, 'but no one has ever mentioned him.'

'Is he nice?' asked Toby, suddenly interested. 'My friend Callum has a grandfather and he gets sweets from him.'

132

'Where is he?' I asked. 'Is he alive?'

'Why don't you see him?' persisted Bea.

'Can we meet him?' asked Toby.

I thought Ma was going to tell us, but in the end she just shook her head and said, 'It's best that you children don't know.'

She pulled her shawl tight around herself as she and Da exchanged a glance. 'I'll go now,' she said quietly.

'Let me come,' pleaded Da. 'I don't want you out on your own.'

Ma shook her head and smiled at him. 'A man out at this time of night looks like trouble, but if a woman is seen on the road they'll not pay much attention.'

Da was beside himself. 'Beatrice then?'

Again Ma shook her head. 'No, I'll not have her out when Parker is searching for our blood and, for all I know, half crazed with drink.' She looked at me. 'Slim can come. I'll take Slim. Bea, you look after your brothers.'

I wasn't at all sure about going with Ma. I wasn't afraid but I was pretty confident the woman I had accidentally thrown a fish at would not be pleased to see me again. I didn't know whether to tell Ma or not but thought perhaps she had had enough surprises for one evening.

We headed off through the woods. We walked for about half an hour. Ma seemed surprisingly certain of the way. When at last we came out of the woods we stood on the large open space in front of the grand house. It was just as I remembered it, except that now dozens of candles shone in each of the windows. Ma didn't stop for a moment. She walked up the stone steps, past the fine columns, and without speaking she opened the huge front door.

A giant doorknocker of brass shaped like an angry lion's head stared down at me.

'Shouldn't we knock?' I whispered, but Ma was already inside, striding across the black and white tiles of the giant room inside. Without a single hesitation she moved towards a pair of large oak doors and opened them. A man in a dark suit appeared behind us and startled me. I was certain we were about to be in dreadful trouble.

'Excuse me,' he began furiously, but then stopped as Ma turned to him. 'Oh, Miss Margaret,' he stammered.

'Good evening, Michael,' she said as if it were the most natural thing in the world to be in this grand place.

What was going on? How did this stranger know Ma's name? Why was he not angry that we had just marched in without asking?

'We weren't expecting you,' he replied, looking flustered.

'I expect not,' replied Ma. 'I want to—'

'Margaret! Is that you? I knew you'd come. I knew it. I said to . . . Come in here,' a voice shouted from inside the dark room.

I peered in and could just make out an old man sitting in a chair by the fire. I couldn't be certain, but I thought it was the man from the garden when

I had had my unfortunate fish incident. I tried to conceal myself behind a large ticking clock.

'Wait here, Slim,' said Ma, moving into the room.

I stayed hidden but stuck my head out just enough to watch her walk in. The room had a vast fireplace and the coals in it were lit. I realized how long it had been since I had seen a fire burning bright! How nice to sit there, I thought.

I don't think the old man saw me. He waved a walking stick in the air and shouted, 'That will be all, Michael.'

The man in the suit, who must have been Michael, bowed and disappeared back where he had come from. Ma moved towards the old fellow. She was about to speak when, instead, she gave a little cry. A woman about Ma's age had been sitting near the old man. It was the one from the garden. Now she got up and moved to Ma. They hugged and smiled enough to make me wonder what was going on.

'Oh, Margaret, I have missed you,' said the woman, holding Ma tight.

'Esther!' declared Ma.

'Finally come to your senses, have you?' barked the old man. I stayed where I was, afraid to move.

Ma turned and closed the door. I tried to hear what was happening but the door was too thick.

The room where I was waiting was bigger than our whole house, but it was odd because no one seemed to live in it. Giant wooden stairs rose up to a second floor, and I thought for a minute about climbing up to see what was there. I wanted to see the rooms where people slept alone with linen on the beds but I didn't dare. Maybe the man called Michael had gone up there and would be cross if I followed. I wasn't at all sure if it was his house or the old man's.

I don't know how long I waited. Maybe half an hour. I stayed by the clock. It was made of dark, shiny wood and ticked in a steady and loud beat. I could feel the pulse against my arm. Da had taught me to tell time but I was too fascinated by the house to pay attention. It was late, I know that. It had all been very exciting and I was tired. The rhythm of the clock filled my head and I was just beginning to feel sleepy when the door to the fireplace room burst open and Ma came out. She seemed upset. The woman called Esther ran after her.

'Margaret! Wait!'

Ma stopped. 'Oh, Esther, it's no use. He won't listen. I didn't know he would be here . . . or you. I thought you were in England. I'm not really sure why I came.'

Esther took Ma's hands. 'I know you don't believe it but he worries about you.'

'He has a strange way of showing it.'

I had kept quiet up until now, but I had got a cramp in my shoulder from leaning there for so long. I shifted a tiny bit and the woman called Esther turned and saw me.

Ma looked at me and held out her hand. I moved forward into the light, fearing the worst.

'Esther, this is my daughter Rosalind.'

Esther looked at me for a long while and then she put out her hand. I shook it, saying, 'They call me Slim.'

'It's a pleasure to meet you,' she replied with a slight smile, and I knew then that she was going to keep our secret. Who was she? Why did Ma know her so well?

Esther turned her attention back to my mother. 'You know he always has to have his own way. He was so angry when you married Patrick. He's a stubborn old fool and he won't rest till you do what he says. Can't you find a way?'

'I love my husband and I'll not leave him,' said Ma.

'Is it true? Is the house torn down?' asked Esther.

'I haven't seen it but Slim here says—'

I nodded. 'I saw him. Mr Crossingham. He had the roof down and was burning everything.'

Esther sighed. 'He never forgave you, Peggy.'

Ma nodded, and for a moment I thought she was going to cry. I could see how exhausted she was.

'Do as Father says,' begged Esther.

Ma shook her head. 'I have a family who depend on me.'

'But what will happen to you?'

I was confused and not at all sure what was happening, but I didn't like the pitying way this woman looked at us.

'We shall be fine.' Ma held her head up. 'Please don't worry. We . . .' She took my hand and squeezed it. 'We shall go to America.'

'America?' said Esther in amazement.

'Yes.' Ma began to sound more certain. 'It's Slim's idea actually and she's quite right. It's a wonderful place. Full of opportunity. We shall go to . . .'

'Oregon,' I added helpfully.

'Yes.'

I was thrilled. It had never occurred to me that we might actually go.

'Esther, come back here this instant,' insisted the old man from beside the fire.

'Meet me in the garden. In our old place,' whispered Esther, and hurried away.

Ma and I left the house. The tall trees hid the moon, but she moved as if she knew exactly where she was going. I didn't know what was going on. Who were these people and how did they know Ma? Down some steps and along a path we came to a small wooden house open on two sides. Ma stepped inside and sat down on a small bench. It was clear that she did not wish to speak so we sat silently. At last we heard a noise on the path and Esther appeared.

'Here – take this.' She produced a small velvet bag with a drawstring, and a wicker basket of food. 'It's all I have.'

Ma hesitated and Esther pushed the bag into her hands. 'You're as stubborn as he is. Take the money, Margaret, and go. You should've left long ago. You married the man; now go with him. Go to America like the child says. Make a new life. There is nothing for you here.'

'Esther!'

Esther smiled. 'I'm jealous, you know. You gave up everything for the man you love while I am still just the same.'

'Come with us,' urged Ma.

Esther shook her head. 'He won't manage without me.'

Ma hugged her. 'You'll always be in my heart.'

'And you in mine.'

Esther turned to me, and offered the basket of food. As I took it she smiled and stroked my cheek. 'Rosalind . . . sorry, Slim – look after your mother.'

'I will,' I said.

I followed Ma out of the garden with a million questions running in my head. 'Who is she, Ma?'

'We don't have time now, Slim,' she replied. 'We must get back to the others.'

'But how do you know her? Was that your father? Is she your sister? Did you live there, in the grand house?' I had so many questions that they all came out in a jumble.

Ma was half running now. 'Soon, Slim – I'll tell you everything soon,' was all the answer I got. 'We have to hurry.'

I don't know what Ma and Da talked about that night. We slept in the woods, and at one point I heard Da say, 'But I must say goodbye to Aedan. He's my brother,'

Ma was very clear. 'No, Patrick, that's why we must just go. If he doesn't know, then he can't get into more trouble.' She sighed and said, 'I can't believe our foolishness.'

Da stroked her belly and, smiling, replied, 'Nothing foolish about it.'

We were all awake before the sun was up. Da was just coming back through the woods. In his hand he held a square piece of soil with grass on it. He held it out to Ma.

'It's turf from our place, Margaret. I cut it out to

take with us. A piece of Ireland to take to America. One day we shall plant it in our new American garden to remind us of home.'

Ma nodded and took the piece of soil. She wrapped it in a handkerchief, placed it in her bag and then, as if it were just another day, she nodded to us all to step forward onto the road to Dublin.

CHAPTER NINE

I'm sure we were quite a sight. Henry's eye was bad. He had a bandage of cloth torn from the bottom of Ma's skirt wound around the right side of his head. We were all filthy from our night in the woods, but Toby led us out with a spring in his step. I think he was even more excited than me about what was happening. As soon as Ma and I got back to the woods she had announced her decision and Toby had started whooping with excitement.

'Ssh!' we all whispered in unison. 'Keep quiet!'

Toby had managed to settle down but I could see it was hard.

Since he'd fetched water in Da's hat he had taken to wearing it. Now he marched along in the giant hat like a tiny man leading a parade.

Bea was the most worried and upset. 'But we've said goodbye to no one,' she kept saying.

'I know, Bea,' Ma would soothe, 'but we have no choice.'

Bea bit her lip to stop her tears. 'I'll not stay,' she said determinedly. 'I shall come back. I shall come back to Ireland.'

'There's nothing to come back for,' replied Henry quietly.

Before we set off Ma had taken the food and hidden it all about us. The basket from Esther had bread, cheese and sausage in it, but Ma didn't want anyone else to know.

'You know how your stomach aches for food and your body hurts?' she said. We all nodded. 'Well, everyone feels like that and they're not thinking properly. I don't want anyone hurting you because they want your food.'

Ma walked with Beatrice and Da. He pushed Uncle Aedan's cart with the printing press on it. Can you believe it? All that trouble it had caused – and do you know what's even more extraordinary? It was Ma who insisted we bring it with us.

'You're right as always, Margaret,' said Da as he pushed the heavy machine along. 'If we can't help make Ireland a nation, then we shall just have to do our best with America.'

'We *are* going to America, aren't we, Da?' I kept asking because I couldn't believe it. It's all very well to dream about something amazing but now it was actually happening.

'That we are, Slim, that we are,' he agreed for the hundredth time. The cut on his face had a great scab on it now. Under his breath he muttered, '*Dia linn*,' and I knew it was serious. Da was not at all religious, but *Dia linn* was 'God be with us' in Irish.

We were not the only ones who had decided to leave. All along the road to Dublin there were people walking away from their homes, trying to escape. You knew they were hungry like us because we all looked the same, our faces a sort of pale yellow.

The children looked very small, like tiny old people made of nothing but bones. By the side of the road we saw whole families who had stopped and given up. They had almost no clothes and just lay down to die.

We walked past four children with a grown-up so ruined by hunger that I couldn't tell if it was a woman or a man. Around their lips I saw a strange band of green.

'Ma, why do they have green stains on their mouths?' I wondered aloud.

'Shush!' she replied.

It was Henry who answered. He had seen it before. 'They've been eating grass. They'll die soon.'

The grass-fed children moaned as we left them behind. It was hard to bear.

On the way there was nowhere to sleep but the ditches by the road. Everywhere we walked, houses were being torn to the ground. You could hear the wail of cats as they too cried out for something to eat or someone to feed them. We walked on, often seeing carts full of grain, butter and bacon heading for Dublin. Great herds of cattle, sheep and pigs trotted past us and all the other people on the road who were starving.

'I told you,' muttered Henry. 'Plenty of food.'

We walked along silently. My bare feet were so caked in dirt they seemed to have doubled in size. We passed a whole village where the fields were now just graves. It was terrible, but still people kept walking towards Dublin. Those who could make it to the sea had nothing left to keep them in Ireland. All anyone could think of was what lay ahead, of America and a new life; a 'life of plenty', so they said.

I don't know how far it was. I know that we walked for two days and that we wouldn't have managed it without the basket of food from the woman called Esther.

'I'm hungry,' complained Toby, so we hid to eat.

The first time we stopped behind a stone wall we could hardly believe what Da was cutting up for us. The most beautiful piece of sausage – and we got a slice each! It probably sounds silly, but I was so hungry I couldn't eat mine at first. I had spent so many hours imagining food that when it was in front of me I could hardly put it in my mouth. Bea hated having food when others had none. It made her cry. We would all have liked to share it but we barely had enough for ourselves.

'Who is Esther?' asked Bea.

I thought Ma wouldn't say but finally she replied so softly that I hardly heard. 'She's my sister.'

'Why do we not know her?' asked Toby. 'We know Da's brother. Maybe they'd like each other.'

Ma smiled. 'I'm sure they would.' And then she told us the story of how she and Da had met and fallen in love.

'Before I became Margaret Hannigan my name was Cardswell.'

'Like the manor house?' I gasped.

Ma nodded. 'Yes, like the manor house. I lived there when I was a little girl with my sister, Esther, and my father, Lord Cardswell.'

None of us could believe what we were hearing.

Henry was shocked. 'Are you English?' he asked.

Ma nodded and he looked away.

'One day, when I was sixteen, a young man came to call. He was poor but he carried some books under his arm, and on his face he wore the world's most beautiful smile.' Ma smiled at Da and he took her hand and kissed it. 'He was offering teaching lessons with "free stories on the side". My father liked him and invited him in. I was in the hall when he arrived. "This is Patrick Hannigan," my father told me. Your da nodded at me and smiled, and in that moment I lost my heart for ever. He began to teach me and Esther all manner of wonderful things. Soon he was coming every day and I knew I would never love another. Despite my father liking your da, he did not think him suitable to marry. He was too poor, he was Irish and he was never going to be anything but a dreamer.'

Da took up the story. 'One day Lord Cardswell

told me not to come to the house again, but it was too late. Your mother and I could not be parted, so we ran away and got married the very next day. Foolish woman, I offered her nothing but a slice of the moon and my heart.'

Bea shook her head as if she couldn't really understand. 'You could have had a fine house and a carriage and all the lovely gowns you wanted?' she asked, amazed.

Ma looked at her. 'Beatrice, none of those things are what make anyone happy.'

'Why did you never tell us?' I asked.

She smiled. 'I didn't want you wishing for a life you could never have.' She looked at all of us and spoke more seriously than I had ever heard her before. 'Never settle for anything other than true love. Be guided by your passions and you won't go wrong. Your da and I may have had very little, but we have been rich just the same. Now let's be off.'

And with that she stood up, brushed down her skirt and headed back out onto the road. Da let out a whistle of appreciation as she walked away, and she looked over her shoulder and laughed at him. It is how I will always remember her.

I think the story made Bea angry. She watched Ma walk away and almost shouted, 'How could anyone give up such a life to live in a small stone house in the woods?'

Da took her by both shoulders and looked into her eyes. 'But, my darling girl, you wouldn't be here at all if your ma had stayed where she was.'

Bea shook him away and began grumpily to carry on walking. I felt sorry for her. Though the trip was hard, my feet were tough from all my time in the woods but Bea had been home more and soon her feet began to bleed. Toby stopped marching. Sometimes he begged to be allowed to ride on the cart but it was heavy enough already, which made Bea even crosser.

'I don't know why we had to bring that machine. It's caused enough trouble. If Henry hadn't used it we would never have had to leave. I hate it.'

Ma had been right about hiding the food. One afternoon, not far from the city, we were crossing a small bridge over a stream. Henry was disobeying Ma and chewing on a small piece of bread. Suddenly a man appeared from beneath the crossing. He was more a pile of rags than a man but he leaped at Henry to get the bread. Henry, his right eye still bandaged, never saw him coming. The man knocked him down, and in a flash Da did something I'd never seen before. He ran over to the fellow and punched him clean on the jaw. The man fell to the ground. Da picked Henry up and recovered his bread from the ground. We walked on in silence.

It was only later that night that Da said, 'I was wrong, Henry. Sometimes you do have to fight.'

CHAPTER TEN

D ublin. It's Irish for 'black pool'. Da told me that they called it that because the black waters of the River Liffey flow from the Wicklow mountains down through the city. What a place it was. I had never seen anything like it. We were a few days at Dublin and I wish I had paid more attention. Now I don't suppose I will ever go there again. What I do remember is that there were ships everywhere.

'Look at that!' gasped Toby as we arrived. He pointed at the giant wooden vessels with three tall masts which crowded the harbour. 'There must be three hundred or more of . . . what do they call them, Henry?'

How Henry loved Toby asking him a question, thinking he knew things because he had been before. Even though he was in pain my big brother puffed his chest out and explained, 'Those are square-rigged sailing ships, Toby.'

'Where are they going?' I asked Da, not wanting Henry to get too grand.

'Every corner of the world, Slim, every corner.' Da smiled.

'I don't care about every corner of the Earth. I just want one corner here so I can sit down,' moaned Bea, who had had enough of walking.

'Soon, very soon,' soothed Ma as Da led the way with our creaking cart.

At last we were crossing the cobbled stones of Custom House Quay. The water lapped at the edge of the huge grey-stoned building. I wasn't sure what 'custom' was, but there must have been a lot of it for the Custom House was even bigger than the manor house; Cardswell Manor would have looked like a cottage beside it.

Everywhere there were people standing in queues, some more than half a mile long.

'What are they waiting for? Is it food?' asked Toby, rather hoping there might be some more.

Da shook his head. 'Tickets,' he explained. 'Tickets for a ship to America.'

Everyone was desperate and ran to get in a queue, any queue, as soon as there was even a rumour of tickets being sold. Agents who worked for the shipping lines swarmed around, making money from desperate people. It was cheaper to go to Canada, but as Da said, that country was still ruled by Britain. If we were going to live somewhere new then we might as well be free. While Ma tried to get food and Da tickets, I was left to guard the printing press.

While we were on the road Da and Henry had already started discussing plans for an Oregon newspaper.

'I think we should call it the *Portland Press*,' declared Da.

'Do you not think we need the word "Irish" in it?' asked Henry. 'Do we not want to help the Irish who have arrived?'

'We do, but not just them. All manner of people will be wanting a paper.'

I wondered who they might be. I wondered how I could help. 'Could I write a story about us?' I asked.

'What do you mean?' said Da.

'This journey,' I said, pointing to the road ahead. 'About what's happened – the police, the house, everything.'

'That's a marvellous idea!'

'It isn't. It's stupid. It's never going to happen,' grumbled Bea.

I stood thinking about writing such a story while I kept an eye on my little brother. Toby had found a fishing line abandoned on the dock and was busy dangling it into the water. The sun glinted off the small waves in the harbour. I looked out to sea. America was out there some-where. I thought America was going to be the answer to all our prayers but the truth is, even with the starving all around, if we had known then what troubles lay ahead we might never have gone.

There were no steamships to America then, just big ships with huge sails waiting for the wind to take them where they needed to go. Almost everyone at the docks wanted to make money so there were a million ways to spend what you had. Everywhere there were advertisements for all manner of things which it was claimed we absolutely *had* to have for the journey – tin plates and cups, suitcases and even special undergarments were all being sold.

'Get your teeth sorted before you set to sea!' shouted a man who seemed to have nothing to do the sorting with but a chair and a pair of dreadful-looking pliers.

'Holloway's Pills and Ointment' seemed to be recommended to cure everything from headaches to liver trouble. They appeared to be a miracle in a bottle. Not only could they sort something simple like a sore throat – but also something complicated called 'dropsical swellings'. I wasn't even sure where such things might appear on your body.

'Ma, Ma.' I pulled at her sleeve as we walked. 'We need to get some of those pills so we can mend Da's cheek and Henry's side,' I insisted.

She smiled at me. 'The cheapest pot is a shilling. We shall just have to make do with what we have. It's too much money to spend.'

'What about the money in the velvet bag?' I asked.

I realized that no one else knew about the bag when Toby's eyes widened and he exclaimed, 'Did your sister give you money as well?'

Ma nodded. 'Yes, your Da has it. It's how we'll get to America.'

At last we found a corner on the steps of the Custom House and we all sat down, exhausted. For a while we none of us did anything except watch what was going on around us. There were so many people and so much noise as everyone pushed and shoved, eager to be off. No one, it seemed, could leave Ireland fast enough and everywhere men were doing what they could to make money. There was a man with a red woollen cap in a row boat who just rowed about all day. You might think he was wasting his time, but there was often an awful scramble to get aboard one of the big ships and people dropped their luggage straight into the water. Well, the rowing man would collect it quick as you like and then wouldn't give it back without being paid first.

A man beside us had already got his tickets but he couldn't read and wasn't even certain what he had bought. 'Do you read?' he asked Da.

Da nodded and looked at the tickets. 'You're going to Canada,' he explained.

The man smiled. 'Good. I have cousins in Canada.'

It didn't take long for the man to tell others about Da's reading, and within half an hour of us arriving people were queuing up, offering him a few pennies to help them with their papers.

Da didn't want the money.

'Don't be ridiculous, Da,' exploded Henry. 'Take the money. We're going to need it.'

We all went silent and I thought they were going to start arguing again.

'Reading is something you should give for free,' insisted Da. 'It's a gift. It's the very thing we shall bring to America – the possibility of books and newspapers, of information.'

'And stories,' Toby reminded him.

'And stories,' he agreed.

Beatrice had had enough. 'You're the one who is ridiculous, Henry. If it weren't for you we wouldn't be in this mess.'

He looked at our sister and then hung his head. 'It's true and I'm sorry. I was trying to help.'

Da patted his hand. 'We all know that, son.'

Ma looked at us all. We were filthy and tired but we were safe. I know that both she and Da were relieved to have got away. 'We're together, that's all that matters,' she said quietly.

In the end Da *did* take the money. He didn't like

it but Ma said they would need to save every penny for the trip ahead. It turned out that it was expensive to go to Oregon. Someone had a pamphlet showing all the things you might need to get there, and Ma kept shaking her head about the journey ahead.

'I don't see why we can't go somewhere closer,' she kept saying, but Uncle Niall was in Oregon and now that we were started towards him nothing was going to stop Da meeting up with his brother. Ma managed to buy some bread and cheese, which was wonderful as the food in the basket had long since run out.

We slept on those steps, sheltered by the arcade of huge stone columns. Da had been to look at a boarding house, but people were charging what they liked even to let you sleep in a cellar. Ma laid out blankets on the marble floor and said, 'Why, it's like a palace,' as if she meant it.

Da smiled at her. 'I should have done better for you, Margaret.'

Ma looked tired but she smiled. 'You have given

me love, Patrick, and our beautiful children, and that will do me.' She reached for his hand and squeezed it, saying, 'I have no regrets and I will always be grateful.'

Toby loved the Custom House. There were lots of other boys his age waiting to leave and they all bounced about playing games. He had been very quiet since Hamlet left us and I know Ma was pleased to see him looking happier.

Above our heads huge stone figures looked down at us.

'You see that?' Da pointed to one of the statues as we lay down to sleep. I looked up at a man carrying what looked like a large fork.

'That is Neptune himself,' he explained, 'the Roman god of the sea, with that giant fork called a trident, which he uses to chase away Famine and Despair.'

Chasing away famine sounded like a very good thing indeed.

It wasn't easy to get any rest. The place was

heaving with people. There were gangs of men unloading cargo from ships which were newly arrived, and there was a never-ending stream of men, women and children carrying what little they had who made their way down to the water night and day. Ma said everyone needed to be careful and mind their money. The minute new people arrived, usually exhausted from their long walk, men known as 'runners' would race towards them. They'd grab whatever bags the people might have, pulling them towards shipping brokers and boarding houses. Sometimes they would grab some poor soul's luggage and not give it back until they paid a dreadful lot of money for their 'service'. Everything was expensive and everyone had advice about how to spend your money.

'Where are you off to?' asked a sailor whom Da had helped fill in a form.

'America,' he replied.

'I'm just back from there,' said the man. 'You mind you don't get "dollared". They take your Irish money and don't give you enough American dollars in return. Happens all the time.'

Even at night the cobblestones on the quay rang with the sound of horses' hoofs and creaking cart-wheels and shouts of men in a hurry.

Da shook his head in wonder. 'I tell you, Slim, if America didn't exist someone would have to invent it. Look at all these people.'

From Dublin and Donegal, from Sligo, Galway and Limerick, from Waterford and Wexford, New Ross, Belfast, Londonderry and Cork, from Tralee, Drogheda, Newry, Kilrush, Westport and Youghal hundreds of people were arriving, all heading for the sea to go to America.

'Why are there so many?' I asked Da.

'The landlords want rid of them,' he explained. 'It costs about seven pounds a year to keep someone in the poorhouse but only half that to send them to America for good.'

The next morning Da begin queuing up to buy

tickets. It wasn't easy. As soon as the departure of a ship was announced there was a great stampede of people desperate to buy a passage. Da tried over and over again without luck. We were there at least three days before he had any success. At last one of the great wooden sailing ships, with three huge masts, arrived at the docks and word went out that she was to sail for New York on the next tide. She was called the *Pegasus*. Da was delighted and ran to join the queue. I ran after him.

'That's the one for us,' he shouted to me, clapping his hands with pleasure. 'Do you know about Pegasus, Slim?'

'Do you mean the ship?' I asked. I knew nothing about ships at all. I'd never even seen the sea before.

Da shook his head. 'No, the winged horse. The ship is named after the great winged horse of ancient Greece. Have I never mentioned him to you?'

I shook my head and he looked appalled.

'Well, what have I been thinking all these years?'

167

he exclaimed. 'You, twelve years old, and Pegasus has never come up. I'm a disgrace as a father.'

Da was supposed to be fighting for tickets like everyone else, but instead he sat straight down on the ground to tell me the story. The crowd had been pushing each other, eager to hand over their money, but Da had a way of getting people to listen.

'Shall I tell you a tale?' he began, and as he spoke the queue calmed and soon everyone had forgotten about their place as they turned to hear him speak.

'Well, Pegasus, he was pure white, that horse. As white as your eyes in the night. But he had something no other horse has ever had, before or since – he had wings. Great white wings which, when they were unfolded, could fly him above the highest mountains in the world as easy as if he were walking.' Da stretched his arms out wide as if he might fly himself.

Then he stopped for a moment to look up at a man standing next to him. 'Do they have mountains in Greece?' he asked. The man seemed about to answer, but Da was off again, answering his own question.

'Of course they do. They have Mount Olympus, which is so lovely that the gods all live there. Now this horse – well, he sorted himself out because his parents weren't great. His father lived in the sea and his mother had snakes in her hair and we've all known a woman like that . . . Well, you can imagine his ma and da didn't really get on, but nevertheless Pegasus, like yourself, Slim' – Da looked at me and smiled – 'he grew up to be a marvel.'

He got to his feet. He was so full of his story now that no one around him could help but listen. Now Da drew me with him as he walked backwards along the queue.

'Why, Pegasus could fly through the sky, and it was that very horse who brought us lightning and thunder from Mount Olympus itself.' Da raised his arms to the sky as if to call down a little lightning himself. 'He's the soaring symbol of wisdom and poetry, which can often be the same thing.' Da whirred round, explaining to everyone.

'This is a great day! Why, to have the privilege of riding in a ship called *Pegasus* all the way to America is like taking to the back of a white winged horse sent by the gods themselves to deliver us to our new home! Nothing, I tell you, nothing on this earth could be luckier!'

Da threw his hands in the air in triumph, and everyone who had heard the story cheered. How they needed to hear something good after the horrors they had all seen. It was to the sound of those cheers that Da found himself at the head of the queue and, a few minutes later, holding his hand aloft with six tickets to America.

We pushed through the crowds to get back to Ma with our great prize.

'Was that true, Da? Is it really good luck to travel in a ship called the *Pegasus*?' I asked breathlessly, trying to keep up as he half ran in his excitement.

He turned and winked at me. 'Well, now, Slim, truth is a funny thing. The point about a tale like that is, it doesn't really matter whether it's true or not. What matters is that we want it to be true.'

CHAPTER ELEVEN

The night before we left Ireland all the grown-ups sat together on the stone steps of the Custom House. They seemed sad, and one of the women began wailing, so Da told funny stories about growing up in Ireland to cheer everyone up. One lad played the fiddle and the men drank whiskey which smelled even worse than poteen.

'It's like that wake we had for Mr O'Connor,' I whispered to Beatrice.

'That's exactly what it is, Slim,' she replied. 'We're having a wake for Ireland.' And for Colin too, I thought, for when I turned to her she was crying.

Five of the women clubbed together and bought biscuits for the children, and as I took my first bite I marvelled at how people could be starving just down the road while we sat eating. Henry gave his biscuit to Toby, who took it with delight, not realizing his older brother didn't want to be thought of as a child any more.

The next morning Ma made me take off the pair of Henry's old trousers I had worn for so long and put on a dress. I don't know where she had got them from but she had one for me, one for Bea, and a sweater for each of the boys. We didn't have much money but Ma was not having us go halfway round the world without 'making an effort'.

'You must look smart so we make a good impression when we arrive in America,' she said, smoothing my long skirt down with her hand.

I was a bit grumpy about the whole thing, so I was sitting on some steps by myself when I heard a little clinking noise. Someone had dropped a coin, a silver coin, and I watched it bounce and roll towards me. I stopped it with my foot and picked it up. There was a picture of Queen Victoria, and on the other side the words ONE SHILLING. It was a shilling. A whole shilling. I had never held such a fortune in my hand. I knew I shouldn't keep it. It belonged to one of the many people sitting singing beside me, but which one? I looked at all the men's faces, but no one seemed to be worrying about a coin. I closed my fist around it. Now, I thought, now I could get that medicine, the Holloway's Pills that solved everything. I put the coin deep in my pocket and went to sleep.

In the morning I was heading off to get my pills but I got distracted by Toby playing the fool, and the next thing I knew there wasn't time.

'Slim! We're off!' cried Da, all excited.

'But I—' I tried, but he grabbed my hand and began to pull me with him.

'Come along! We're off! Off to America!'

It did sound wonderful.

It was May 1847 and I remember the moment we stepped off Ireland. We had to climb a wooden gangplank that led from the dock up to the deck. Everyone was pushing and shoving to get the best space on board. People seemed to be climbing over each other in a kind of muddle but Da wouldn't rush. I put one foot on the wooden plank and he stopped me, placing a hand on my shoulder.

'Take a minute, Slim. That's the last touch of Ireland beneath your foot.' He turned me to face him. 'Remember where you came from, my darling girl. A people who don't have a knowledge of their past is like a tree without roots. This was your home. The place that made you. Take time to say goodbye.'

A man behind Da had been about to shove him out of the way, but he heard what my father said and stopped too. I saw him swallow hard, trying not to cry.

Da began to sing in Irish,

'*Siúil, siúil, siúil a rún
Siúil go socair agus siúil go ciúin
Siúil go doras agus éalaigh liom
Is go dté tú mo mhúirn'n slán.*'

One by one everyone around us joined in:

'Go, go, go, *my love,*
Go quietly and peacefully,
Go to the door and flee with me,
And may you go safely, my dear.'

And it was to the sound of raised Irish voices
that I stepped off the land where I was born.

The truth is, I was too excited about what lay
ahead to think too much about what we were saying
goodbye to. My heart was thumping with the new-
ness of everything. Everything was unfamiliar – even
the smell, which was like something heavy filling
your nose. A mixture of old wood, rope and something sticky called tar.

I think we were about a hundred passengers on
the boat, maybe a few more – it seemed like a lot.
And there were a dozen or so men to sail the thing.
It wasn't big for the number of people, but I thought it
would be fine. We were used to a small space.

The crew were shouting instructions as we boarded. 'Find your berth. One per family,' yelled a man in navy trousers and matching sweater.

'Where?' asked Beatrice, who hated the noise and didn't want to be there at all.

'Down below!' He pointed down some steep stairs to the dark belly of the ship. We were to live on what we quickly learned was known as the 'tween deck, a low deck between the upper deck out in the open and the hold below in the dark, where all the food and luggage was stored. Just like everyone else, the captain was making money and we were to travel in no greater comfort than the slaves from Africa who had gone to America before us. I don't know how Da persuaded the sailors to lift the heavy press onto the boat, but lift it they did. Perhaps he had told more stories. Whatever he had done the printing machine, still in the cart that Uncle Aedan had once used for charcoal, made its way onto the ship and under a cover on the deck.

As soon as the press had arrived Toby had

unexpectedly become concerned in a way that we hadn't seen before. Up until then he had been having a nice time, playing with the other little boys who were leaving and excited about the idea of sailing anywhere.

'I don't think we should take Da's printing machine with us,' he suddenly kept saying. 'I think we should leave it behind.' He really became very anxious, pulling on Da's sleeve. 'Please, Da, you have to leave it behind.'

More and more people were coming aboard, and with each fresh arrival Toby became more and more anxious – until at last he broke down sobbing. 'Please, Da!'

Da picked him up and held him. 'What is it, Toby? What's the matter?'

He could hardly speak for crying. 'There's . . . too . . . m-m-many people,' he finally managed to say. 'The m-m-machine is really heavy and we'll s-s-s-sink!'

Da took him to chat with one of the crew, who

explained that the ship was made of sturdy stuff and wasn't going to end up under the waves.

'Don't you worry, my lad,' he said. 'I've a very fierce wife here in Dublin and she would be furious with me if I drowned, so I won't take the risk.'

We made our way 'below'. All the passengers were in together. The berths were made up of bunks of rough wood, one lower and one higher, each about six foot square. They were built into the ship's timbers on either side of the hold, with a gangway down the middle. Ma, Da, Bea, me and Toby were all in one lower bunk.

Bea stood looking at it. 'I don't see how we'll all fit,' she said crossly.

'I want to sleep with Ma,' said Toby, who was feeling better.

'Ma will want to sleep next to Da,' I said.

'I don't see why,' said Toby. 'She does that all the time.'

I didn't like the dark or the smell of the boat. It was a heavy scent which cut the back of the throat.

There were no windows or portholes on the 'tween deck. Nothing to let the air in. The only light came from the hatch above the steep ladder leading to the top deck.

'All right, Slim?' asked Ma.

'It's too dark,' I replied.

She reached into her bag and pulled out a candle. 'Not to worry – we'll light a candle and soon have it cosy.'

'No candles!' screamed a sailor from above. 'No fire at all below. Captain's orders.'

'Well' – Ma shrugged, putting the candle away again – 'at least the dark means we can't see how filthy everything is.'

'She's an old ship and I've met Captain Walker,' explained Da. 'I don't get the impression he's a man to worry about cleaning either himself or his ship.'

The place was still filthy from the tobacco and cotton the crew had brought back from New York, and probably still had dirt from the last set of people who had made their way to America. The bunks had mattresses which had once been filled with straw, but great rips in the fabric meant a lot of the stuffing had fallen to the floor. Ma patched what she could and spread out a blanket for us to lie on.

'It will have to do,' she said, and for the first time I thought she didn't sound as if she believed it herself.

The ceiling was so low that Da banged his head as he stood up. At the far end of the sleeping deck a cow gave a low moo. There were a few animals on their way with us. They were to provide milk and they seemed to have as much sleeping space as we did.

'Well,' said Da, smiling and rubbing his head, 'we shall just have to stay on deck in the fresh air till we see the blessed sight of America.'

I wondered if they would let me sleep on the deck.

Henry was the only one of our family not in the lower bunk – there wasn't room, so he had a place above us, sharing with three brothers called Byrne who had come from somewhere near the Wicklow mountains. They had lost their parents to the famine and now they were off to America to buy a farm. The oldest brother, Sean, was a serious fellow who acted like he was the father. He was forever minding the manners of his younger brothers.

'Liam, get out of the way of the lady,' he scolded as Bea tried to get past. 'We're to a place called Sonoma in California,' he told Da.

The youngest, Liam, grinned. 'My brother has some wild notion about growing fruit.'

'You may laugh,' said Sean seriously, 'but I'm telling you, grapes are going to be the thing.'

I had never even heard of grapes. Mostly what I remember about the Byrne boys is that they all itched something chronic. You could hear them all night scratching away at their skin. Liam had scabs and sores all over his arms and legs from the trouble. Ma wanted Henry to sleep somewhere else but there was no more room. Every inch was packed with people.

We climbed up the steep ladder to the deck. Ma was struggling and holding her belly. Da turned to help her up.

'What will it be like, Da?' asked Toby. 'America?'

'Like?' exclaimed Da. 'Why, it's a place of wonder like no other on earth. We shall know when we are near, for there are so many fish in the sea you can just reach your hand out and pull one from the water. Pigeons roost by the thousands in trees; so many that when they take off, they darken the sky like night suddenly falling. There are wild turkeys so fat that when you shoot them they fall to the ground and their skin bursts open for you to help yourself. There are strawberries so high a horse would stain its knees red just tramping through them.'

Everyone around Da smiled at the thought of so much wonder and silently congratulated themselves on their excellent decision to go to such a place.

'Prepare to cast off!' called Captain Walker.

The captain was small and slightly lame, with a

huge pair of white whiskers which almost hid the lower part of his face. He wore wire spectacles and a large black coat with wide lapels and shiny buttons. His white shirt wasn't at all clean and he wore a peaked cap. Despite his small size, his voice was loud and he boomed out orders to his men. Everywhere sailors were pulling ropes and heaving sails up as the *Pegasus* prepared to leave.

Everyone was looking at the land. Toby and I realized that no one was paying attention to us so we snuck off to explore. Apart from the steps down to the 'tween deck there was another set at the front of the ship, which I later learned was called the bow. No one was about so Toby and I crept down to have a look. We found a wonderful cabin with windows looking out to the harbour. The room was about ten feet square, with a low ceiling relieved by a skylight. The ceiling was covered in charts rolled up and held by tapes to the beams. On another hook was a small bag with the captain's spectacles, rule, pencil and compass. Below was a berth concealed from view by flowery curtains with a white cotton fringe. Opposite was a table with a decanter and an old prayer book, and above, on two brass hooks, was a dangerous-looking gun which Da told me later was called a blunderbuss. To me it was like a cave of wonders, for to one side there were narrow shelves with jars of sugar, preserves, bottled porter, spices and other foodstuffs, and in a small recess stood a crock of butter, a small cheese and a little keg of fish called sprats. This was the sort of food I had dreamed of in the worst days of the hunger. Perhaps all this plenty had come from America.

I was moving closer to have a look when Toby called out, 'Look, a bird!' He pointed to a rusty cage which swung from a hook in the skylight. Inside was a bright yellow bird.

'Maybe it can sing! Or speak!' wondered Toby as we crept up to it.

It was then that someone appeared behind us saying, 'You shouldn't be in here.'

I turned to find a giant person behind us. He was

the size of two men and he more than filled the doorway. His head was huge and seemed the wrong shape. He had the most enormous jaw, and his whole body was so firm it could've been made by Uncle Aedan in the forge. He stood with his giant hands hanging down by his sides and his whole body stooped forward. When I first saw him I thought he was one of those people with dark skin I had heard about, but as I looked closer I saw that he was covered in soot. He wore a red flannel shirt and loose blue trousers which had probably always been too short for his long legs.

'Aren't you vast!' exclaimed Toby without thinking.

'Who are you?' asked the giant.

I pulled Toby behind me so he wouldn't get into trouble.

'I'm Slim Hannigan and this is my brother Toby. We're going to America. Who are you?'

The huge fellow took his time before replying. 'I'm Jack. I'm the cabin boy.'

'You don't look like a boy,' commented Toby, who didn't appear to have noticed that we might be in trouble.

Jack nodded and announced with some pride, 'I'm fifteen.'

He was the same age as Henry but twice the size.

'This is the captain's cabin. You shouldn't be in here,' he repeated.

'We wanted to see the bird,' I explained.

'It's a canary.' Suddenly Jack smiled. It was a lovely smile and you could see he was nice. I smiled back. He looked at the bird and said softly, 'I like the canary. She's called Norma.'

We all nodded in agreement. We all liked the bird.

'You have to go.'

'You're in the way,' I said, pointing to the door.

He grinned and moved.

We climbed back up on to the deck, with Jack following. The next moment he received an order from Captain Walker and he was off to work. He was astonishing. Despite his size he could climb the rigging as if it were a flat road. I never met anyone stronger than Jack. His job seemed to be to do all the work no one else liked the look of, and on that trip I soon got used to seeing a flash of red above as he leaped about the ropes from sail to sail.

The wings of this *Pegasus* were actually sails the size of houses, and the sailors clambered about getting ready to release them to the wind. A small steamboat was tied to the front of the ship, ready to pull us out into the open water. All the passengers tried to get to the rail to say one last goodbye. The wooden deck was packed with people, tripping over the dozens of bags and barrels that still hadn't been taken below. Small babies played below the long skirts of the women, who pulled their shawls tight over their heads as if the wind blew already. There were people of all ages – some so old that to my young eye they looked as though they shouldn't be going anywhere but the grave.

A great black belch of steam came up from the small boat, which was ready to pull us away from the harbour. It made dark clouds in the bright blue sky. There were a lot of people on the land watching us go. The huge thick ropes holding us to the dock were about to be let go when there was a commotion on the dock. A group of six men on horseback rode violently towards the *Pegasus*, not worrying about the crowd of onlookers in their way. A woman screamed as she pulled her child out of the way, while a man tripped and fell into the water trying to avoid them.

'Stay the ship!' called a man in a black cloak.

'Don't let them slip!' called another, who seemed to be a policeman.

In that moment I think all the Hannigan family knew who it was. Parker Crossingham leaped from his horse and, with a flash of scarlet from the lining of his cloak, ran towards the man on the dock, who was about to let the final rope go that held us to Ireland.

Ma gave a sharp intake of breath and put her hand over her mouth in horror. 'He wants Henry,' she gasped.

Crossingham was quick, and we thought for a moment that he would manage to hold *Pegasus* back, but it was too late. The rope slipped from the land and as if we were indeed carried by a magical winged horse, we were away. Away to America.

CHAPTER TWELVE

Crossingham stood there, black as thunder against the light grey of the Custom House, and looked straight at us. He shook his fist in fury, but now that we were under way the crowd took over, the men on the land raised their hats and the women began waving white handkerchiefs. You could hear a long and loud 'Farewell!' from the crowd, and the passengers all shouted back and waved. Now some of those on the dock began to wail and wring their hands with sadness at saying goodbye for ever. They moved forward, and soon Parker Crossingham was lost in the great swell of people.

Da put his arm around Ma, who had tears streaming down her face. He called out to the land:

'Roll on, thou dark and deep blue ocean, roll!
Ten thousand fleets sweep over thee in vain;
Man marks the earth with ruin – his control
Stops with the shore; – upon the watery plain.'

I looked at Ma and smiled at her, but it was Toby who pointed out the obvious to all of us.

'Ma, how is it that we've all been starving for so long and I've lost my belly but you have a new one?'

I looked at Ma and noticed that she did indeed have a large belly. How odd, I thought, that we were always hungry and yet her stomach was growing. I knew she often gave us her own meal so I couldn't think how that had happened.

Da ruffled his hair. 'Shall we tell them, Peggy?' he asked Ma. She nodded.

'There's a new Hannigan on the way,' he said proudly.

I think of all of us, I was the most appalled, but I decided that now wasn't the right time to say anything.

The topsails were let loose and billowed out. It wasn't long before the wind took the great canvas sheets and we were heading north with the lovely land of my birth on our left. I think Ma and Da would have been sadder than they seemed, but they were very shaken by Crossingham's unexpected appearance. The thought of Henry being arrested was so frightening that they couldn't wait to get as far away as possible.

We watched the shore for ages, with the sailors pointing out the mountains of Mourne, purple and deep blue in the distance. The sea was calm and everyone began to settle down to life on board. We said goodbye to land at some place called Malin Head, and turned to face the great Atlantic Ocean and the weeks of travel that lay ahead.

The mate, a man called John, who seemed to be in charge when Captain Walker was not, was holding up a strange quarter-circle of brass called a quadrant. It had a sort of eyehole through which he checked the sun and the shadows to send us in the right direction. The water ahead looked so wide and empty; I hoped he knew what he was doing.

Jack, the cabin boy, handed out food. It was all kept in sacks on the deck below where we slept and was given out each day – a pound of meal for all the grown-ups, half a pound for those under fourteen and a third for those under seven. Jack was slow and careful as measuring gave him a headache.

Each family had to do their own cooking at fires on the foredeck. You'd think it might be dangerous cooking at an open fire on a wooden ship, but there were two of them, each contained within a large wooden case lined with bricks, with the coals held back by two or three iron bars at the front. The fires quickly became the place where people spent their time, and the talk was all about the New World we were heading for.

'I'm to California,' declared one man, and Da would shake his head.

'Not for me. That's for gamblers and risk-takers.'

'And grapes!' I added thinking about the Byrne brothers.

Da smiled at me. 'I'm a family man,' he continued, 'We're off to Oregon, and when we get there, we are promised one square mile of land almost for free. Can you imagine such a thing? Imagine how many potatoes you could grow.'

The man who thought California best lowered his voice as he warned, 'I hear tell Oregon is swarming with wild Indians who try to kill anyone who dares to enter their land. They have an axe called a tommyhawk and they like nothing better than taking the top of your head clean off as a souvenir.'

Just when it looked like an argument might happen over the benefits of Oregon or California, Da laughed. 'Well, now, wouldn't that be an adventure, to meet an Indian? I tell you, I don't think it matters which place we choose. I think they both sound a wonderful spot where dreams can come true.'

Toby was terrified of any talk of Indians, but I loved those stories. I remember I got into terrible trouble for teasing Toby by sneaking up behind him, pretending to be a crazy, wild Indian about to take his scalp.

'Stop that hollering,' Ma called, but I think she was secretly pleased that at least two of her children were behaving normally. The same was not true of Henry or Beatrice. Both were very quiet; Henry hardly spoke at all. He would lie in his bunk staring at the ceiling as the ship lurched further and further away from home.

We started to get to know the others on the boat. There was a Mrs Kavanagh who had a new baby. Mrs Kavanagh looked no older than our Bea. Both she and her little one cried a lot. There didn't seem to be a Mr Kavanagh, for she was all alone. Perhaps he had died. No one liked to ask. Mrs Kavanagh kept to herself. She was pretty, with a lovely blue dress and a straw hat with a matching blue ribbon. It looked expensive, so it was hard to understand what she was doing down in the hold with all of us.

'Can I get you anything, Mrs Kavanagh?' I would ask.

'A little hot water in a cup, Slim, if it's no trouble,' she would reply as she tried to stop her tears. She spoke carefully, like Ma, with the same sort of accent. 'I've no skill with babies,' she would weep, and Ma would lend a hand. They liked each other, I'm sure of it.

On the bunk opposite us was Mr Hughes, a great brute of a man. He was good looking except that his face had lots of little marks from the pox, which was a sickness no one wanted to catch.

'I'm a carpenter,' he announced to Da, and nearly crushed my poor father's hand with his huge handshake. 'This is my wife, Mrs Hughes.'

His wife was tiny – not much bigger than me. Everyone on board was thin but – and I don't mean to be unkind – Mrs Hughes looked worse than anyone. There was so little of her that her long dress hung from her tiny bones as if she were nothing but a peg.

'And these are my girls, Louise and Leann.'

The girls were twins. They must have been about four years old and as alike as two shamrocks by the road. Next to Mr Hughes, Mrs Hughes and the children looked like a doll collection. She was the most cheerful woman you ever saw, with a smile in her eyes, she was always beaming at everyone.

'Isn't this delightful!' she would say about pretty much everything.

I think she was in shock. Like so many she had lost family to the famine – her father and mother and brother.

'Forced from our home,' boomed Mr Hughes, 'but at least that pig of a landlord paid for everything. The whole journey. Just wanted shot of us.'

Mrs Hughes nodded in agreement and said, still smiling, 'He appeared with the tickets on Friday morning.'

'Do you mean yesterday?' asked Ma, amazed.

Mrs Hughes nodded again. 'I know. Isn't it delightful? One morning you think you're going to clean the house and the next you're off to America.'

'Do you have a plan?' asked Da.

Mr and Mrs Hughes looked at each other blankly at the thought of a plan.

'No,' whispered Mrs Hughes, looking at the floor. 'No plan, and I've not enough clothes for the girls.'

'I expect you haven't had time for a plan,' I suggested.

'We're not at all worried,' declared Mr Hughes, even though his wife looked terrified. He put his giant arm around her tiny body as if she were a glass he might drink from. 'We shall make our fortune in the New World, make no mistake,' he assured us.

Mr Hughes was not one for reading, so he was also certain that America had streets made of gold and that the journey across the sea would take no more than a week. He wasn't a man to disagree with. Mr Hughes also didn't like to wait, and some-times he pushed ahead of everyone so his wife could make him a hot drink. Da said it wasn't worth the trouble to ask him to wait. Whatever was happening you could always rely on hearing Mr and Mrs Hughes say, 'It is a piece of luck, so it is, coming away from Ireland like this.' They repeated it to each other over and over as if that would make it true.

'It must be hard to have come away with nothing,' said Ma, sympathizing with Mrs Hughes. They were kind words because we had almost nothing as well.

I had my box with Uncle Niall's letter and the map in it; Da had his knife and coat in which he was pleased to find in a pocket a book of Shakespeare; Ma had her shawl and her piece of Irish turf wrapped in a cloth. Beatrice had brought a book of her drawings and a pencil and she would spend hours imagining new wardrobes for herself. Toby wore Da's hat, and Henry? I don't think Henry had anything.

Time passed with everyone just trying to manage the basics. There was always someone at the fires making a 'stirabout' or trying to bake cakes on anything they could make into a griddle. It was a good thing that we were all so hungry because I don't think the food was very good. There was some strange mess of water, barley, rye and peas, and a biscuit, hard as a rock, which the Byrne brothers called 'blahs' and the sailors said was a 'pantile'. The only way you could eat these biscuits was to put them in a canvas bag, pound them with an iron pin and mix them with water. Sometimes the sailors baked them, and then they were known as a 'dandy-funk'. Sounds all right, but the truth is they were full of maggots and every other kind of insect, and for the first few days I couldn't make myself eat them. Odd that you can be starving and fussy at the same time. I wasn't alone. There were two pigs on board and they refused the biscuit as well. The sailors had coffee, I think, but we had water. It tasted terrible but we were glad of it all the same.

Mrs Kavanagh didn't seem to know anything about making food so Ma spent time teaching her the basics.

'You'll have to learn,' she said. 'Did you not cook at home?'

Mrs Kavanagh shook her head.

'Where are you heading?' Ma asked gently.

'I have a sister in California,' she replied.

'And the rest of your family?'

'They . . . they . . .' Tears fell down Mrs Kavanagh's face.

'Not happy about the baby, were they?' soothed Ma. 'Ah, well, more fool them. She's a beautiful baby. Now, you'll not get to California, either of you, if you can't cook. When I married Mr Hannigan I had no idea, but I quickly learned. So . . .'

While Ma gave cooking lessons I started chatting a fair bit with Jack, the cabin boy. Well, probably I did most of the chatting as he was a boy of few words. When he wasn't working he liked to stand at the back of the ship – the stern, it was called – and watch the white foamy water rush away behind us. It was nice. I used to stand at the railings with him holding onto the polished wood as we steamed on.

Jack was from Liverpool in England. He had signed on with the *Pegasus* when he was fourteen and had already been to America twice.

'What's it like?' I asked excitedly.

He shook his head. 'Don't know.'

'Don't know?' I repeated.

'Stayed on the ship.'

'Why?'

Jack looked away from me. 'Too scared,' he muttered.

I showed him my wooden box and the map inside.

'Oregon,' he repeated when I told where we were going. 'I know about Oregon,' and he went to get a most beautiful piece of wood to show me.

'From Oregon,' he said carefully as he handed it to me.

I never saw anything like that piece of wood. It

wasn't just one solid bit but lots of small, intricate pieces which made a beautiful pattern. It was about six inches long and four inches wide, like a sort of wooden brick. On one side the carpenter who had made it had managed to create a delicate picture of a small group of green trees with great wide brown trunks. The trees stood by a river and a man.

Jack pointed to the picture. 'My da,' he said with certainty.

The rest of the wood was decorated with a repeated pattern of tiny squares in half a dozen different types of wood. It was the most complicated and beautiful thing I had ever seen.

Holding the brick in his hands, Jack declared, 'This box is my treasure. From my da.'

I looked at the piece of wood and wasn't sure what he was talking about. It didn't look at all like a box. There was no lid, no way of opening it. I took it down below to show Da, and Jack followed me.

'It looks Chinese,' my father said.

Henry stirred himself enough to have a look over the edge of his bunk. He took it in both hands and turned it over and over. 'It's not a box, it's just a piece of wood,' he announced.

Jack shook his head. 'It's a box,' he assured my brother.

'But how do you open it?' asked Henry.

'It's a trick.'

'Show me,' insisted Henry.

Jack refused. 'In Oregon. Make my fortune in Oregon.'

Henry didn't believe him, but our da said maybe it was a magic box. He had heard of such things. So we left it at that.

Jack and I went back to our posts at the back of the ship.

'You think the box is magic?' he asked after a while.

'I don't know,' I replied. 'But one thing's for sure. If you want to find out and go to Oregon, you will have to get off the ship.'

It didn't take long to settle down to life on board the *Pegasus*. Mostly we lay about on the deck, where Da often told stories out loud. I think hardly anyone could read so they liked to hear his tales.

'They're just a slice of the moon,' Da would say before he started, and soon that's what people would ask for – a slice of the moon. The sailors would sit with their legs straight out, wearing a strange thimble on the ball of the thumb fastened by a leather strap as they mended sails with coarse needles and long threads. They always seemed to be busy tarring ropes or fixing things but they loved to listen, just like the rest of us.

The boys seemed to have nothing better to do than tease each other. The youngest Byrne brother, Liam, the one who itched the most – he was about seventeen, I think – had a battered old top hat which he wore night and day. Toby, still in Da's hat, admired it very much. It was considered great sport by all the boys to capture such a fine topper, and one day, during a bit of rough wrestling, it blew into the water. Liam took it well and found a blue and white striped nightcap from somewhere which he seemed to wear with equal pleasure. Everyone knew he was sweet on Bea. He was always hanging about trying to have a word with her or fetching her hot water before she even knew she wanted some. For the first part of the journey Bea always sat by herself. She wasn't the least bit interested in Liam or anyone. In fact I think his niceness made her cross and sometimes she was quite rude to him.

'Don't you have something better to do?' she would snap as he fetched her a blanket to keep her warm on deck.

He shook his head and his brothers laughed. 'Liam the lover boy!' they called out.

It made Bea blush. I thought it was stupid and that people ought to have better things to do!

The truth is, Bea was still too sad to pay Liam much attention. She hardly spoke. What with Henry lying silent in his bunk and Bea keeping her own company on deck, I think Ma and Da had a difficult time.

'Tell me about one of those glorious dresses you might one day wear,' Da would try, but she wouldn't even be drawn on that. She would shake her head and not reply. I know she wanted to go back to Ireland and every mile we travelled further away made her more sad. At night we lay packed so tight in our bunk that you couldn't tell which were your own arms and legs, and I could hear her crying.

One morning Ma had had enough. She didn't often get cross, but when she did no one had any choice but to listen. She insisted Henry get up and that Bea sit with the family while we all had breakfast on deck. We had been sitting in silence when Ma suddenly stood up and declared, 'That will do, all of you. We're in this together, Hannigans, and soon we'll be welcoming another member of the family. I think it would be very nice when your brother or sister turns up that everyone at least try to look a little bit pleased. Imagine arriving in this world to all your miserable faces. The baby will cry for days.'

The thought made me laugh and once I started I couldn't stop. Bea tried not to smile but she couldn't help herself and then Henry joined in. It was a funny idea – a baby arriving to a miserable family – and soon we were all laughing. It was a lovely sound.

We were just finishing our meal when the ship gave a little lurch and the cloth covering the printing press fell off, revealing the marvellous machine. Lots of people gathered round and Liam Byrne wanted to know how it worked. Bea would have nothing to do with it, but for the first time Henry seemed interested in what was happening.

Da started to explain about the ink and the letters, but then he looked at Henry, saying, 'Actually, my son knows. He has printed fine papers on this machine. He has printed words intended to stir the heart.'

I could see Henry swell with pride as the crowd parted to let him through. Even Bea reluctantly smiled to see him so pleased to hear Da's praise.

'This wonderful machine,' began Henry, 'was made

by my father and my uncle Aedan, and it is going to America to help change the world. On it we shall print fine newspapers with the information that people need to make a great democracy. With this machine we shall help make a country where all men will be equal.'

'And women!' I shouted, and everyone laughed.

Henry showed how you had to lay out all the tiny metal letters in the big box in a special order so that they were easy to find. Then you thought of the sentence you wanted to write and found each letter, plus strips of plain metal for the spaces between the words. These were all put together in a row, and then you made your next sentence in the same way. Finally it was all screwed tight in a large frame to put into the press itself. Jack loved it, and although his hands were large he began practising every day. We had no paper or ink, but he and I would spend hours pretending that we were printing. What wonderful stories we imagined flying off our magic machine!

After that Henry seemed a little better. I saw him and Da talking again, and was pleased. The breeze that had pushed us up the channel left us, and soon the crew were kept busy doing something called 'tacking'. It was hard work as it involved the ship turning one way and then the other to try and get wind in the sails. We zigzagged across the ocean for days. You would hear Captain Walker call out, ''Bout ship!' – and round we'd go. The rolling of the ship made a few people feel unwell and the bunks became busier during the day. Liam Byrne had the sickness worse than anyone. He could hardly move from his bunk.

Mr Hughes didn't like the tacking. It made him think we were going the wrong way. 'I don't understand it,' he said to Da. 'Sun sets in the west. America is in the west then why are we running away from the sun as hard as we can?'

In the distance we could see other ships heading the same way. Da said they came from Liverpool in

England, where Jack was from, and somewhere called Aberystwyth.

Captain Walker was a touch grumpy and didn't seem to want any company. He drew a line on the wood to stop passengers going on to the afterdeck. He was serious because the penalty was stoppage of a whole day's water. Da said maybe we should all vote for someone to be in charge, so everyone chose Mr Hughes, who looked big enough to deal with anything. He kept order, making the boys behave and stopping men from smoking below. A quarrel was soon settled if Mr Hughes had a word. He liked being in charge.

I liked to be on deck. I thought the sea was the most wonderful thing I had ever seen, even better than I had imagined that day in the woods with Da. There was always something new to look at. No wonder Raleigh, the potato man, had wanted to be an explorer. One day, when the sails were still and Captain Walker kept muttering about 'being becalmed', I saw a creature on the surface of the flat water which seemed to have a tiny sail on its back. The sun was setting and it was almost pink in the light.

Suddenly Jack was standing beside me. I never heard him come up. Even though he was huge he moved silently about the place. 'Portuguese man-of-war,' he said slowly, as if he wasn't sure about talking at all. 'Long way north. Must've drifted.'

'How incredible to have your own sails to take you to America,' I said.

Jack looked at me and then looked back at the creature in the sea. He nodded. He had been at sea since he was Toby's age, but I think it had never occurred to him that having your own sails might be nice.

Henry started to seek out Jack's company too. His right eye was no better and it was clear he would never see from it again. The Byrne brothers teased him about it, and it made him a bit crazy. I think we all realized that just because he and Da were speaking again, it didn't mean Henry wasn't suddenly going to be good. He knew he had got us all into trouble, but that didn't suddenly make him a transformed character. He started daring himself to do dangerous things, as if to prove that being blind in one eye wasn't going to stop him doing as he pleased. Ma thought it was the blow to the head that had made him foolish. He had been left with blinding head-aches which appeared out of the blue and left him weak and tired.

Despite them, he got Jack to teach him how to climb the rigging and he often went out onto the bowsprit. This was a fat wooden pole which stuck out from the front of the ship. It held the edge of one of the triangular sails out over the ocean. It was a dangerous and silly place to be. Da would call him back and give Henry a good shake but I think we all knew Henry was never going to do exactly as he was told.

When the sun shone people could get fresh air, wash their clothing, clean themselves and cook their food. The journey was not too bad then, but when the weather turned it was awful. The first time that the clouds darkened and Captain Walker said a big storm was coming, I remember he frightened us all by saying that there was nothing to do but 'lower all the sails and trust to God'.

As the weather got worse, he refused to allow anyone on deck. We were all sent down to our bunks. He even covered the hatch with a giant piece of canvas so that we passed our day in complete darkness. You could hear people praying and crying as the heaving waves tore at the old ship. The wooden boards of the *Pegasus* were made waterproof by something called 'caulking', which meant putting the sticky tar you could smell everywhere in the gaps between them. It was fine in good weather, but when the sea became rough it had a strange effect. Sometimes a space between two planks closed up suddenly and without any warning. I remember Mrs Kavanagh was lying on her bunk when it happened. Her long skirt caught as the planks closed together all of a sudden. She lay trapped like that for hours until the ship went over the other way.

You had to watch for the boat suddenly turning round. Someone as light as myself could be tossed straight over to the other side of the hold if you didn't hang on.

Ma held Mrs Kavanagh's baby while she lay there, unable to move. Da said the baby was 'a sweet little thing', but I just thought it annoying.

'Do you not like babies, Slim?' asked Ma.

'Not at all,' I replied.

Ma smiled but she looked sad. I wish I had never said it. It was a stupid thing to say as I knew a baby was coming. I should have been more cheerful, but the truth is, I was a bit jealous of the baby already. It was hard enough getting Ma's attention with three brothers and sisters. Now there were going to be four and I wasn't at all sure Ma would have any time for me.

After the planks released Mrs Kavanagh she refused to sleep in her dress again. She lay in her bloomers and undershirt, saying, 'I'd rather the men see my underwear than ever get caught like that again.'

Bea had never seen such fine garments. They were trimmed with lace and made of the softest cotton. 'Imagine having such finery to wear under your clothes where no one can see them!' she whispered to Ma.

'I suspect Mrs Kavanagh's clothes tell a story,' Ma whispered back. 'I suspect she was once richer than she is now.' Just like Ma, I thought.

We were all together in the hold for some days and it was scary. I remember one dreadful moment when some planks parted and water rushed into the lower deck. Everyone screamed and I know we all thought the *Pegasus* would go down to the bottom of the sea. She righted herself again, but now there were several feet of sea water on deck. Two of the bunks fell down and no one could do anything to fix them. Our feet became too damp to ever dry out, and because we were all together all day, everyone got lice. We all itched and no one could cook. All the meals got wet from the damp weather and nothing could be heated up. In one quick break in the rain Mr Hughes led a cooking party, but the captain soon had the fires put out. Jack threw a bucket of water on them from the rigging and the men descended into the hold half blinded by steam with all the supper burned on the outside and raw in the middle.

Mr Hughes's little wife hated the dark, and after two days of no light, she had had enough. 'I can't stand it. I can't stand it,' she kept repeating.

Both her little girls were crying. 'I hate the dark. Light a candle, Ma, please,' they begged.

I slept on the edge of our bunk and I was lying there next to Ma, Da, Bea and Toby one night. They had all managed to fall asleep, but I was being pressed against the wooden side and kept waking up. Just like everyone else, I was frightened and the darkness made it worse. As I lay there I heard a noise: I couldn't be sure but I thought it was Mrs Hughes searching for something. Suddenly I heard her strike a match, and in the tiny flash of light I saw that she had stuck the candle between two boards.

'No, Mrs Hughes,' I whispered urgently. 'You mustn't. Captain Walker said no candles. No candles at all down below.'

Mr Hughes sat up beside his wife. 'Are you telling my wife what to do?' he demanded.

'No, I . . .' It was very difficult. Mr Hughes was in charge and I didn't feel I could go against him. I lay back down as Mrs Hughes lit the candle; it flared into life. It was nice. The pale yellow light flickered and it really was better than lying in the dark. It was scary down below in the bad weather and the candle made things seem less frightening. I could now see the boards that were making such terrible creaking noises and I was less afraid.

I don't know how long we lay there with the light burning. The ship twisted and turned, and then suddenly it gave one of those sudden movements which you could never predict. I had just closed my eyes to sleep when the jerking movement made me sit up and I saw the boards holding the candle part and let it loose. The white wax light shot from its place and flew across the deck. You would have thought every-thing was too damp to catch fire, but the candle landed on the hem of a dress hanging from a bunk. It didn't seem to take even a moment for a blaze to begin.

'Da! Da!' I called.

Mrs Hughes looked horrified but she didn't move. The fire spread so fast that it took a moment for everyone to understand what was happening.

Smoke began to billow from the flames as Da jumped up from the bunk. 'Henry!' he called. 'Peggy, get the children out.'

There was a terrible scramble as everyone pushed for the deck. Ma slipped and fell against the steps as people tried to get past her into the fresh air. Bea and I got her up. Toby was crying and the noise from everyone shouting was terrible. Da and Mr Hughes raced to the deck shouting, 'Fire!'

Jack appeared and, seeing what was happening, ran to fetch buckets. Captain Walker raced out of his cabin in his nightgown and was soon organizing a line of people to pass buckets of sea water to douse the fire. Once the blaze was put out there was a dreadful silence.

The captain strode over to us. He looked slightly comical in his nightgown and nightcap, but there was nothing funny about his voice. He was very angry. 'Who was responsible for this?' he demanded. 'Who?'

No one wanted to say. I didn't know if everyone knew that it was Mrs Hughes, but Mr Hughes was not someone anyone wanted to go against. I thought she should have told the truth but she just looked out to sea as if it were nothing to do with her. Mr Hughes put his arm around her and stared at me to make sure I kept quiet. The captain went back to bed in a terrible temper and we all went below to see the damage. The smell was terrible. It cut the back of your throat. Sadly it was Mrs Kavanagh whose dress had been burned and now she had almost nothing to wear. The women gave her what they could and she ended up dressed in a jumble of clothes, none of which looked quite right.

Mr Hughes had burned his hand badly, and once order had been restored Da went to see if the captain had any medicine in his cabin. I slipped along behind him because I wanted to see the yellow bird again.

When we went in Captain Walker noticed me looking at it. 'Do you like my bird?' he asked. I nodded. 'It's called—'

'Norma,' I said without thinking.

The captain frowned. 'How did you know that?'

I thought I was going to get into trouble, but Da distracted him. 'Ah, surely Norma from the great opera by Bellini?'

Captain Walker looked surprised. 'Yes – how did you know?'

'It had to be. I was invited to a grand house once and heard someone sing it. So wonderful. When she pleads to the goddess of the moon for peace . . .' Da turned to me. 'You should hear it one day, my darling Slim.' He put out both hands as if to plead to the moon and said quietly,

'Pure Goddess, whose silver covers
These sacred ancient plants,
we turn to your lovely face
unclouded and without veil . . .'

He looked almost tearful. 'I've never seen it but I believe the moment she prepares to leap into the flames at the end is very affecting.'

The captain nodded and swallowed hard. 'My wife loved it. We saw it in London. Just the once, but she never forgot it.'

'Beautiful,' said Da as if he had come to see the captain to talk about nothing else.

Captain Walker gave a great sigh and stared at his bird. Not looking at either of us, he asked, 'Can I do something for you, Mr Hannigan?'

'Do you have any ointment for a burn?' Da asked.

The captain shook his head. 'Not for the passengers. Crew only.'

Da nodded his head in agreement. 'I see the point

223

of that, but it's for Mr Hughes. I've had a look and the injury is quite bad. I think it will get infected if we don't sort it, and then he won't be able to help keep order. No good for you, Captain. No good at all.'

The captain thought about this and, still looking at Norma, pointed to a box of medicines which Da picked up. He smiled at me and we left.

Da took it on deck and looked through it with Ma. '*Castor oil, Epsom salts, hartshorn . . .*' he read out from the labels on the jars. 'Where are the instructions? This is incomprehensible.' He looked at all the medicines and sighed. 'It's ridiculous. We have all this stuff and no idea how to use any of it.' He turned to me and said, 'This, Slim, is why people need printing. They need information.'

'We shouldn't use medicine we don't know,' said Ma, checking the bottles. 'We'll use the old remedies.'

She got a cloth soaked in some vinegar and tied it to Mr Hughes's hand. It seemed to help, or at least the pain didn't get any worse. He could barely bring himself to say thank you but he was a bit nicer to us all. After that everyone seemed to think Ma and Da knew about healing and went to them for every little sore or headache. Ma did know a lot of ways to make people better and she started writing some of them down. Those who could write began copying out her words to take with them on their journey.

'You see, Henry,' Da enthused, 'if we could just get printing, this is just the sort of thing that would be fantastic to give out.'

Liam Byrne was better but as soon as the seasickness was gone, two of the women in the furthest bunks became ill with some kind of fever. It was odd and sudden. Ma gave them flour porridge with a few drops of something called laudanum, which helped them to sleep. When they were awake they kept calling out for more water. That was when the next problem was discovered. The drinking water was kept in wooden barrels on the lowest deck, but several of them had leaked.

The water wasn't good anyway. Captain Walker

had bought the barrels cheap from a man who had used them to store wine. It meant the water tasted terrible – bitter and muddy. I know Da and the mate, John, talked about improving it somehow – with charcoal, I think – but some of it was too far gone. John pumped out the water from one of the casks and it looked like the stuff from the ditches outside Dublin where people had died.

Now more passengers were becoming ill. Eight people lay in their beds, six with the strange fever and two with something called dysentery, which made them want what we called the *leithreas* or chamber pot the whole time. There was nothing more than buckets to use and only sea water to wash with. I had never been one to worry about being clean, but even I was uncomfortable. The salt in the water dried in a sort of crust on the skin and made me itch.

One man lay in his bed moaning and calling, 'Beef and wine, I need beef and wine for a cure.'

Well, he might as well have asked for a slice of the moon.

226

The food too had spoiled. One day the mate opened a provisions box to find the ham inside alive with maggots. He had no choice but to throw it overboard, and even then we looked at it with longing. I had quickly got past thinking that maggots might stop you eating anything.

Mr Hughes's hand was very painful and I think it didn't make him easy to deal with. When his wife got sick he became very angry and went to the captain. 'I need more food and water for my wife and children,' he demanded.

'You have your rations,' he was told.

Mr Hughes raised his voice and said he would break into the hold where the food was kept and take it for himself. The captain stared at him. Then he turned and went into his cabin. I thought maybe he was going to get that keg of sprats and the cheese I knew he had, but instead he came back carrying the old blunderbuss. Without another word he pointed the gun just above Mr Hughes's head and fired. Well, it was like a cannon going off and everyone dived onto the deck. I landed on an old piece of sailcloth next to Mrs Kavanagh and neither one of us moved for a while. When I finally looked up I saw Henry and Toby crouched down behind a barrel and Liam Byrne grinning. I couldn't think what there was to be happy about until I noticed he had his arm around Bea and was enjoying every minute. She suddenly realized what was happening and shook him off. After that there was grumbling, but no one dared challenge the captain again. A small hole in one of the sails reminded everyone not to ask him too many questions.

More people wanted laudanum to sleep, but Ma knew there wasn't much. 'We need to use it only when necessary,' she said, firmly refusing to give it out to just anyone.

Meanwhile the *Pegasus* was making very slow progress across the sea. Da said the wind was not on our side and the captain announced there would be even less water given out every day.

'The journey is going to take longer than expected,' he announced, 'so you will use sea water for cooking,' which made everything taste horrible.

One day little Mrs Hughes and I were standing at the back of the boat, watching the water move slowly away from us. We hadn't seen land for days and days, and all around us there was nothing but the biggest amount of water anyone has ever seen all in one place. Mrs Hughes knew that I hadn't told on her about the candle and since then had taken to spending time with me. I took her to show her my favourite place on the boat. It was wonderful to stand there. You never knew what you might see. All sorts of creatures lived in the ocean. Sometimes you saw a dolphin break through the water or flying fish that seemed to dance on the surface. That day we saw a great beast of a thing following the boat, looming in and out of the surface. It was a great, grey thing, abo ut twelve foot long with a bright white underbelly. Sometimes it stayed below the surface and all you could see was a large triangular fin sticking up above the water line. Other times it lifted its head showing off a huge mouth which seemed almost fixed in a grin around rows of razor sharp teeth.

'A shark,' said one of the sailors.

Mrs Hughes put her hand to her chest and declared it was 'a forerunner of death'.

I didn't understand what that meant or how a shark might know such a thing, but I kept going back to look and it never left us all day.

That afternoon, for the first time, one of the sailors got sick and the life on the 'tween deck began to get worse. Some of the patients who had been getting better became ill again. Poor Mrs Kavanagh's baby – there wasn't enough of her to resist the illness. Bea sat with her trying to cool her with a damp cloth, but her little feet had swollen to double their normal size and were covered with the most awful black spots.

Ma and Bea did what they could and I thought everything was going to be fine but the baby, that tiny little thing, well . . . it died. It just stopped breathing and lay there all floppy like a rag doll. None of the women but most especially Mrs Kavanagh and Bea could stop crying, and that made everyone feel terrible. The captain was afraid of more people getting the fever so he told the sailors to bury her at sea straight away. I watched her tiny body drop from a plank of wood into the deep water where the shark lived. She was the first to die but she certainly wasn't the last.

CHAPTER THIRTEEN

Bea sat with Mrs Kavanagh as she sorted her baby's few things. Ma was too busy dealing with the sick. She made all of us scrub the bunks every day and shake out the lice from the blankets.

'We have to keep clean so the sickness can't take hold,' she said. She looked exhausted. Her belly was so large now that it was hard for her to move. Da kept trying to get her to lie down but she would shake her head and move to help someone else. There was a young priest on board who seemed not much older than Liam Byrne. He spent all his time praying beside the bunks of people who were sick. Everyone was so busy trying to manage that I don't think anyone even knew what day of the week it was. One day the mate John told us it was Sunday so the priest tried to get everyone to have some sort of mass. He called for everyone who could manage to come up on the deck and sing. I think we were all supposed to be Catholic but hardly anyone had the heart. I remember him reading aloud from the Bible. A few people were gathered around him, but the wind blew in the wrong direction and his words of comfort were lost in the air.

About twenty of the passengers were sick now and their relatives were too upset to think of anything else. We tried to help each other but there was one group who made Da cross. There were about eight young men who were travelling without family. None of them got sick and they didn't seem to understand how awful it all was. If anything they looked bored by all the illness around them. One evening they started singing and tried to get some of the women to dance with them. A man from Galway tried to sweep my sister Bea up into his arms but she pushed him away. He shrugged and pulled one of Mrs Hughes's little girls up to dance. I don't remember if it was Louise or Leann but she started to dance happily making everyone smile, but then she suddenly collapsed. Mrs Hughes ran to her and for a while the child just lay still as though she were dead. Then she awoke screaming terribly and writhing about in pain. It was awful to watch.

Now the illness became more and more frightening. No one knew when or who it might turn on. A woman warming a drink at the fire for her husband suddenly dropped down quite senseless and had to be carried below.

Bea was the first in our family to take to her bed. We were sitting by the fire when Ma reached out and put her hand on Bea's head.

'You look pale, Beatrice,' she said anxiously.

'I've a terrible headache,' Bea admitted, getting up to go, but as she did she fell forward and would have fainted onto the deck if Da had not caught her.

'Help me, Henry,' he called, and the two of them picked her up and carried her below.

'Ma!' cried Toby. He was frightened and ran into her arms.

She hugged. 'It's all right, Toby, stay with Slim. She'll look after you.' And she put Toby into my arms.

I didn't know what to do. I was scared too and had no idea how to look after him. I just squeezed him close and it felt odd. I didn't like the responsibility but Ma had work to do.

Bea soon had the most awful pain in her bones. Her feet began to swell and then her limbs up the body. She was covered in red and purple spots which turned into terrible sores with liquid running from them. Ma and Da were beside themselves with worry, and even Henry spent all his time fetching water for her, which he had carefully boiled to make it safe. Water was what everyone wanted but there was never enough to stop anyone being thirsty. All through the boat you could hear cries of 'Water – for God's sake, some water!'

Mrs Hughes's daughter recovered but she was

sick herself now. I got a headache and didn't know if it was the fever or just worrying about Bea. I didn't say anything because Ma was already so frantic with worry and I didn't want to make it worse. I remember lying in my bunk looking over at Mrs Hughes on the other side of the boat. Everywhere was filthy and it made it difficult to breathe. On the deck a layer of muck had formed so thick that you could see footprints in it. Poor Mrs Hughes's head and face were swollen so big that she seemed twice the size she usually was. I'd never seen anyone's skin so white. Mr Hughes stood beside her holding a rosary he had got from the priest. He mumbled his prayers over and over but it did no good, for the next morning she too was dead. The sailors wrapped her in canvas and lowered her into the ocean.

Mr Hughes stood looking out to sea, a daughter in each arm. As his wife's body disappeared from view he lifted his head. The rosary was still clenched in his fist and he called out to the heavens, 'By this cross, Mary, I swear to revenge your death – as soon as I earn the price of my passage home, I'll go back and shoot the man who murdered you, and that's the landlord.'

A lot of people talked about their 'landlords' and blamed them for what we were going through. I hadn't thought about ours. 'Did we have a landlord, Henry?' I asked.

'Yes,' he said. 'Lord Cardswell.'

'But wasn't he . . . I mean, isn't he . . . ?'

But Henry had no time to chat. He, Da and Liam were too busy trying to help some of those recovering to get air on deck.

My head felt confused. Lord Cardswell was the old man in the grand house, but he was Ma's father, or so I thought – so did that mean that her own father, my grandfather, had sent the terrible Parker Crossingham to . . . I tried to make sense of it all.

Those who were a little better sat on the deck, their faces yellow and withered, with terrible dark circles around their sunken eyes. Da got Toby to go round with a damp cloth to wipe the fever from them but he hated doing it. He was afraid and didn't want to touch anyone. I went with him and tried to be brave, but the truth is I was scared too and didn't like the feeling of their damp skin. None of the children played any more and Toby followed me around as Hamlet the pig had once followed him.

Even the air didn't feel healthy, for now we were surrounded by thick fog. Jack sounded a loud horn all the time in case another ship was nearby and we might hit it. How gloomy it was. We could not see, and between every blast of the foghorn you could hear the cries of the patients below. The fever made some of them quite mad and they would shout out in a crazy way.

I don't remember the order of people dying after that. It was terrible but we almost got used to it. One little girl whose parents had already gone into the ocean soon followed her mother and father, but everyone just shook their heads as they tried to carry on living. By now about half the passengers, maybe fifty people, were sick. So many had died that the sailors had run out of old sails to put the bodies in. They began sending people to their grave in two meal sacks with a weight fastened at the foot.

I couldn't bear it and tried not to think about what was happening. I sat on the floor, practising over and over putting the box of silver letters together as if I were working the printing press. Toby leaned against me, not wanting to be alone for a moment. I dreamed of helping Henry and Da with their newspaper when we got to Oregon.

When he wasn't working, Jack would sit with us as well. How he loved to sort the tiny letters with his giant hands.

'Make a story,' he would say as he held out a handful of silver.

'Once upon a time, a long time ago,' I began, and as I spoke I sorted out the letters with their spaces on the wooden deck, 'there lived a giant who had no friends.' Jack looked at me and Toby sniggered. 'He had no friends because people were foolish not to realize how nice he was.' Jack smiled as I made up a story about a giant called Jack and his friend, a small girl called Slim who found a wonderful box which, when you said the magic words 'Hard about!' opened to reveal whatever sort of food you wished for.

Jack would neaten all the letters I had laid out, and when he was done I'd get up with our finished blocks, fit them into the press and pretend to churn out page after page. Jack loved that, and would work the handle of the machine for me when it got too heavy. He wasn't one for conversation and he probably wasn't one for books, but he smiled and smiled as we pretended.

At last, when no one could manage any more, the weather turned calm and those who were able to crawled up onto the deck. They lay about in a jumble, arms twisted under and over each other, women with shawls over their heads leaning up against men, whether married or not. One old man just sat in despair, his hat pulled low over his head, his hands in prayer. Even the children were completely still.

I think everyone would have stayed that way, but the captain came up from the cabin and after looking about gave the word to 'double-reef topsail and make all snug'. I didn't know what it meant but everyone said we should get ready for bad weather. As if we hadn't had enough trouble. So many sailors had fallen sick that some of the healthy passengers now had to give a hand in the rigging. Both Toby and Henry helped, even though Toby was really too small. They climbed up with Liam Byrne, Da and Jack. How I longed for my old trousers so I could help. I was stronger than Toby but had to stand there, helpless, in my long skirt, watching the preparations and getting more and more angry.

Ma watched me, and one day she took the skirt from me. 'I need to fix that,' she said quietly. She sat on the deck with needle and thread for about an hour, and when she was done she held up a pair of trousers for me. It was so kind I wanted to weep.

I barely dared to ask, 'Do they have pockets?' Ma nodded and my happiness was complete.

Soon the sky became black again, and the rain descended in torrents. The water rose in tremendous waves and the captain sent us all below. Jack was at the wheel, the only one strong enough to hold *Pegasus* steady. I waved to him as we went down into the hold but he stared straight ahead through the falling rain. His wet hair clung to his head and his hands were white with the strain of holding the wheel.

'Good luck, Jack!' I called, but he didn't hear me.

Once more we were tossed about, one minute carried up by an angry billow, the next plunging into a deep hole. The roaring wind was drowned by the tremendous noise of thunder and lightning. The temperature dropped and we were cold.

The whole family huddled in the lower bunk and Ma pulled Mrs Kavanagh in to be with us. There was hardly room with Ma's belly but we were glad of the warmth of each other. The ship rolled from side to side as the sea swelled. The timber planks buckled and bulged, then shrieked and shuddered.

Each time we thought it must surely be the end the *Pegasus* righted herself once more. Toby was terrified and clung onto me like he would never let go.

'Slim, Slim,' he moaned, but you could hardly hear him for the sound of the sea and the cries of the other children. A mountainous wave rose up and the wind howled out his fear. The ship was propelled to the lip of a wave and then hovered there. For a brief second, time was suspended as we waited to be dropped down into the jaws of a whirlpool, where we expected to be swallowed whole in a final, terrible squeak of timber.

Just when everyone thought they could take no more, the storm died away. It was late afternoon when we were allowed to climb back up on to the deck. How odd it was after all the noise and commotion to find everything looking so calm and beautiful. The sun was setting and the orange, red and pink colours which glowed on the water made it seem as though we were gliding through a sea of liquid fire. The afternoon was clear, with a gentle breeze making a ripple on the surface of the water. Down below, calm was restored and a woman no one had even known was sick was found dead in her berth.

By morning the wind had dropped so completely that the water looked like a piece of clear green glass. You couldn't believe it was the same sea. Now everyone got on with jobs. Washing was done and soon the rigging of the ship was covered with the passengers' linen hanging out to dry. Most of it was just rags but everyone did what they could. We tried fishing with anything that could be made into a line. Padlocks and bolts were used for weights, with wire hooks made from scraps. Even with such simple gear quite a lot of fish were caught and soon my hand was cut from pulling on the line.

Everyone was so happy to have fresh food that one of the men took up a fiddle and another began to dance a jig in his long boots. He wore a light blue flannel shirt and a green scarf, and seemed so handsome and happy. Henry joined in and the two fellows tried to outdo each other with skill. Henry was not such a good dancer but he had wonderful energy and made everyone grin as he leaped about. It wasn't long before everyone was standing in a circle shouting out encouragement. Toby, who had hardly left me since Bea had fallen ill, suddenly got up and joined in. Henry grabbed his hands and my brothers tried to out-dance each other.

It was so nice until Jack suddenly tumbled to the floor. We had seen it too many times. Someone well one minute and quite senseless and apparently dead the next. Everyone liked Jack – we all knew that he had taken the wheel to get us through the storm and he was always so nice and cheerful. The mood now was terrible and my heart pounded.

The music stopped as I ran towards him. 'No! Jack! Jack!'

He didn't answer. His eyes were closed and there was no response even when I shook his giant huge shoulder. I couldn't bear it. He was my friend.

'He's too big to be sick,' I yelled as the men came to carry him below. He was so big that it took six of them to get him to his berth.

'I want to go with him,' I called, but Ma thought it wasn't right.

'We've got our lovely fish supper,' she tried, but I didn't want any. It should have been a delicious treat after weeks of biscuit and bad water, but it meant nothing to me if Jack was not there to share it.

No one said very much as they ate. Everyone was exhausted and the poor members of the crew who were still well had to work doubly hard. There was hardly any wind and they had to tack over and over again. The overworked mate seemed to be everywhere dealing with food one minute and the next stretched across a yard, reefing a topsail.

I think we all thought we had left death behind, but with incredible speed the two oldest Byrne brothers, who had had such plans, both passed away, leaving Liam in his striped nightcap to say goodbye alone. How odd that the one who had been so seasick had survived the fever. A few who had been ill again appeared on deck, weak and weary. We were all desperate for fresh water. Bea seemed a little better at last, but Ma looked exhausted from tending to her. Mrs Kavanagh just sat on her bunk not moving. She missed her baby, and sometimes rocked from side to side as if still holding her. She sat with her straw hat looking ready to leave. I remember thinking that it was a cheerful-looking thing for someone so sad.

Da sat on the edge of the bunk looking exhausted while Ma tried to see to those around her. He was not a strong man and helping the crew had tired him out. 'Surely we have been through the valley of the shadow of death,' he sighed, but it was not over yet.

Despite all her looking after so many sick, Ma had kept well. Bea was getting better and Henry, Toby and I seemed to have escaped. We itched with lice but the ship's fever had not caught us. When Ma began to let out low moans I thought she must have caught the sickness and Bea and I tried to make her comfortable. Da was helping on deck and Toby ran to fetch him. Ma clung onto my hand – I didn't know what was happening.

'Laudanum?' I shouted to Bea. 'Shall we get the laudanum?' I felt panic grip my throat at the thought of Ma being ill. She was everything to us and we couldn't manage without her.

'Bea – not Ma, not *Ma*. It can't be Ma who is ill,' I cried.

Bea shook her head while she helped Ma lie down. 'It's not the fever. It's the baby, you idiot. It's coming!'

I felt so foolish. She was having the baby. Well, I had no idea what to do. Da raced down the steps, and soon all the women who were well enough were helping. They sent Da and me back up on deck to boil water, and only Bea was allowed to stay below. Da paced up and down, listening all the while for noises from the hold. At last there was a great cry from a baby and a cheer went up on deck.

A little while later Bea appeared, smiling. 'You've to come down now,' she called.

We went down one at a time to see the new member of the Hannigan family who lay in Ma's arms. Even I thought it was quite a sweet little thing. It was a girl. I thought we probably had enough girls.

'A little sister for you, Slim,' said Ma. 'She'll look up to you.'

I looked again at the baby. That hadn't occurred to me, that she might look up to me. I gave a little smile. Perhaps I could teach her a thing or two. Maybe it wouldn't be so bad.

'Look, Peg, an American baby!' declared Da with delight.

'But we're not in America,' said Toby.

'Well, sure and we're on our way,' replied Da. 'She can't be a baby of the sea, now, can she?'

Da was practically dancing with delight. He announced to all who would listen that, as we had all been through so much, the new American

Hannigan child should be called Hero. She was the Hannigan hero. She was the hero of our great adventure.

Everyone thought this very fine, and even the captain sent down a little whiskey to wet the baby's head. I couldn't stop grinning. I don't suppose I was all that bothered about the baby but I was so happy that Ma didn't have the fever; that she was going to be all right. I saw that some of the women were whispering with Da, who looked serious, but I was too busy taking a turn to hold the baby to pay attention.

While I sat on the bunk with my new sister, Ma lay in her bunk, trying to smile at me. 'I'm sorry, Slim,' she said. 'I know you're not keen on a baby.'

I shrugged. 'It'll be fine, sure it will,' I said, trying to sound confident. I had never held a baby before and was terrified I might do something wrong.

Ma smiled as Bea took baby Hero from me. Then she took my hand and said, 'Whatever happens, Slim, you know I depend on you. I rely on you to do the right thing for the family.' She gave me a long hard look. Then she took off her Claddagh ring and slipped it onto my finger. It was too big and only fitted on my thumb.

'Remember,' she said, 'the heart is for love, the hands for friendship and the crown for loyalty.'

I wasn't sure why she was giving me her ring, but I nodded. She pulled me down to kiss me on the head.

I felt grown up then, as if she trusted me. I felt so happy – but in the night, while I was asleep, everything changed. I awoke to crying. Henry, who never cried, sat beside me sobbing and Toby was inconsolable.

Ma was dead. It was not the fever that had taken her from us, but having the baby.

'She just wasn't strong enough,' said Mrs Kavanagh, who knew all about losing the most precious thing you could imagine.

All I could think was that I should have bought some of Mr Holloway's pills. The money I had found on the Custom House steps was still in my pocket and the coin seemed to burn against my leg. Perhaps Ma had had the dropsical swellings and I could have made her better.

CHAPTER FOURTEEN

M a had done so much to help that there wasn't a soul on board who didn't gather on the deck to say goodbye. She was laid out in a meal sack and placed on the wood of one of the hatches. The priest, who had done his best for the whole journey, looked exhausted. He said a few words, but I could hardly hear him. I hurt inside worse than any hunger had ever been. Worse than any seasickness or fever could ever be. Then everyone began to sing as four of the sailors lifted her to the railings. It was an old hymn I knew well called *Be Thou My Vision*. Everyone sang in Irish, but I couldn't manage any of it.

'*Be thou my battle-shield, be thou my sword.*
Be thou my dignity, be thou my delight.

253

Be thou my shelter, be thou my stronghold.
Mayst thou raise me up to the company of
    the angels.'

I didn't want Ma to be an angel. I wanted her to come with us to America. I felt numb inside. One of the sailors turned to look at me and then dropped his head with such sadness. Henry stood beside me squeezing my hand. His poor right eye was never going to see again and a slow stream of tears fell down just the left side of his face. Bea held the new baby in one arm while the other held Toby steady. Da was asked if he wanted to say something but he shook his head. He couldn't speak. We could none of us speak. Then the men tilted the hatch and my precious mother slipped from us into the sea.

Da stood there for hours watching the spot where she had disappeared until it was too dark to see the water at all. I stayed beside him, but for the first time in my life I didn't feel I could take his hand or even touch him. Toby lay on the bunk below, sobbing in Bea's arms, while Henry went to the bow of the boat and did nothing but look ahead for sight of America.

The baby lay on the blanket on our bunk. When she began to cry, Mrs Kavanagh picked her up. 'I have milk from my own baby,' she said. She held my new sister and fed her, and I didn't understand any of it. My heart was broken. None of us knew what to do.

Da said nothing. As it got dark I moved near him. He was still standing by that wooden railing where we had said goodbye to Ma. He had his back to me so at first I didn't see that he was carving something into the wood with his big knife. I touched him on the arm, and he was so startled that he jumped, and I watched his knife fly from his hand into the water. He stared at it as if he could not bear to lose one more precious thing. Then he looked at me for a long moment and turned to go below. Without meaning to, I knew I had done a bad thing. I stared at the wooden railing and there, in a half-finished heart, were the names *Pat & Peg*, just like in our little house in Ireland. How could we go to America without Ma? I wondered. How could we ever be safe again?

I didn't dare go below and face Da so I stayed on deck until the light faded and the stars came out. It was cold and late. I went to the back of the boat but it wasn't the same without Jack. No one was paying me any attention, so even though Ma had told me not to I went to sit beside Jack as he slept in his berth.

He still had the fever and called out, 'Ma! Where are you, Ma?'

The giant boy wanted his mother and I wanted mine. I put my head on his chest and tried to cry, but no tears came. Instead I kept taking great gulps of air and shuddering. At last the rhythm of Jack's heart steadied me and I felt calmer.

I stayed all night, and when he tried to get up sweating with fever I put my hand on his and said, 'Jack, it's me, Slim. You need to lie down now.'

He seemed to know me, for he let me settle him down again. The captain came in at one point and I thought he was going to yell at me, but he nodded and let me stay.

The next morning Jack seemed a little better and I went to fetch him some water. While I waited for my turn at the kettle one of the sailors came over.

'Captain Walker wants to see you Slim,' he announced.

I was expecting trouble. The captain was not kindly except to Jack and the canary – but now he was nice to me too. Jack had served with him for three voyages and I think he was fond of him and grateful to me. He opened a locker near his berth and took out a raw egg in its shell. I hadn't seen an egg since we had left Ballysmaragaid. Captain Walker held it up to the light and tried to look through the shell to see if it was good. He shook his head. I saw that there was a small box of them in his cupboard. He put the first egg back, and then tried another and another until he found one that pleased him, which he then gave to me as a present.

I looked at the egg in my hand and thought of the one I had broken and never given to Mrs O'Connor. For the first time I wept and wept. Tears poured down my face as if I had swallowed the ocean itself.

CHAPTER FIFTEEN

We saw land long before we reached it. Ma had been gone from us a week when Toby first cried out from the rigging that he could 'see New York!' Everyone laughed because when Toby shouted it was so loud they could probably hear him across the water in the city itself. People immediately began to run to the bows to have a look. I chased after Bea and we both noticed Henry was out on the bowsprit again, dancing over the waves on the narrow piece of wood. We knew Da wasn't right because he never said a word about it.

By now almost everyone was at the front of the ship pushing and shoving for the best view of the land. Captain Walker called out for order, but it took a while for there to be calm. Every child was

259

lifted up to see New York. Liam, the remaining Byrne boy, lifted Bea high in the air with delight, and only put her down when she hit him on the head. Everyone laughed.

It was good to hear laughter but we didn't join in. My family was in too much pain. Henry stood alone out on the bowsprit while Toby clung to me. Bea held little Hero and Da stood by himself, looking at nothing. We had left as a family of six and we were still six, but the baby was no replacement for Ma. I think I hated the baby then. I looked at her and knew that her arrival had taken away Ma. It wasn't her fault but I blamed her anyway. Bea tried to make me hold Hero a little but I turned away.

We should have been happy. We had been at sea for seven terrible weeks. We had been through terrible times, frightening weather, and now at last the waters were calm, the decks level and the ship was still. How we had longed for that when we were at sea. The sky was clear and blue, the air was fresh, and everything looked so beautiful – but our hearts were heavy. Even though this was what we had journeyed for, it was hard for anyone to feel any kind of pleasure. A third of those who had left Dublin with us had died, including three of the crew.

We had got used to the wild open water of the Atlantic, but now the great ocean narrowed down to a much smaller piece of calmness. We sailed between somewhere the captain called Staten Island on the left and Brooklyn on the right. Staten Island looked nice, with lots of pretty houses, but all eyes were now on New York itself. I'd never seen anything like the size of it and even I, in all my grief, was gripped by how it looked. 'It's beautiful . . .' I whispered.

'But Ma will never see it,' said Toby.

Bea turned away. 'I never wanted to see it at all,' she muttered and hugged the baby as she went below.

Ma will never see it. The words hit me hard. We should have been excited but there was not one of us who would not have traded the whole sight of America for one more hour with Ma.

Once again we were hungry. The journey had taken too long and there was no food left but I didn't even think about it. I was so sad I didn't mind if I never ate again.

The bay ahead was crowded with what must have been every kind of ship in the world. There were tiny tug boats, a large, grim-looking man-of-war, barges, canal boats and hundreds of sailing ships like the *Pegasus*. Flags of every country in the world fluttered from masts in bright colours as dozens of ferry boats crossed and re-crossed the water. Ships were constantly entering and leaving. Not even Dublin had prepared us for the energy and activity of the place. In the distance we saw a great river that seemed to flow on as far as the sky, while another to the right was lost in a forest of masts and houses. This was America – and it was amazing.

Everyone began rushing around to get ready. Whatever our grief we couldn't stay on the *Pegasus*.

Bea was busy with the baby, while Toby would not let go of my hand.

'Toby!' I cried, losing my temper and shaking him off. He looked so upset that I felt bad. 'I'm sorry. I'm sorry. Help Bea – help Bea with the baby,' I suggested.

Toby looked at me with such sad eyes that I had to turn away and busy myself with gathering up our blankets. We hadn't owned much but what little we had was scattered after so long at sea. As I was tidying I found a piece of cloth under our bunk. I opened it and inside was the piece of Irish turf Da had dug up for Ma. I put my face towards it and thought I could smell the sweet grass of home. It was unbearable. I wrapped it up again and placed it carefully in our tiny bundle of belongings.

Henry would not come below. I had called to him but he ignored me, staying out at the front of the ship by himself. Bea gave baby Hero to Toby, and now he clung onto her instead. She seemed to like it and not knowing she had no ma, she slept peacefully. And Da? Da still did nothing. Everyone else on board tried to wash, the men to shave. The women dressed their children in the best clothes they had. Da sat on the top step and didn't move.

'Da, you should shave like the others,' I tried, but he did not or would not hear me. 'We need to make a good impression.' I tried to sound like a miniature Ma but it had no effect.

After a while the captain called us all on deck. 'As we've had the fever on board we shall drop anchor here in the bay,' he announced. 'We shall stay here till the doctor says we can go ashore.'

'It's called "quarantine",' explained one of the sailors. 'They don't want us bringing the sickness into New York.'

We were so close to the land that we could see horses and carriages moving about – and yet still we were not able to get there. All that journeying, and still we had to wait. A few people were not quite well yet and the doctor needed to decide what should happen to them. Jack had recovered. He sat on the deck drinking tea and smiling at me but I had no smiles in me to give in return.

That night I stood on the deck for the last time at the back of the boat. Ma was behind us in all that deep ocean and I couldn't bear to let her go. I don't know how long I stood there before I thought I heard Jack approaching, but when I turned I saw it was Henry. My big brother seemed to have got bigger since we had left Ireland and had a scrubby little beard. I was surprised he wanted to stand with me. He didn't speak at first. The sun was setting and the sky glowed with a beautiful pink light.

'The sky looks bigger,' he said quietly.

And he was right. It did seem bigger than any Irish sky.

We stood there until night fell and the stars came out. They too seemed bigger and brighter. I don't think I had ever seen so many. Henry gave a deep sigh.

'Is it one of your headaches?' I asked, concerned.

'No, no . . . It's just . . . so beautiful,' he said. 'Surely this is a land of plenty that it can afford so many lights in the sky?'

It was a fairy-tale sight as they reflected off the dark water of the harbour. We could just see the buildings on the shore, but the countless rows of lights and the many-coloured lamps of the ferry boats darting back and forth made it seem as though a party was about to happen.

Henry sniffed the air. 'Smell that, Slim? That is the smell of opportunity,' he said. He took another breath. 'We should stop here. No need to go any further.'

I shook my head. New York did indeed look a wonder but it wasn't the plan. 'We're to go to Oregon,' I said firmly.

'We could make our fortune here.' Henry turned to look at me and I could see he was serious. 'We're all tired, Slim. I'm too tired to be in charge, and Da . . .'

He didn't finish his sentence. My brother looked

terrible so I reached out to touch his hand, saying, 'Ma wouldn't want us to give up.'

He pulled away sharply. 'Don't you mention her,' he huffed and walked off.

'Da says we're going to Oregon, so that's where we are going,' I called after him. I had Uncle Niall's letter in my box of precious things with the map and no thought of going anywhere else.

But the truth was mostly now Da didn't say anything. He sat at the top of the steps. Some of the passengers complained he was in the way but it didn't make him shift. He didn't even get up to see the sights. Bea took little Hero from Toby and tried to hand her to Da, but he shook his head and looked at the floor.

'She needs you,' pleaded Bea.

'We all do,' I said, but he still said nothing.

I sat with him for a while. 'You have to help us, Da,' I whispered.

'I can't,' he said quietly. 'I don't have my knife.'

I looked at him. Was this my fault?

We all had to be examined by the doctor but it didn't take long. Even the people who were still a little sick were nodded through. As soon as he had cleared everyone and said we could make for the shore an astonishing thing happened. Before the captain had even hauled in the anchor, about a dozen small boats appeared around the *Pegasus*. Men began to pull themselves aboard in any way they could. They were all shouting and yelling. Some offered us rooms in boarding houses for 'practically no money at all' while others wanted us to 'buy a ticket for Albany immediately so you'll not be delayed'.

They said they were Irishmen and they sounded Irish. They said they wanted to help us, but great fights broke out between them. Captain Walker got Jack to stand between them. He was such a giant of a lad that it soon stopped the fisticuffs.

Mr Hughes seemed to have made friends with one of the salesmen. He kept trying to persuade everyone to give their money to this one particular man, saying, 'utterly reliable fellow' and clapping him on the back.

Everyone was making plans and I thought we ought to as well. I fetched Bea and she sent Toby to find Henry. Mrs Kavanagh took the baby while we all sat down around Da for a Hannigan family meeting. Da still sat, not moving. He had an odd look in his eye which frightened me. I knew there was no point in asking him what we should do but I also knew that we should do *something*.

'Do you think maybe we should get a ticket or go to a boarding house or something?' I asked the others. 'I mean, we need to do something. We'll be off the boat soon.'

'Do you think Da has the fever?' asked Toby, frowning at our father sitting by himself.

I didn't think so, but the very thought made me shiver. Losing him too was more than I could manage to think about.

'How much money do we have?' asked Bea, trying to be practical.

I had no idea. I didn't even know where our money was. All I had was the shilling in my pocket and I wasn't sure whether I should tell the others about it. I thought they might be cross that I hadn't spent it before now.

'There's a man says we can come to his mother's house,' said Henry. 'He'll take our things and we can have food when we get there.'

'Do you trust him?' asked Bea.

It hadn't occurred to me that some of the men selling things were not to be trusted.

Henry shrugged. He wasn't sure. I think we all knew that none of us had any idea about anything, and we certainly didn't know the price of anything.

'Well, for a start we need to find Ma's velvet bag of money,' I said, getting up to look.

We split up. Henry searched in her bunk, I looked in the cart with the printing press while Bea checked Da's coat and Toby crawled about looking in Da's pockets while he just sat there. We couldn't find it anywhere. I didn't know what to do. We had no money and perhaps Da did have the fever. What would we do then? We couldn't manage without Da.

We Hannigans gathered again to discuss what to do next.

'I think we should ask Captain Walker to take us home,' declared Bea.

Toby began to cry. 'I don't want to go back to the sea, I don't want to go back to the sea.'

'Don't be daft, Bea,' I scoffed. 'Go back to what? Having Henry arrested by the police? Besides, we've no house there any more, there was no food – and what about Parker Crossingham? You think he would leave you alone now we don't have Ma to protect you?'

I felt a new kind of sickness, this time with worry.

Bea sighed. She knew I was right. 'All right, well . . .' She looked out to the big city waiting for us. 'We shall need somewhere to sleep,' she said, gazing across to where little Hero, our new baby sister, lay on Mrs Kavanagh's shoulder not knowing a trouble in the world.

'The baby needs to go somewhere,' agreed Henry.

'And so she will,' I said, trying to sound as if I knew anything at all. 'I think you are forgetting that this is the land of plenty. This is the land of promise. We shall find something splendid.'

'Marvellous,' groaned Henry. 'Another slice of the bloody moon.'

America was a big place. Da had told me that. I was sure there had to be room for us in some house or other. I had my shilling, which seemed a fortune to me. *I* would look after everyone. I rubbed Ma's ring with my forefinger and tried to find courage in it. Ma had trusted me. I needed to do this.

Mrs Kavanagh had been nursing the baby. She handed Hero to Bea with tears in her eyes.

'If you get milk and a small length of rubber tubing you can use that to feed her. And make sure you hold her on your shoulder afterwards to settle her down and . . .'

'It'll be fine,' Bea assured her. We were sorry to say goodbye, but she was excited. She had been so sad but now she almost smiled as she showed me a neatly printed piece of card. 'Look what Mr Hughes got for me. Half price, he said, and someone cheap to take my luggage and all.' Mrs Kavanagh couldn't read but she was happy with her ticket. It showed a picture of a steamboat, a railroad car, and a coach and horses. 'This piece of printing will take me all the way to my sister. Isn't it wonderful?'

We agreed that it was and hugged her goodbye. She had been good to us even in the midst of her own great sadness and we were sorry to see her go. I tried again to find the bag of money. I went through Da's coat one more time but there was nothing. If only we could have bought a ticket to take us all the way to Uncle Niall. If only we had a fine piece of printing like Mrs Kavanagh.

As *Pegasus* reached the wooden dockside, more

men climbed aboard. It was overwhelming. We had arrived somewhere called the Third Ward. Like Dublin, it was a place where everyone was selling something. There must have been a hundred or more men, all saying the same sorts of things. Most of them wore green waistcoats.

'See this?' said one man, pointing to his waistcoat. 'The green of Ireland come to welcome you.'

'Limerick is it you're come from?' another asked. 'Well, if my old mother wasn't from Limerick . . .'

'I'm telling you, this is the palace of boarding houses. Why, the President himself would want to stay there. They charge but a small sum for the most delicious meals you ever had in your life. Better than my grandmother used to make. I don't know how they do it.'

'You'll be needing dollars, but you shouldn't trust just anyone with your money. Who better than a man of Ireland to . . .'

Everyone was trying to sell us something, but

when they realized we had no money they quickly moved on to the next person. Luggage was collected up and put aboard carriages while the passengers made their way slowly down the gangplank. Despite our best efforts we must all have looked filthy. There wasn't one of us who wasn't exhausted from the journey and not a little bewildered by the incredible noise of the place with orders shouted in languages from countries I never even heard of.

The only one of the Byrne brothers to survive seemed a little lost. Liam had made the long journey in the care of his older brothers, but now they lay in the great ocean and he had to face this huge city all alone. He still wore the blue-and-white nightcap but it had become ragged and made him look sad. He came to say goodbye and tried to hold Bea's hand. She smiled and shook her head as she gently pulled away. He nodded and looked at the ground before he waved and was off. How odd to say goodbye to people we had come to know so well. I thought maybe we should follow him, but he was soon lost in the great mass of people. Perhaps a thousand people had arrived on the tide. The ship beside us had come from Germany. I had got to like Captain Walker, but when I saw the Germans coming ashore looking healthy and cheerful after the same voyage across the ocean, I began to wonder how well we had been looked after.

I didn't know what Ma and Da's plans had been for when we reached New York and Da could not tell me. He stood just looking blankly at the ground, not saying a word and not even seeming to notice that we had arrived. People ask me now how we managed, but there was nothing else to be done. We children would have to sort things.

Jack and a couple of the sailors helped us get the printing press down onto the dock, where it stood on Uncle Aedan's old handcart. Suddenly the machine shifted and seemed about to slip from the cart – and I saw Da look up. It was the first time I had seen him interested in anything since Ma died. I know that Henry noticed it too.

'Da, help us,' he tried. But it was no use. Da looked away again and was lost.

As soon as Bea saw the machine being delivered to the quayside she shook her head and stamped her foot. 'We are in enough trouble,' she said fiercely. 'We have nowhere to go and we are *not* taking that wretched machine with us.'

I put my hands on my hips and stood my ground. 'You shush now, Beatrice Hannigan. This machine is one of the reasons we have come. We have work to do here in America and we didn't bring this all the way here to give up now. You mind the baby and we'll mind everything else.'

I think she was surprised to have been spoken to like that by her little sister. She went to say something else but Henry gave her a look and that was the end of it.

Toby didn't like the arguing so he went to stand by Bea, who held the baby on one side and put her arm round him. Henry and I tucked the rest of what little we had around the metal press and the box of letters.

'It'll be fine,' Henry kept saying. 'Just fine.'

Jack stood awkwardly in front of me as if he wanted to say something.

'You came ashore, Jack – well done,' I said, and took his big hand in mine. I squeezed it and he turned to head back to the ship. I had thought we would have said more of a goodbye but he seemed to be in a hurry. I looked at my family. I knew Henry had been trying to be the man in Da's place, but once we had finished arranging everything and we stood having to decide what was next, he looked uncertain. His one good eye was wide open as he looked about at all the activity in this brand-new city. He leaned against the cart and I knew he was having one of his headaches but wouldn't say.

'What shall we do now?' he whispered.

I looked at my family. My father could not help us. His face looked so empty of any understanding that he could've landed on the moon for all he seemed to know. Toby looked so small just waiting to be told what to do, while Bea rocked the baby, who had taken up crying. Henry looked pale. Someone needed to take charge and it wasn't going to be him.

'Well, we shall walk,' I said firmly.

'Which way?' he asked.

Just then Jack came running back. He was so huge that the ground almost shook under his feet. He was carrying a small bag.

'You all right, Jack?' I asked.

He nodded and put his bag on the cart. He reached in and pulled out his chunk of decorated wood. 'Oregon,' he mumbled. 'Magic box. Oregon.' He looked at me and then added, 'Please.'

'You want to come with us?' I asked, a little confused.

He nodded and grinned.

No one else in our group was even smiling so it felt good to see and I nodded back. He picked up the handlebars of the cart with his giant hands as if it were the lightest thing on earth and looked at me, waiting for instructions. I realized that no one else was going to make a decision so I turned and faced the nearest street that led away from the water.

'This way,' I announced with great certainty, and off we started – the five Hannigan kids, Da and Jack. Jack pushed the handcart while we all walked alongside. I looked at his wide shoulders beside me. I was glad of his company, for though I led the way with a confident step, truth be told, I had absolutely no idea where I was going.

CHAPTER SIXTEEN

We must have looked a strange sight. The huge boy with the printing press in an old Irish farm cart, me, a girl in boy's trousers and all of us barefoot, apart from Da, who shuffled along in his worn-out boots. It was hard to keep together. The streets were so busy and there seemed to be a lot of shouting. A girl in an old shawl stood on a corner calling out, 'Hot corn!' as she tried to persuade us to buy some for a penny. It smelled good, but now we didn't have Mrs Kavanagh to help I knew Hero would need milk and I only had my one shilling. We walked on. I had never seen a little girl selling things in the street like that, but soon we saw all sorts trying to get us to part with money for matches, toothpicks, cigars, flowers and even songs.

Newsboys shouted about the big stories of the day.

Bea was carrying Hero and the baby would not stop crying. It was late now and I knew it wouldn't be long before dark came.

'We should just knock on a door,' Toby suggested. 'People will want to help.'

'True enough,' I said, remembering how kind everyone had been when Mr O'Connor died back home.

I looked along the street. I had never seen so many doors and wasn't at all sure which one to try. At last I saw a nice little house with a notice hanging on the door which read, ROOMS FOR RENT.

Just the thing, I thought.

'Go and knock,' I said to Henry.

I thought he was going to refuse, but he pulled his shoulders back and stepped up to knock. A woman came to the door and Henry started to say hello, but as soon as he opened his mouth she pointed to a sign in the window and slammed the door shut.

I looked at the notice: it read NINA, but I had no idea what that meant.

'How rude!' exploded Henry. 'Did you see that? Just slammed it in my face! What kind of a welcome is that?' he yelled at the closed door.

I think we were all a little shocked. This wasn't the America Niall had written about.

I thought Henry was going to knock the door down so I grabbed his arm and pulled him away. 'Come along. We'll try somewhere else. Perhaps she was not well, that woman.'

We walked on. We saw many doors to many houses and kept meaning to knock on another, but that woman had put us off. The further we got into the city the busier it became. Everyone seemed to be rushing to get somewhere. There were horses and carts carrying coal or milk or anything you could think of that might want carrying. We saw carriages with glimpses of fine gentlemen and others trotting along in top hats. Those driving with no passengers called out, 'Take you home for a dollar!' – but not to us. Anyone would've known just by looking that we didn't have a dollar.

Giant signs shaped like gloves showed the way to shops and the pavement was crowded with things you could buy. It all seemed fantastic to us. After the small streets that led away from the docks, we finally reached a very wide avenue. It appeared to stretch for miles and we nearly lost ourselves in the roar. I didn't know it then but this was a place called Broadway. What a sight! These were the biggest buildings I had ever seen in my life. They were built of the most beautiful stone, some five or six storeys high above ground, with cellars below the pavement. In the windows were the grandest things you could imagine – jewels, silks, satins, laces, ribbons, anything you might want for a house, silverware, toys, paintings and beautiful objects of every description. One window was filled with ladies' dresses in silk and gentlemen's shoes so polished you could see your face in them.

Henry could hardly believe it. 'I shall have shoes

like that one day,' he said, standing so close to the window that his breath covered up the sight.

I looked down at his bare feet. We had none of us ever had shoes and I didn't know if I should like it. Henry looked at the fog of breath he had made on the window and slowly drew a shamrock in it with his finger. We stood there for a moment together and then walked on.

No one was interested in us, for the street had people of every description. There were fine gentlemen in broadcloth, ladies in silks and jewels all mingling with beggars in squalid rags. This was America.

Bea stood with her mouth open at it all. 'Is it what you imagined, Slim?' she asked, leaning down to me.

I shook my head. 'I never saw anything so grand in all my life.'

The bustle and uproar was so loud it was impossible to chat in a normal way. All along the street whole trains of people were being pulled along by horses in something called omnibuses. We had never seen them before. Certainly they didn't have such a thing in Dublin.

Bea was terrified of crossing the busy road and would never have made it if Jack had not left the cart and gone back for her. Overwhelmed by the sounds, we turned down a smaller street and soon our surroundings changed. The place seemed much poorer. The pavement was almost gone and the streets were full of holes.

The cart was heavy and more difficult to push in such a street. Suddenly Jack gave a cry as one wheel fell into the biggest hole we had seen. The press tipped to one side and the weight of it meant none of us could right it. Just then three dark skinned men ran towards us. We had never seen a man with a black face up close before, and Bea screamed. I was fascinated and wanted to touch their skin. It was beautiful. Shiny like the night sky.

The men put their hands up and laughed.

'I beg your pardon,' muttered Bea, flustered by it all.

'It's all right,' they said. 'Let us help you.'

The three men, Jack and Henry heaved at the cart until it was safe back on the street again.

'You're new to town?' asked one of the men.

'Just arrived,' said Henry with a little swagger, as if he were ready to be in charge.

'You're very black,' said Toby.

I shushed him while Bea added, 'I don't think you're supposed to say, Toby.'

The men smiled. 'We are from Africa and we work at the American Museum,' said one. 'Come see us some time. You'll be amazed.'

'Why?' asked Toby, who was already amazed.

The largest of the three men leaned down to him. 'Why, because there you will find such things as you thought existed only in stories.'

'Like what?' Toby's eyes were wide with excitement.

'The wonders of the world,' continued the man

with a huge smile. 'You can see Tom Thumb, the world's smallest man to ever walk alone.' He patted Toby on the head. 'Smaller even than you yet a fully grown man.'

'There's a woman with a beard,' said another of the men.

'And a mermaid from Fiji!' said the last.

'No!' screamed Toby with delight as he practically jumped up and down. 'I want to see that!' He pulled on my hand as if I might make it happen.

'Sure and there's no such things,' scoffed Henry.

The men smiled. 'Better come and see for yourself,' they suggested.

All the while we chatted Da sat on the kerb of the pavement staring at his hands. The sun was beginning to hide behind the tall buildings and shadows fell across the street. It was getting late.

'We need somewhere to stay,' I said.

The tall man sucked his teeth in thought before saying, 'Maybe try down the Bowery. I reckon you get rooms down there.' And then they all waved goodbye.

'Imagine that,' enthused Toby. 'A mermaid and a woman with a beard! What a place New York is!'

Jack helped Da up and we walked on. *What a place indeed*, I thought. If there really were such things here, then there would be no trouble filling the pages of a newspaper.

CHAPTER SEVENTEEN

We headed down the street the men had suggested and you could see that the place was getting poorer. Some of the buildings in these streets were of brick but others were much flimsier, one- and two-storey places made of wood that leaned on each other at funny angles. After a while we came to a large open area where five streets met together, like little rivers emptying into a bay. It was called Five Points. In the centre was a small triangular space surrounded by a wooden fence on which old clothes had been hung out to dry. An unusual-looking man with very narrow eyes and an odd little silk hat stood fussing over them. Even though we had not come far, this was not fancy like Broadway. The smell was terrible and you had to wade through the dirt as you walked.

Here, all the buildings looked worn out, the windows and doors sagged at their hinges, but everywhere people were still going about their business. If we hadn't seen black people before we met the ones from the American Museum, now they seemed to be everywhere. Toby kept pointing till I told him to keep his hands in his pockets. A shop called D. BRENNAN GROCERY AND LIQUORS was doing a fine trade in all manner of things and outside stood a large group of young men hollering and drinking. Children in nothing more than a few bits of cloth were picking through some rubbish in the street to see what they could find while a woman bought milk from a man with a donkey and cart.

By now it was late in the afternoon. We were hungry and tired and I knew we had to find something soon. Bea was singing quietly to the baby: *'Be thou my shelter, be thou my stronghold.'*

That was when Henry spotted the youngest Byrne brother outside of Brennan's. I wouldn't have recognized him except he saw Bea and called out to her.

'Beatrice! It's me, Liam.' He hurried over. 'Hello, Hannigans! Welcome to Paradise Square!'

He looked so different. His face still carried the scars and scabs from the terrible itching but he looked smarter. He had a new hat – a soft, slouched sort of thing with a small peak – and a tight jacket with a waistcoat underneath. In his mouth was a cigar, and he reminded me of Parker Crossingham. I thought he looked ridiculous but I could see that Henry was impressed.

'Where did you get those clothes?' he asked.

Liam laughed. 'Did you not see the grand shops? I stopped and spent some money. Told the man I wanted him to make me into a real New Yorker!'

Liam was only a year older than Henry but he clearly thought his new clothes made him more of a man. Henry didn't want him to think he couldn't manage in the new city, so he swaggered over to shake Liam's hand and it would've looked impressive if he hadn't tripped over a small pig on the way.

Liam laughed. 'Damned pigs. They're all over.' He reached down to help Henry up and dust him off.

'I'd like a pig,' exclaimed Toby, and he would have run off to catch one if Bea hadn't stopped him.

'Where are you heading?' Liam asked.

'Why, we're off to—' began Henry, not wanting to say we had no idea, but I had no such shyness.

'We don't know, Liam,' I said clearly. 'We've nowhere to go. We're tired and Da is not right.'

He looked at Da, who didn't even seem to notice that we had stopped. Liam was only half a day ahead of us in the streets of the city but he already seemed to know a great deal more than we did. He stood with his feet wide apart and tried to look at us with a pitying glance as he took a puff on his cigar. He clearly wasn't used to it and it made him choke a little. Bea turned away, trying not to laugh.

Toby had no problem saying what we were all thinking. 'You look different.'

Liam grinned and patted his pocket. 'I've got money. A bucket of money.'

'I thought the money was for a farm?' I said.

He laughed. 'And what would you be wanting to farm here in this great city?' he asked. 'Who wants to be ploughing when you can live the high life here in New York?' He pulled a silver coin from his pocket and flipped it in the air towards Henry, who caught it as Liam declared, 'Money! In New York that's all you need! I've not been here five minutes and already I've got myself a fancy place with my name on the door and everything so the whole world knows where I live.'

Henry turned the coin over in his hand. 'This doesn't look like money to me,' he said suspiciously.

Liam shook his head. 'Henry Hannigan, do you know nothing?'

Henry blushed because that was the truth. We none of us knew anything.

'That's American money,' continued Liam, pointing to the coin. 'That is a dollar. That one coin is worth four English shillings. You can spend your money from home but everyone will know that you're just arrived.'

We hadn't even thought about American money, and all gathered round to see this vast sum lying in Henry's hand. Apart from Da, Jack was the only one who didn't seem interested. He stood by the cart looking suspiciously at anyone who came near. I could see he was afraid of all these new things but I wasn't. The silver coin sparkled in Henry's hand.

'Can I hold it?' I asked, and Henry reluctantly passed it over. I held the coin close to my eye and saw that it had a picture of an eagle on one side and a woman sitting down with a flag on the other.

'Why do they have different money?' asked Toby.

'I have no idea,' I replied. 'Da . . .'

I turned to my father, but he was leaning against the front of the shop and not paying us any attention. A smart-looking man holding a handkerchief to his nose walked past and stared at us. Liam put his tongue out to him and pretended to raise his fists. The man scuttled away and Liam smiled.

'Look at that! The rich coming down here to see how the poor live,' he sneered. 'Well, I'll show them. Give me a couple of months and I'll be swanking around too.'

I think Liam was showing off for Bea's benefit, but she was unimpressed and just then Hero began to cry again. Bea jiggled her up and down and declared, 'Well, we're not staying that long but we do need somewhere now. So if you could stop showing off, Liam Byrne, and help us, I know I at least would appreciate it.'

Liam blushed and nodded. 'Come with me,' he said. 'I'm in Mulberry Bend, which is full up, but I could ask in the shop. Someone will know about a space.'

'And get some milk for the baby while you're in

there,' ordered Bea, bossing him about. 'And a piece of rubber tubing so I can feed her.'

Liam nodded again and went to get the things for Hero. We stood silently waiting. We were exhausted.

Liam returned with the requested things. 'I've asked in the shop about a room. They say you need to try the Old Brewery. It's this way,' he said shyly, handing the milk to Bea.

He led the way quickly and I hurried to keep up.

'Liam, what does N-I-N-A mean?' I asked, half running.

He looked at me. 'N-I-N-A?' he repeated.

I nodded. 'A woman had it on a sign in her window. She was awfully rude to us even though she said she had rooms to rent.'

Liam looked grim. 'It means No Irish Need Apply.'

I couldn't understand this at all. 'What do you mean? No Irish?'

He chewed down on his cigar and replied, 'I've been talking to the men in Brennan's. There's plenty don't like us here. That's why we Irish must stick together.'

'Who doesn't like us?' panted Toby, trying to keep up.

'Why would they not like us?' I asked. Uncle Niall had never mentioned this. No one had ever mentioned this but Liam did not answer my question.

'Here it is,' he said. 'The Old Brewery.'

He pointed to a large building with three floors and perhaps a fourth, right up under the roof. Maybe it had been a fine place once but now it looked as though a baby's cough might blow it down. The windows were broken and patched with paper and rags. Three stone steps led up to a wide front door with great cracks running from top to bottom. A man was standing in the wrecked doorway holding a piece of paper, arguing with another fellow who seemed to be in charge.

'I don't understand,' said the man with the paper.

The other fellow had a thick accent and was hard to understand. 'I'm ze landlord,' he said. 'It eez my house. You haff been staying here and zats your bill, you domkop.'

The man stared at the piece of paper. It was clear he couldn't read. 'How much does it say?'

'Eighteen dollars.'

He looked confused. 'But didn't you say sixpence per meal and thruppence for bed?'

The landlord nodded. 'Yes, zat makes seventy-five cents per day for all of you in two rooms wiz all your meals. You haff been here eight days, so eighteen dollars.'

Bea shook her head. 'Seventy-five cents a day for eight days doesn't add up to eighteen dollars.'

I was about to step forward and argue too but Henry told us to shush.

We waited till the landlord had finished his business and Liam introduced us with a flourish.

'Mr Van Hoffen, Liam Byrne, you just let me have that place up at Mulberry Bend.'

'Zo?' replied the man.

Liam took his hat off and continued, 'These people are my friends. They need a place to stay.'

Mr Van Hoffen looked at us. 'You have money?' he barked.

Liam gave a small laugh as if it was a ridiculous question. 'Of course, they have money. Lots of money,' he cried.

We didn't have any money – but I'm sure he said it because he was sweet on Bea. Hero was crying more than ever now and I decided that whatever room the man had we would take it. He looked uncertain and I'm not surprised. We were a very odd-looking group, but Liam suddenly pulled a small stack of the American coins from his pocket and made a great show of putting them in my hand.

The landlord heard the rattle of the money and nodded reluctantly. He was a large, fat fellow, with a beard still showing signs of his last meal. His breath was terrible.

'I am not storing zat!' He pointed at the cart. Jack squared his shoulders as if there might be a fight, but Liam didn't seem to notice.

'No indeed,' he said cheerfully. 'Jack, Henry, you come with me. I've just the place for your machine. You ladies' – he bowed to Bea and me, sweeping off his hat – 'you ladies, make yourselves comfortable in your new home.'

'Idiot!' declared Bea as he led Jack and Henry off with the printing press. I didn't like to let it or them go out of my sight, but the landlord was heading into the building. It was nearly dark out and I knew we had to sleep somewhere so we followed. Hero was crying up a storm and Toby was snivelling as well. I was shaking with fear. We had no one to protect us except Da, and he was a world away from being able to do that. The landlord led us down some stairs into a cellar. He kept telling Da things about rules and money but Da wasn't listening. It was dark and the smell was terrible: worse than the buckets we all peed in on the ship. The staircase was rickety, and it groaned and trembled beneath our feet. We passed three small children asleep on the stairs who Mr Van Hoffen kicked out of the way as we headed down into the gloom.

The cellar was divided into about twenty rooms. This was where the men who once made beer had kept their machinery. Now, amongst the old pieces of equipment, the place was full of people. One room was filled with a whole family who lay on the floor staring up at us as we passed.

'Den of thieves,' muttered the landlord. He went down a few more steps. It was so dark we could hardly make the man out as we tried to follow. Suddenly a rat the size of a cat ran over my foot. Bea gasped and exclaimed, 'We can't stay here, Slim!'

'It's just temporary,' I whispered back. 'We'll sort something else in the morning. We have to have something. It'll be all right.'

It didn't *feel* all right, but I kept repeating to

myself that Ma had trusted me to do my best and this was it. I rubbed her ring with my thumb.

We carried on down a dark corridor, tripping up over who knew what as we went. It seemed to twist and wind for ever – until at last the landlord stopped and opened a door. I was the closest to him and looked in. The room was small, with a low ceiling which looked as though it would only just be above Da's head. Only the faintest bit of light from the street struggled in. The walls were patched with pieces of pasteboard and the floor was covered with dirt. An old straw mattress was the only furniture. A black, cast-iron stove stood against the wall, the door hanging off at one corner.

'Seventy cents for ze week,' said the landlord to Da.

I hesitated. It was truly horrible – the smell was so bad it burned the back of my throat – but it was all there was and I wasn't at all sure how much money Liam had put in my hand. Da didn't answer.

'Make up your mind,' growled the landlord. 'I 'ave plenty of ozzers who vill vant it. There is more boats coming in, you know. It eez zis or the stones in the street.'

'We need food as well,' I said, determined not to cry.

The landlord turned to look at me. I think he was surprised I had spoken at all. He looked at me long and hard and then said, 'You can haff bread and milk for ze same again.'

'For all of us,' I insisted.

The landlord looked at me and I thought he was going to kick me too, but at last he nodded. I turned away to count my money and saw that Liam had put five of the dollar coins in my hand. I put three in my pocket and turned to give the rest to the man. He said he'd bring me the change but I doubted it and I was too tired to worry about it now. I was learning fast about who you could trust. Finally he nodded and snarled, 'No trouble now. Not a peep or you vill be out,' before leaving us alone.

Da sat down heavily on the filthy mattress. Bea, Toby and I all turned to each other with a sigh. Another giant rat ran across the floor. Hero was crying so we got on with trying to work out how to use the tubing to feed her. At last we managed to get milk in her mouth and she began to gurgle happily. At least she had no idea where we were or that Ma was not with us.

'I thought this was the land of plenty,' complained Henry that night as we ate the tiny amount of bread and milk we had been given for our money. Jack sat quietly on the floor with his back against the wall. Liam had not returned and I was glad. Bea had never liked the old Liam and I didn't think I liked the new one, even though he had helped me out.

'Oregon,' said Da suddenly.

I nodded. 'That's right. There's plenty in Oregon. Pigs and all sorts.'

'I'll need my knife,' he said.

'Tell us again about Oregon, Da,' said Toby

happily jumping up to put his arm around Da's neck but the moment was gone. Da shook Toby off and stared at the wall. I looked at him not knowing what we could do.

'I'll get your knife for you, Da, don't you worry,' I said. 'Then we'll be off to Oregon.'

I chewed on my bread and tried to sound confident, but in my heart I couldn't imagine for a moment that we might ever get there.

CHAPTER EIGHTEEN

I awoke in our new home to the sound of Da muttering out loud. He was lying on the bare floor staring up at the ceiling and repeating aloud some words that I did not know then.

'To *die*, to *sleep* –
No *more*; and by a sleep, to say we end
The heart-ache, and the thousand natural
   shocks
That flesh is heir to? 'Tis a consummation . . .'

I know that speech now. It was one of Da's favourites but I didn't care about that. All I knew was that my wonderful father was not right at all. Ma's death was terrible for all of us –

but for him, well, it was as if he had died with her.

Bea was sitting with Jack's beautiful piece of wood on her lap. She kept turning it over and over in her hands. She looked at me. 'Do you think there is a treasure inside?' she wondered. 'A treasure would be wonderful.' She studied it. 'If I had a treasure, even a small one, I'd build us a house where it's warm all the time and you don't even have to light a fire.' Bea smiled at me, and with absolute certainty said, 'I shall have such a place one day, Slim. We shall be so snug inside in the winter that we might even have to open a window to let the air in.'

I gazed at my lovely dreaming sister. Her hair, which she had always kept so nice, hung down around her face in great matted pieces.

Toby was still asleep but Henry and Jack were both gone again and I had no idea where. Baby Hero was stirring and getting ready to cry. She would need more milk. I knew I probably should go out and find my way back to the shop but I was afraid to go out by myself. I got up and looked at the oven with its useless door hanging off at one corner. It wasn't cold yet but we would need to mend it to heat food for the baby. I was pretty sure she couldn't manage on just cold milk. Somehow I doubted the landlord was going to be helpful. Perhaps we should find out how to get to Oregon straight away, but Ma had said it was expensive and all I had was the three dollars left from Liam and my silver shilling. My head ached with trying to work out what to do, so I did nothing.

We must have sat for an hour or so until Henry appeared in the doorway. He looked quite wild – as though he had not slept. Jack came in behind him, awkward and as though he had been up to no good. He avoided my eye and crouched down near the stove as if he hoped it might suddenly give off some heat.

'New York is a very wicked place,' Henry announced in a way that I couldn't tell if he thought this was a good or a bad thing. He reached inside his jacket and produced some milk and a large piece of cheese.

'Where did you get that?' I asked, but Henry shrugged and took a great glug of milk before tearing off lumps of cheese for Bea, Jack and me. Then he sat chewing on what was left. I got up and put a little in Da's hands and he sat breaking it into smaller and smaller pieces.

'We took it,' Jack suddenly declared honestly.

'Stole it?' Bea asked horrified.

Jack nodded. Bea turned on Henry. 'Have you not caused enough trouble with the law for a lifetime without making things worse?'

'We have to eat,' mumbled Henry.

Toby woke up and was hungry so we asked no more questions. Hero was awake now too. We tried to give her some milk but she wouldn't stop crying.

'Maybe it's because the milk is cold,' suggested Bea.

'What do I know?' I muttered. 'I don't know about babies.'

I did know that we had no way to heat anything up. I took some milk and went to see if anyone else in the building had a stove. I went out into the corridor and as I did so I thought I could hear singing from further into the darkness of the basement. I was scared and rubbed Ma's ring as I stumbled towards the sound. Making my way through the dark, I came to the very end of the narrow passage, where I found a door. I could still hear a woman singing.

'*Happy soul! thy days are ended,*
Leave thy trials here below:
Go, by angel guards attended,
To the breast of Jesus, go!'

The door was open and I looked in. It was even smaller than the place where we were resting. A meal of bones and crusts was set on an old packing box which was drawn close up to the stove. A small fire was trying to stay alight in the stove and a kerosene lamp provided the faintest of lights. By this feeble glow I noticed that on the wall near the stove was a small shelf with a clock and a calendar. Beside it stood a wooden screen which was decorated with the strangest pieces of paper. At first they just looked like letters, but when I looked closer I saw that this was no ordinary writing but odd drawings in brilliant colours. I had never seen anything like them but somehow they made the dreadful room seem more like someone's home.

The woman was sitting on the only chair in the room. She was singing to a little girl who sat on her lap.

'Hello!' I called.

She stopped and turned to me. 'Is it day out there?' she asked.

'Sorry?' I replied.

'I need to know if the day has come. I need to mark my calendar.'

I hadn't been outside, but a very faint light shone into our miserable room. 'I think so,' I said.

The woman put the child down and went to cross off a day on her calendar with the short stub of a pencil. Then she turned to me. Although her face was half hidden by the huge frill of the cap she wore, I saw that somehow she had lost the greater part of her nose. Her once pretty face had a great gap in it. What made it seem so much worse was that the child who clung to her skirts was so pretty. She was maybe three or four, with long dark ringlets but with eyes the shape of almonds.

'My name is Elsie,' said the little girl, smiling, and my first thought was that she was much too lovely to be in such a place. Then I remembered that my own family were just next door; none of us wanted to be here.

'I'm Slim, Slim Hannigan. We're next door, but there's no stove and I wondered if I might heat some milk – for my baby sister?'

The woman didn't answer at first and then she said, 'Are you a girl?' I nodded. 'Why do you dress like a boy?' she asked.

'It's more comfortable,' I replied shoving my hands in my pockets to show that I could.

The woman nodded as if she understood. Then she added, 'No one comes in here. No one visits.' I knew straight away she was Irish.

'We're from Ballysmaragaid,' I explained. 'Do you know it?'

She looked as though she might smile but stopped herself. She nodded. 'Ballysmaragaid,' she repeated, 'We were the next *clachan*.' With that she got up and fetched me a small pan. I poured in the milk and she took it from me to set it on the heat. Elsie watched me with big eyes, as if having a visitor was something new and exciting. I stood chatting and telling the woman about our journey and how we had just arrived. Once the milk was warm and I turned to go I realised I didn't know her name.

'I'm Mrs Liu,' she said. Funny name for an Irish woman.

When I got back to our room Henry was

explaining that he had been out looking for work but jobs were hard to find.

'They don't want the Irish,' he said quietly once Hero had been persuaded back to sleep with the warm milk. 'Everywhere I went there are signs saying No Irish Need Apply and everyone called me Patrick or Paddy.'

'Da's name is Patrick,' said Toby.

'They think all the Irish are called Patrick,' replied Henry.

Toby thought about that. 'That's silly,' he decided. 'Slim can't be called Patrick.'

'No, she's called Bridget,' explained Henry. 'Irish girls are all called Bridget and boys are all Patrick.'

Toby shook his head. 'Well, that would be very confusing if you were trying to organize something.' He turned to Da. 'I'm right, aren't I, Da? It would be too confusing if we all had the same name.'

But Da did not answer. He had stopped spouting Shakespeare and once more he sat staring at the wall.

Even though it was not winter the cellar was cold. We were sitting there shivering, not at all sure what to do next, when suddenly Liam Byrne popped his head round the door.

'Hello there, Hannigans. Safe night, was it?'

Bea looked up, and didn't look as though she was going to be pleased by his reappearance until he said, 'I've brought you some ham!' and produced a great chunk of meat. I thought Bea was going to refuse it but it looked too good. She almost smiled at him as she took it and I thought what a marvellous thing it was to have money. Bea didn't like Liam, but was putting up with him because he bought things.

'Liam, do you think the landlord might fix the stove? It's cold for the baby,' I asked.

He gave a sort of snort as a reply. 'Old Van Hoffen? I do not. That old Knickerbocker.'

'What's a Knickerbocker?' asked Toby, for whom the whole world had seemed strange ever since he had woken up.

Liam took his time to explain. 'He's descended from the first Dutch settlers so he thinks that makes him God Almighty. He looks down on everyone. They say he has a coach with his own coat of arms even though his father used to sell fish in the street.'

He looked at Henry and rubbed his hands together. 'Anyway, enough about that.' He lowered his voice and spoke as if he didn't want anyone outside the room to hear. 'Right, Henry, my boy, I've heard a little rumbling about an "opportunity" so I reckon we need to be off and making ourselves a little . . . money. The pot my brothers left me is not going to last for ever.'

Henry's eyes widened. 'What kind of opportunity?' he asked. He too was uncertain about this new Liam but I could tell he didn't want to be thought of as soft.

Liam looked at Bea and tapped the side of his nose with his finger. 'Men's work. Nothing to worry the ladies with.'

I didn't know what he was talking about. Henry was not a man but he moved to the door. Jack too slowly got to his feet to go with them.

Liam frowned at him. 'You stay here. We need brains on this operation.'

Jack's big face looked so hurt, but without another word Liam headed out into the street. Henry looked awkward.

'He didn't mean it, Jack. The thing is, you need to stay here and look after the girls. Someone needs to stay with them and Toby and Da. All right?' Jack nodded.

Henry was nearly out of the door after Liam when he turned back to me. He grabbed me by the arm and whispered, 'Where's the money?'

'What money?' I said. I knew what he meant but I didn't want to give it to him.

'From last night,' he said, looking irritated. 'Liam gave you five dollars. You only spent two. I need some of that money. I can't be borrowing off Liam all the time. It looks bad.'

I reached into my pocket for the three dollars we had left. I thought Henry would only take one, but he grabbed all three and stuffed them in his pocket. He could see I looked shocked which I think made him cross. He pulled his shoulders back and spoke making sure Da could hear him.

'I need to be the man now,' he said firmly. 'You have to trust me.'

'But, Henry . . .' I tried, and he did his best to be nice, but he was showing off in front of Da.

'It's all right, Slim. I'll be back with food for us all,' he added.

'And some wood?' asked Bea.

Henry nodded. 'And some wood.'

Then he left. He left us with nothing.

CHAPTER NINETEEN

Those first few days Bea, Toby, Da, me and the baby all stayed in that room. Jack would go out scavenging and come back with bits and pieces of food. We never asked him where he got it. Then, much later, Henry would come back from wherever he'd been with milk and scraps of wood from broken furniture. We managed to prop the stove door shut with an old chair leg and kept warm as best we could.

I didn't like being stuck in the cellar but Bea didn't want me to go out exploring. 'It's too big a city,' she kept saying.

One morning Toby was gone too when I woke up and I didn't dare go and look for him. I felt scared of how big New York was but at the same time I was getting tired of being in that dreadful dark place; it was like being back on the *Pegasus* in a storm. If Toby, who was younger than me, dared go out then I ought to be bolder. I decided to start by wandering out into the corridor again from time to time.

I'd got to know a little more about the woman with the sad nose. She never left her room so I would wander down the hall in the morning and chat with her. She was Irish like us but she was called Mrs Liu because she was married to the unusual-looking man who sold old clothes at Five Points who it turned out was Chinese. I had never met a Chinese person before – but then I'd never met anyone like Mrs Liu either. She'd had her nose bitten off by a dog when someone had heard her Irish voice and not liked it at all. This seemed unbelievable. Bad enough people might slam a door in your face, but to let their dog have a bite of your nose . . . I didn't understand how anyone could behave like that, but Henry said there were lots of people who didn't want us; people who said we weren't welcome and that we could never be Americans. I wasn't at all sure I wanted to be American.

Mrs Liu kept a calendar while she waited for her brother. She had come from Ireland with him but there had been no work in the city.

'He was a potato farmer,' she cried. 'What does he know of getting a job in a place like this?'

He had heard of work somewhere inland, building a canal, and gone off. He had told her he would be gone three weeks and she had the date of his return marked on her calendar – a date that had passed months ago. She had no way of finding out where he might be.

'I just want some news. Any news,' she wept as she sat on her only chair. She missed Ireland and wondered how things were back home. It occurred to me that there might be new people coming off the boats who would know. Perhaps I could find out for her to thank her for letting us use her oven to heat the milk.

She smiled at me. 'It's not like home, where you know your neighbours,' she sighed.

'You have to go out, Mrs Liu. You won't meet anyone sitting here. If I hadn't come in you wouldn't know us at all,' I said brightly. 'You never know there might be someone right next door from your own village.' I was standing by the wooden screen with the strange pictures and thinking they probably held a story. Mrs Liu looked so miserable. I wished Da had been there to tell one of his tales but I didn't think I could get him off the bed in our room. I wondered if I might tell one myself – I doubted I could think of anything to interest a grown-up. I looked at little Elsie. 'Shall I tell you a tale?' I asked.

Elsie nodded and came over to take my hand. I sat down on the floor with her ready to begin, even though I wasn't at all sure what was going to come out of my mouth. Just then Jack wandered in from next door. He loved a story, and straight away sat down to listen too.

'I'll tell you a story about a man living . . .'

'Yes?' said Mrs Liu, pulling her chair closer.

I felt a bit panicked as I didn't really have a story

to tell but I carried on, hoping that one might come to me. 'Well, right here in New York. He had . . . what do you call it when you have more than one room?'

'An apartment?' suggested Mrs Liu.

I clicked my fingers and pointed at her in agreement. I don't know where the story came from but Da was right: stories were just out there if you looked for them. If you opened your mind they fell right into your head.

'That's exactly right. An apartment – a fancy place, not like this at all, if you don't mind me saying – and he lived there for ten years or more. Now, you know how these fancy places have plates on the door to tell you the name of who lives where? I haven't seen them but I know Liam Byrne has one . . . well, one day he happened to notice the name of his next-door neighbour. He was amazed to find it was the same as his own. A few months later he happened to see the neighbour and for the first time he spoke to him saying wasn't it a remarkable thing that two people with the same name should live side by side for years without knowing each other? This bit of conversation started more chat and soon the two men discovered that they were brothers – sons of the same parents.'

'No!' exclaimed Mrs Liu.

I nodded. 'Oh yes. These brothers had not met for many years, and for fully twelve years had lived side by side as neighbours, without knowing each other because they never took the time.'

'Was there ever such a thing!' said Mrs Liu in wonder. 'Is it true?'

I stood up and said confidently, 'Well, now, truth is a funny thing, Mrs Liu. The thing about a tale like that is that it doesn't really matter whether it's true or not. What matters is that we *want* it to be true.'

'Indeed,' she agreed.

I wanted Da to be there but he was still in our room, still silent. Just then there was a great clattering and a loud whooping on the stairs – which could only be Toby with his incredibly strong voice.

Jack got to his feet and looked out into the corridor.

'Da! Da!' Toby called. Footsteps thudded down the hall as he ran towards us. I jumped up and went out into the passageway, only to find that my little brother was being pursued by a giant pig. I thought at first he was in trouble with some wild creature, but he didn't sound frightened at all. We followed him into our room, where he carried on calling out but I saw that Da didn't even look up.

'I found him! I found him!' Toby shouted out, loud enough for people back in Ireland to hear his excitement.

Bea was demanding to know, 'Found who?'

'Hamlet!' cried Toby, turning to the pig to give it a hug.

Where Hamlet back in Ballysmaragaid had been small and soft pink and smooth haired, this pig was quite large, with surprisingly long hair. It was also sandy coloured, with great patches of black and brown. It had one long black ear and one pale one,

one black leg and three light ones. The Hamlet I had known had been pale pink all over. This looked like no pig I had ever seen. It had so many patches of colour it was as if its mother had not been able to make up her mind what kind of child she wanted. Even its nose had streaks of different colours. It was hard to know where Toby had found it, but both he and the pig had filthy feet.

Toby was almost crying he was so happy. 'Da! You were right! You said Hamlet was going on a grand adventure and that we might meet again, and sure enough, here he is!'

Da was still staring at the wall. He didn't seem to notice any of us, least of all the pig.

Bea spoke carefully as she looked at the creature, which was now sniffing in every corner. 'It doesn't really look like Hamlet, Toby,' she tried.

Toby agreed with her. 'I know. I think the journey has been hard on him. Imagine him being on a boat all by himself! But I knew as soon as he looked at me.'

'But the spots . . .' continued Bea.

Toby looked serious. 'I think they must be from the sickness. Like the people on the boat. Maybe he had the lice like Liam. Thank goodness he's all right now. He must have had some of that *lady numb* that Ma gave people.'

'Laudanum,' corrected Bea.

'Yes,' said Toby.

I should have liked some laudanum. It made people go to sleep and not worry. I could see Ma going about the boat handing out little drops of the stuff to calm the sick. How I missed her and wanted to feel her soothing hand on my head.

Even though this pig looked nothing like Hamlet, Toby was not going to be talked round that it might be some other animal than the pet he had known. 'The minute we set eyes on each other,' he said confidently, 'I knew it was Hamlet and he knew it was me.'

He grinned. He was as happy as we had ever seen him and neither Bea nor I could bear to spoil it.

Toby grabbed the new Hamlet by the neck and slumped down on the floor, hugging the creature for all his life. Jack smiled and rummaged about looking for a scrap of something to give the new pet.

I went and sat next to Bea on the mattress. Since Da had become so distant Bea and I seemed to be getting on better. As if she didn't think I was such an idiot.

'I don't even think it's a boy,' she whispered.

'No,' I said.

'We've hardly any food for us,' she continued. 'How are we going to manage the pig?'

CHAPTER TWENTY

The next morning I could stand the cellar no longer. Henry came back each evening with food and milk, though he was becoming strange and secretive again. I wanted to know how he was managing to make the three dollars last but he didn't tell me anything.

'Where have you been?' I asked, but he refused to say. Without Da or Ma to help I couldn't get him to come back to his old self again and tell us what he was up to. Then one morning he left a note saying, *Back in a few days*. He left enough money for the rent and some food but no hint of where he had gone or why. I was furious.

Jack watched as Bea and I tried once more to look for Ma's missing money purse but it was no good. Already we had been in New York much longer than I had thought we would. I had imagined we would be on our way to Oregon now and I was beginning to get restless.

'You all right, Slim?' asked Jack, his kind face full of worry.

'We need to get out of here. This is not a life for any of us. This is not what we came for. We're supposed to be in Oregon by that great big river.' I wanted to cry but there wasn't time.

Bea did her best with little Hero but I thought I had heard the baby cough in the night. The room was terrible and getting worse. Each day some kind of brown liquid oozed down the wall behind the stove. I didn't know what it was but it smelled terrible, as if it had come straight from a drain in the street above. We were going to get sick if we stayed.

'We need to go out and find Henry,' I said. 'He can't just leave us here.'

Bea was too afraid to leave the cellar, and

although Toby now played in the street all day with his pig, he wasn't old enough to be walking around the city. Da lay on the mattress. We needed him to come back to us and tell us what to do. I tried to turn his head to look at me.

'Da! You have to wake up now! We need your help! I know you're sad and everything, we all are but we're still here and we need you.'

He was facing me but I don't think he really saw me.

I shook his shoulders. 'Da, please! Please!'

Bea came and pulled me from him. 'It's no use, Slim. No use at all.'

She was right. Da's eyes were blank. He didn't even seem to know we were in New York.

I got up and went to the door. Bea looked afraid. 'Where are you going?'

'Well,' I said, 'I'm going out to look for Henry. He can't be far. I'll bring him home and we shall make a plan.'

I wanted to cry at how impossible it all sounded

but I was determined to be brave. I twisted Ma's Claddagh ring on my thumb and said, 'You stay here with Da and the baby. Let me see what I can find.'

'Shouldn't you wait? Henry can't be long . . .'

'Well, you never know with Henry.' I sighed. I was going to take Jack with me but I could see how frightened Bea was. 'Jack will stay with you. I'll be back soon.'

Bea tried to be brave and got to her feet. 'I'm older – I'll go.'

Just then Hero began to murmur. She was so tiny. I still felt bad about what I had said to Ma about not liking babies.

'Please, Bea, I can't look after the baby. I just can't. Stay here with Jack. He'll protect you.'

Jack nodded slowly and smiled. He was a good fellow. I knew he would take care of them.

Bea looked at me and then at Hero. 'All right,' she said reluctantly. 'But be careful.'

I think Bea had always found me annoying. I was

the little sister who never quite did as she was told, but things were different now. She reached out and pulled me in for a hug. I rested my head against her dress and she smelled of Ma. It was both wonderful and terrible at the same time.

The stairs creaked and groaned as I climbed up from the cellar. An old woman I had never seen before lay across one step. It was so dark I couldn't tell if she was asleep or dead. I tried to poke her but she didn't move, so I had to step over her to reach the outside. It was so awful in that building. How I longed for some fresh air. All around me I could hear babies crying, people moaning, and our neighbour, Mrs Liu, singing her hymn over and over.

Outside I took a great gulp of air. How I longed for the green fields of Ireland. New York was nothing like home. It was nothing like anywhere I had ever been. I walked along, trying not to trip up in the holes which were everywhere in the street. The drain from a large building poured with horrible stuff into an open man-hole. The hole was about four feet wide and a waterfall of waste poured into it. Nearby, at Five Points, Mr Liu had laid out all his second-hand clothes on the metal railing and was busy trying to persuade a woman that the cold was coming and she would need a coat. He also had a little wooden table covered with broken bits of sweets, which he was selling for a penny a piece. I would have loved a sweet but we needed to keep every penny we had.

I had no idea where to begin looking for Henry so I just picked a path and began walking. Every few feet there was a sign above a door which read DISTILLERY. I didn't know what they were except they were places where men and women seemed to be drinking and talking too loudly. Even first thing in the morning they were full up.

Having said I would go and find my brother I suddenly felt terrified. I was twelve years old. I was a girl. What on earth could I do? I wasn't the only child my age out and about, but I seemed to be the only one who was looking for news. All the others were lounging about on street corners, wearing nothing but rags and their faces and hands were filthy. There didn't seem to be any grown-ups in charge of them or any school where they were supposed to be inside learning. Two nice-looking women in long black skirts were trying to talk to a group of them. They said they were from some 'mission', but as soon as they came near the children ran away.

I didn't really know what to do or where to go so I headed back to the big street called Broadway. I knew Henry had liked the shops and thought perhaps he might be looking in the grand windows. If he wasn't then I might be able to make my way down to the docks and see if anyone had any news of my brother.

Broadway was just as wonderful in the bright light of day as it had been that late afternoon when we first saw it. There were people everywhere, and for a while I quite forgot what I was supposed to be doing as I stared at all the wonderful things for sale in the shop windows. The sights were glorious. I stood for ages watching the fountain in a large green park where water jetted fifty feet into the air. Smart ladies and gentlemen wandered slowly as if they had nothing better to do, and a girl about my age ran past. She was wearing a pure white dress and boots buttoned at the ankle that shone like a mirror. How Bea would love such a dress. The girl was playing with a hoop which had run away ahead of her. She called to her mother with excitement as she tried to catch it. I wondered if she were ever hungry.

Another palace of a building overlooked the park and two giant American flags fluttered from the roof. I stood and looked at them waving overhead, the stars and stripes bright against a blue sky. They were just like Uncle Niall's drawing. I had to pinch myself. I was here. I was in America. It was all so new and overwhelming but I loved the look of the flags. They seemed so proud and perfect. Surely we would be all right here? I told myself. This was the land of plenty. This was the land Uncle Niall had written about.

I kept walking, drawn by more flags fluttering. This time they flew from the roof of a corner building which was covered in giant paintings. You couldn't help but notice it. The paintings were huge and were of animals from all over the world. As I stood almost breaking my neck to look up I saw a marvellous thing. A bright coloured balloon with a basket underneath lifted off from the roof. The passengers – two women and a man – waved down to the street and I grinned, waving back like mad. How wonderful to fly off into the sky like that in a balloon. What a country this was! And what a building! A large sign read THE AMERICAN MUSEUM and I wished I had brought Toby with me. This was that place those African men had told us about, where things you might think only existed in stories could be found. It had even more wonders than we had been told about. There were advertisements for giants and midgets, jugglers and magicians, a circus made entirely of fleas, a loom run by a dog, the trunk of a tree under which Jesus' disciples had sat before the

Last Supper, trained bears, a dancing Indian woman called Fu-Hum-Me. And someone called Feejee who didn't dance as she was the mermaid and had no legs. It was twenty-five cents to go in and see such sights – how I longed to give it a try. It was all I could think about. I made a promise to myself that before I left this great city I would find the money to go and see such wonders. With great reluctance I left the building and walked on.

The noise and busyness all around me was over-whelming. There hardly seemed to be anywhere that didn't have building work going on as if the city were endlessly knocking itself down and starting again with something new. I couldn't believe how many vehicles were making their way up and down the road – carriages, wagons, carts and omnibuses, all pulled by horses, and trucks pushed by hand; so many that every now and then they became jammed together and there would be the most helpless confusion. No one moved and the police had to come and sort it all out. Everyone would be shouting and to me it looked as though the mess could never be sorted. That someone would surely be injured or a horse might die. But eventually the police did manage to arrange it so that soon everyone was moving along again.

I knew nothing about big city life, so I stepped out into the street without looking. Only to be very nearly run down by a carriage pulled by a white horse which came racing towards me. There were two people in the carriage – a man with the most astonishing blue check trousers and bright yellow hat. He had a thin moustache which curled up like another smile above his lips. He carried a dog on his lap and shaded them both with a small umbrella which matched his trousers. He was nowhere near as astonishing as the driver. In charge of the carriage was a woman in a long bright red dress wearing a man's top hat and carrying a long whip. She did not sit down to drive but stood upright with a great beam on her face and shouting at the horse to 'Go faster'. I didn't think I had ever seen a woman drive a horse at all. As the carriage disappeared in a great cloud of dust I remember smiling and thinking one day I too might drive like that.

I was so busy dreaming that I didn't think to step back onto the pavement. I was still in the street when suddenly a horse brushed past my shoulder and the wheel of a large carriage clipped my foot. I fell headlong into the road, banging my head on a stone. When I turned to look up, it was into the hoof of a horse hovering above me. Instantly the traffic fell into a terrible mess, but I was too shaken to move. A huge vehicle pulled by two large horses had nearly hit me. The driver jumped down from his seat but as he did I saw that he wore a large black cloak. I was dazed and it reminded me of Parker Crossingham. Not thinking clearly, I leaped up in panic. The driver tried to grab me – I think – to see if I was all right, but I couldn't make sense of any of it. I shook him off and began to run. All at once the city didn't seem exciting or grand or anything but a very long way from home. I thought about Ma dying and Da not speaking and poor baby Hero and Toby thinking that the pig was Hamlet and nobody daring to say, and a great sob rose up in my throat. I wanted to shout that I was only twelve and the city was too big for me.

CHAPTER TWENTY-ONE

'Don't run!' the driver shouted after me, but I couldn't stop. I ran and ran until I thought my lungs would burst. If I could have run back to Ireland, I would have. I didn't want to be here. I didn't want to be this far from home. I felt alone and scared. Tears poured down my face so fast that I could hardly see. At last I couldn't run any more. I stopped. My heart was pounding and my legs ached. I looked around, not knowing where I was, and saw a little further on the most incredible church.

We had never been a religious family. Da said religion caused nothing but trouble but even he would have thought this was quite a place. The spire was so high that from the ground it looked as though it could reach right up through the clouds and touch the hand of God. I needed some peace: the traffic was still pounding along Broadway and I was desperate to get away from it. I pulled at one of the vast wooden doors and managed to get it ajar so that I could squeeze my way inside. Instantly I was transported. I had never seen anywhere so beautiful. Vast arches of stone soared above my head, and above the altar was surely the most spectacular window in the world. It was made of coloured glass and had pictures of what I knew to be Jesus and his men. They almost all had beards and one had a lion. I liked the idea of having a lion to come with you everywhere you went. Perhaps I would not be so afraid if a lion were at my side.

There was a small area by the side of the church where candles were flickering. I watched a woman take a fresh one and light it. It took a second to catch and then glowed with a soft flame. She had her back to me but I could see her shoulders shake as she began to sob. She wiped her eyes and then, as she turned back to face me, I realized that I knew her. It was Mrs Kavanagh from the *Pegasus*.

I went straight up to her. 'Mrs Kavanagh! It's me – Slim.'

For a moment she looked as if she didn't know me, then looked around and quickly pulled me down to sit in one of the bench seats. 'Slim!'

I thought she was going to hug me, but instead she stroked my face and smiled. I was very confused. What was she doing here? She had bought a ticket to take her straight to California. I had seen it with my own eyes.

'Shouldn't you be on your way to see your sister? In California?' I asked.

She tried to hold back the tears. She could hardly tell me what had happened. 'Yes,' she finally managed, 'but my ticket . . . it was a cheat. There was no train or boat or coach with horses. I paid all my money and all I got was a pretty picture which wasn't worth anything. When I tried to use it everyone just laughed.'

I was shocked. 'But Mr Hughes – he told you it was all right . . .'

Mrs Kavanagh nodded. 'It was a lie, and now all my money is gone and I don't know how I shall ever get to see my sister. Here I am in New York with nothing and I don't know anyone to go to for help.'

Now she broke down and cried. She cried and cried, and I didn't know what to do. I knew just how she felt but I wasn't sure this was the time to say so. We had little enough space in our terrible room at the Old Brewery but I knew I couldn't leave her. I thought about her baby dying and I wondered if it was with Ma now.

Somehow I found my way back to our dreadful home. It took ages as I kept taking wrong turnings and by the time we got there it was dark. I think Mrs Kavanagh was too tired and upset to see how awful it was. 'Beatrice!' she cried.

'Mrs Kavanagh!' and they fell into each other's arms with delight. How Mrs Kavanagh lit up at the sight of my little sister Hero. Straight away she took the baby in her arms and began to nurse her. She couldn't help but notice that Da was just sitting on the old mattress.

'Hello, Mr Hannigan,' she tried.

I thought for the first time that he glanced up at us, but then he went back to looking at the wall again.

'Grief,' she said. 'It's a dreadful thing.'

It was late. Toby had been out playing with his pig but now he was back and hungry.

'Did you not find Henry?' asked Bea.

I shook my head. 'It's such a big place. There's so much to see. You ought to come with me, Bea. The place where the African men said . . .'

Bea looked cross with me. 'You didn't look for him, did you?'

I felt ashamed of myself. 'I got distracted,' I muttered, 'but I did find Mrs Kavanagh.'

Now Jack went looking but after an hour or more when he too had not returned I became restless. We had no money. Well, that's not entirely true. I still had my lucky shilling in my pocket and I thought now was probably the time to spend it. I looked at our little group which was growing in size and knew something needed to be done.

'I'll go out again,' I said.

But Bea had had enough. 'We should go to Oregon and leave him behind. He's never been anything but trouble,' she said. 'Will he never learn?'

'He's our brother, Bea.' I headed to the door. 'Don't worry. This time I'll find him. I'll make it up to you. I won't look at anything else, I promise.'

Both Bea and Mrs Kavanagh thought I should stay but I had made up my mind.

As I left our room I jumped at a noise. Mr Liu, the Chinaman, was standing in the dark corridor, appearing as if from nowhere. I couldn't think how he had got there. There was no door to our place so we would certainly have seen him if he had walked past, yet there he was. I stared at him. I hadn't really noticed his clothes before. He wore a small black silk hat fitted close to his head with a tiny silk bobble on top. The collar of his shiny black jacket was square and fitted close up round his neck. The picture of a red dragon was embroidered across the shoulders. It matched his silky bright red trousers, which billowed out over black slippers. All his clothes were worn and old yet he looked wonderful to me. His long black hair was pulled back into a ponytail that fell almost to his waist. He had an odd, sharp way of speaking, as if he didn't want to use too many words.

'Your brother Henry?' he said as if he knew what I was thinking. I hadn't even realized he knew our names.

I nodded.

'You try Bowery. He be on Bowery.'

Then he turned and disappeared into the room where his wife without a nose and their pretty child lived. I turned towards the stairs. Night had fallen. It was just as dark outside as it was in our cellar. I was more frightened than I had ever been but I could hear Hero crying. I knew I had to do something. I took a deep breath and went back out into the night.

CHAPTER TWENTY-TWO

I asked a few people and it didn't take long to find the place Mr Liu had recommended. I already knew New York was a place of wonder but the Bowery was another world again. All the big shops, factories and offices had closed as the clocks struck five, and now the streets were packed with people looking for fun. It was as though I had walked into a carnival. Lights blazed from every window while the omnibuses were now lit with coloured lights that seemed to go on as far as the eye could see. It was probably not the place for anyone who was hungry and had no money. There were restaurants everywhere, with waiters trying to persuade people inside by calling out descriptions of their delicious food and their cheap prices.

'Fatted capons the size of turkeys!' yelled one man, while another shouted about the quality of his steaks. One restaurant had a large block of ice in the window, inside which two large fish, each with a lemon in its mouth, appeared to be swimming downwards, forming a V, with a red lobster between them. I was so hungry. I hadn't eaten since the morning and everything looked good. Food tempted me everywhere I looked. Even if you didn't want to go inside to eat there was every kind of delicious thing available in the street. Every ten steps or so there was someone selling hot gingerbread or oysters or apple pie, ice cream, baked pears – and things I had never even heard of, like yams.

An old woman selling clams stood by her street cart calling out:

'Here's clams, here's clams, here's clams today,
They late came from Rockaway.
They're good to roast, they're good to fry,
They're good to make a clam pot pie.
Here they go.'

All life was here, from the beggar picking through bones in a pail of rubbish to the millionaire buying an apple from a stand.

I still had my precious shilling in my pocket. I wanted to spend it so much it almost felt hot – but there wasn't time. The crowd of people hardly noticed me. No one was interested in a little girl, but everywhere I heard men and women speaking like Da with an Irish accent.

One woman stopped me and said, '*Weißt du wo ist der Arzt?*' She said it again: '*Weißt du wo ist der Arzt?*' and would have repeated it a third time, but a young man walking with a big black dog interrupted, saying, 'She's not German.' He turned to me and asked, 'You're not, are you? German?'

I shook my head and said nothing. I didn't want to say I was Irish in case his dog was the sort that didn't like Irish people and tried to bite my nose. I walked on, feeling a bit shaken. Maybe it really *wasn't* safe out here. It felt so strange. There were all sorts of signs I couldn't read; arrows pointing to places with *Lager Bier* and *Großes Konzert; Eintritt frei*. There were gardens full of people drinking beer, and I had no idea who was German and who was Irish. All I knew was that I didn't see Henry amongst them. I saw a man who looked like a pirate, and a funny chattering fellow in a flat hat with a monkey on his shoulder. How Da would have made up stories about these people. How Da would . . . my poor da. It was all I could think about. What were we going to do?

I passed a place where, for three cents, a customer could suck beer from a barrel through a rubber tube till they ran out of breath! Whatever anyone might have wanted to buy was for sale. All along the street there were men shouting about their cheap prices, how everything was so low in price that they were 'on the verge of ruin', that they were throwing their goods away for the benefit of the customers! Those who had nothing to sell were buying cheap lottery tickets in the 'exchanges' in the hope that they might make their fortune and join the rich up on Madison

Avenue or Broadway. Others had already lost every-thing and were coming out of the shops called pawnbrokers, where anything could be sold. Even the shirt off your back.

Mrs Liu had told me about those places; because before she married Mr Liu she had been to them herself. They always had a sign of three gold balls above the door and the windows were full of sad treasures that desperate people had sold for tiny amounts of money.

I slipped past a narrow opening down to a cellar where a concert of some kind was in full blast. Air rushed up from the steps, hot and smelling horrible. I could hear the sound of loud partying coming from below. I stood for a moment wondering if Henry could be in such a place, but I didn't dare go down so I walked on. A crowd had gathered in the next corner to watch two dogs fight, and a policeman wearing his gold badge of office on a plain suit was trying to settle everyone down. Just then a wild cry of 'Stop thief!' came from an alleyway and

354

everyone's attention turned. Even the dogs gave up and slipped away into the dark.

I was so busy watching all the excitement that I nearly tripped over a beggar sitting on the pavement. He called out, 'Help for a blind man! Will no one help a blind man?' His hat lay in front of him on the ground ready to accept coins from kind strangers. A smart-looking woman passing on the arm of a gentleman threw a coin in and walked on. I noticed that the blind man's eyes suddenly seemed better, for he picked the coin up and checked to see how much it was worth. Ahead, in the middle of the street, a band of musicians began playing, and the noise grew loud enough to drown out the Punch and Judy show on the next corner. I was somewhere between terrified and excited the whole time.

I drifted past a theatre where a minstrel show was advertised. I stopped to look at the pictures and thought how odd the black men in them looked. Not at all like the lovely three who had helped us with our cart when we first arrived. These somehow didn't look real.

I passed an alley beside a restaurant. A boy in a ragged pair of trousers was bringing out a large serving plate from a kitchen door. I could see the remains of a cooked chicken and some potatoes and I could hardly speak as, without a thought, he scraped it into a bin. I waited till he had gone back in and ran over to look inside the bin. I couldn't believe my luck. There, lying on some old cabbage leaves, was at least half a chicken and three potatoes. What kind of a person could throw such a feast away? I looked round and saw that no one was looking into the dark alley, so I reached into the bin and pulled out the food. How I wanted to eat it all straight away, but more than that I wanted to see the faces of everyone at home when I returned with such a feast. I stuffed the food in my pockets and practically ran in case the kitchen boy returned, having realized how foolish he had been.

I ran through the crowds and kept going till I

was out of breath. I stopped, panting, on a street corner, and as I stood there a new sound filled the air. It sounded just like the Captain's blunderbuss on the *Pegasus*. Along almost the entire length of this street I saw people firing guns at places called shooting galleries; places where anyone who could manage to hit a bull's-eye might win a prize. You didn't even have to step inside to have a go. Anyone could just pay and fire a gun at one of the targets right from the street. And what things there were to aim at! There was a bright yellow lion with a wide mouth which, if hit in the right spot, would bellow a truly royal roar. Or a trumpeter who you had to shoot in the heart in order to make him raise his trumpet to his lips and send forth a blast loud enough to wake every Bowery baby in existence.

A crowd of barefoot and penniless boys were gathered to watch people give it a try.

'Only five cents a shot,' cried one of the stall-holders, 'and a knife to be given to the man who hits the bull's-eye.'

That was when I saw the knife you could win. I had never seen anything like it. Da's knife had been a fine piece of steel, but it had just been one sharp blade and a wooden handle. This prize knife was quite another matter. It was advertised as 'the Finest Penknife Ever Made', and so it looked. It was about eight inches long with a beautiful bone handle, but instead of having just one blade it appeared to be almost an entire tool box in one glorious instrument. The sharp blade could fold away into the handle and other marvellous tools could then be opened. There was some sort of corkscrew piece of metal, a small hook, a big hook, a small saw and a flat blade for doing heaven knows what. I knew in that moment that this was the knife Da needed. With such a knife in his hands he would be sure to smile again. I thought about his knife flying off the boat into the sea and I knew it was my fault; that I needed to make things right. This was the very gift to bring Da back from the dark place in his mind. I was hungry, but there was not the food in the world that was going to stop me winning this knife for my wonderful father. I stopped thinking about Bea and Toby and the baby and Mrs Kavanagh and I certainly stopped thinking about finding Henry, as I stepped forward through the crowd.

I was small and easily made my way to the front of the counter, where a group of young men wearing black silk hats and with their hair all oiled were standing around laughing. One of them had just fired at a target, very nearly hitting the stallholder, who was furious. I tried to get the man's attention, but no one was expecting a small girl to be out on a Saturday night shooting anything. My shoulders were pushed and pressed by the crowd – until at last I called out, bold as you like, 'Excuse me! I'd like to have a go!'

There was a moment's silence as everyone looked around to see where the voice had come from. Then one of the young men spotted me and pointed. 'It's a girl! Ha! A little girl in boy's trousers wants to have a go!'

Now everyone began pointing and laughing about the girl who wanted to shoot a bull's-eye. The owner of the gallery wandered over. It was late and he was tired, but I reckoned he would take money from anyone.

'Five cents a go,' he repeated.

I reached into my pocket and pulled out the precious coin that had rolled towards me all that time ago at the Custom House in Dublin. 'I have an English shilling.' I held it up to the light. 'How many cents is that?'

The owner waved his hand at me. 'Get off with you. This is not a place for girls.'

I had made up my mind and was not leaving without the knife. 'I've got money,' I insisted. 'I want to have a go. I want to win the knife.'

The owner bent down and looked at me. 'How old are you?' he asked.

'Twelve,' I replied, which was surely old enough to do anything.

By now a crowd was beginning to gather, and

perhaps the stallholder thought he might make more business out of everyone wanting to see a girl shoot. He sucked on his teeth for a moment and then said, 'All right, Mrs Twelve Years Old, you can have a go . . .' He looked around at the large crowd. 'On the house!' he added with a flick of his hand. A cheer went up.

I had never heard such an expression. 'What does that mean?' I asked. 'On the house?'

'It's free, you young fool,' explained the nearest man in the crowd. 'Go on. Give it a try. Nothing to lose.'

Now the owner was enjoying himself. 'Roll up, roll up,' he called out in a loud voice. 'Come and watch the little girl try to make the lion roar.'

He reached for a rifle, loaded it and handed it to me. The gun was almost as long as I was tall. I tried to lift the wooden end to my shoulder as I had seen others do, but it was so heavy that the metal barrel swung round, and for a brief second pointed at the crowd. There was a great yell as people ducked out of the way before I finally managed to turn back to face the lion. I thought about the one in the church. The one on the stained-glass window and how I had wished for a lion by my side. How things changed, for now I lifted the gun again, holding the trigger with my right hand and the barrel with my left, and pointed at the great creature. Then the strangest thing happened.

'Put your elbow on the counter,' whispered a voice in my ear. I looked round but I couldn't see anyone. A hand reached out and helped me settle the weight of the gun against my body.

'Now look down the barrel of the gun and aim at the lion,' continued the voice.

The crowd were all waiting, so I lowered my head and put my right eye level with the long piece of metal that ran along the top of the gun.

'It will hit back at your shoulder when you fire,' said the voice, 'so try and stand as steady as you can.'

I pushed my legs apart and tried to dig into the pavement.

'Get on with it!' someone shouted.

Now I closed my left eye so that the lion's face entirely filled the sight in my right. I put my right forefinger on the trigger and took a deep breath.

'Now fire!' said my new invisible friend.

It only took seconds, but to me that moment of firing a gun for the first time seemed to last for ever. I squeezed my finger against the trigger with all my might. It was really hard and the gun slightly moved. I could hardly focus as I brought the end of the rifle back to the lion's face – and before you knew it there was a massive bang and I fell back onto my bottom on the pavement. The gun dropped from my hands and cracked down on the ground beside me. There was a dreadful silence, and then I heard it: the great roar of the lion followed by the even louder roar of the crowd. A hand reached down to pick me up off the ground. I turned to see who was helping me, and was horrified to see the burned and scarred face of Henry's old friend Kyle.

CHAPTER TWENTY-THREE

I scrambled to get on my feet by myself but Kyle wouldn't let go of my arm.

'Kyle, I . . . what are you doing here?' I demanded.

He sneered at me and squeezed hard on my shoulder. 'You Hannigans think you're the only ones can take a boat? Did Henry think he was going to leave me to take all the blame with the police?'

He leaned in close and I could see all the tight white markings where his face hadn't healed properly.

'Go get your prize,' he encouraged, and I recognized now that his was the voice that had helped me. I picked up the gun and headed back to the counter. By now the crowd were cheering and patting me on the back. The owner was not at all pleased, but he had no choice with so many people watching. He took the penknife from where it had been on display and fetched a small leather bag. He placed the knife inside and carefully handed it to me. He could not bring himself to smile.

'Well done,' he said almost grinding his teeth. He leant down so the crowd wouldn't hear, 'Now don't come back.'

I nodded and, in a daze, took the bag. I almost began to cry. I knew I held in my hands the greatest prize ever given. I opened the small bag and looked down at the beautiful knife, and carried on staring as I left the great mass of people behind and walked away.

Kyle moved to stand in my way and put out his hand. 'I'll have that,' he said.

I knew he had helped me but there was no way anyone other than Da was having the knife. I shook my head and put it behind my back.

'What are you going to do with such a knife?' he asked. 'You're just a girl.'

'It's a present for my father. He's not well,' I explained.

Kyle did his best to look sympathetic. 'Is he not? Oh, what a shame!' Then he gave a small laugh and grabbed for the prize. 'Well, your poor da is not getting it. Now give it to me.' He pulled me closer and suddenly sniffed loudly. 'Wait a minute!' he declared, sniffing again. 'You smell of chicken!'

It was bad enough that he might take the knife from me but he wasn't having our dinner as well! It was terrible but without thinking I stomped straight down hard on his foot and turned to run away.

He howled with pain. I could hear him hobbling after me, shouting, 'You'd never have won that without me!'

Kyle was much bigger than me, but I was quick and determined. I ran back past all the beer drinking and the mermaids. I ran and ran until I reached Broadway, where once again, without looking, I sprinted out into the street. This time the carriage hit my shoulder square on. I collapsed onto the ground and there was a terrible sound of horses whinnying and people shouting. I think I was knocked out for a minute, for when I looked up it was into the kindly face of an old man. He was neatly dressed, and what hair he had was white, including his beard which sat neatly round his throat and under his chin.

He looked at me with his blue eyes and chuckled. 'Well, well, if you're not determined to be run over by someone today.'

He helped me to sit up and immediately I began to panic. 'The knife! The knife! Where's the knife?'

The man held up my prize in his hand. 'Is this what you are looking for?' he asked.

I nodded. I wasn't feeling at all well. 'It's for my father.'

The man smiled. 'It's beautiful. How did you come by it?'

I held the knife tight. 'I won it! I didn't steal it! Honest, the man said I could have a go and everyone was laughing at a girl shooting, but I shot the lion right in the mouth with my gun and I won!'

The man put his hand up to stop me going on. 'I believe you. I didn't think you were a pickpocket.'

I had never heard of such a thing. 'Sure this city is full of new things,' I said. 'What's a pickpocket?'

The old man's voice sounded very serious. 'People who steal from other people's pockets. I don't like them. I don't like them at all. If I catch them I go straight to the police.'

I couldn't imagine how you could steal from someone else's pocket or why you would do such a thing.

'It's awfully late. Shouldn't you be home? Your mother . . .'

'I don't have a mother,' I whispered, hardly bearing to say it. 'I mean, I did, but she's gone now.'

'Well, then you'd better let me take you home to your father.'

Suddenly I was suspicious. 'How do you know I have one of them?'

He pointed at the knife. 'The present? For your father, you said. I always like to pay attention to what I am told. He will be very proud of you.'

The thought that Da might be pleased was too much, and now the tears began to come. I tried to dry them away with my sleeve, but as soon as I got rid of one it was followed by another. I didn't want to cry but my eyes would not listen.

The man looked at me and gently suggested, 'I'll take you home.'

I shook my head. 'I'm not supposed to talk to strangers,' I explained.

'Hmm.' The man thought for a moment. 'Well, first of all we are not strangers for we have met before.'

'We have?' I said, bewildered.

'Yes. You had the good fortune not to be hit by the circumvolution of the wheels of my carriage earlier today on Broadway. We seem destined to meet.'

I looked at his dark cloak and realized he was

369

the driver who had tried to help me up from the road before, the one I'd thought was Parker Crossingham.

'I'm sorry I ran,' I said.

'Indeed.' The driver put his hand out to shake mine. 'Well, as we are not strangers we had better know each other's appellations.'

I had no idea what he was talking about.

'Names,' he explained. 'Our monikers. My name is Horace . . . and you are?'

'They call me Slim.'

'Slim,' he repeated. 'What a delightful designator, a name of names.' Horace clapped his hands together as if everything were now settled in the most pleasing way. 'Isn't that splendid? Superbly splendid, in fact.'

'What is?'

'That we are now friends.' Once more the old fellow clapped his hands with pleasure. Then he leaned forward and asked in a serious voice, 'Do you have many friends in New York, Slim?'

I shook my head.

'I thought not,' he said gravely. 'Shall we be friends?'

I looked at him. He had the nicest face and really kind eyes. I didn't know if he was one of the ones we could trust but I thought so. I nodded, and Horace smiled and nodded back.

'Well, Slim, always a pleasure to be your first friend in this great city. Do you have a patronym? A surname.'

'Hannigan,' I said.

He considered this for a moment. 'Hannigan, indeed – and you are the Hannigans of . . . ?'

It was taking me a while to get used to the way the man spoke. I had never heard anything like it. He smiled. 'Where do you live, Slim?'

'The Old Brewery. Not for long, you understand, but for the moment—'

'Indeed,' he interrupted, helping me up. 'The Hannigans of the Old Brewery. Well, well. Now perhaps you will allow me to escort you to meet my dearest chums, Romeo and Juliet, who very nearly made an impression on you.'

'Who?' I asked, confused. I was sure they were the names of people in one of the plays Da used to love so much.

'My horses. They nearly ran you over and are bound to be sorry.'

Horace walked me over to where he had stopped his carriage in a hurry. It was a beautiful thing, with two large wheels at the back and two slightly smaller ones at the front. It was bright yellow with a narrow seat for the driver, and behind that a covered part with a door and a window through to two wider, more comfortable benches for passengers. Two horses stood in front, snorting, one brown and one almost black with a white mark on her forehead.

Horace stood beside the black horse. 'This is Juliet,' he said. Then he turned to the horse and announced, 'Juliet, this is my new friend, Slim.'

Then he turned to the brown horse. 'This is Romeo. Romeo, this is my new friend, Slim.' He pretended to reach for Romeo's ear to whisper in it, 'Be careful. She's very good with a gun. Shot a lion only this evening.'

'Is this your carriage?' I asked.

Horace smiled. 'It is indeed.'

'How is it that you have such a fine carriage?' I said in wonder, looking at the beautiful shiny paint and leather seats. 'Are you rich?'

Horace laughed. 'Not exactly, but I work very hard. This is America, Slim. When you work very hard you get nice things. Now let's pop you home.'

'Can I sit with you?' I asked.

Without another word he helped me up onto the narrow seat and then swung up beside me. I thought it looked a nice job, driving a carriage. I remembered the woman I had seen driving earlier and wondered if I might ever have a go. 'Is it nice, driving a carriage?'

Horace smiled. 'It is, although usually I have a fellow who does it for me and he says it's too hot in the summer and too cold in the winter. But then, some people are always unhappy.'

'My da is unhappy.'

'Is he now? I'm sorry to hear that.'

Horace made a gentle clicking sound, and that was all it took to persuade the horses to head for Five Points. They walked slowly through the streets, and honestly, I felt like a queen. The light from the gas lamps glowed as people hurried home.

'Broadway!' sighed Horace beside me. 'Doesn't matter how often I drive up and down here I never get tired of it. Most remarkable street in the world. Look at those lamps. Nineteen thousand gas lamps just on this one street, and that's not even counting the lights private parties put out in the street themselves. And if you think that's a lot, consider the fact that as many as twenty thousand vehicles travel up and down this thoroughfare every day. I've not been everywhere, but I bet there's nothing else like it in the world.'

He was right. There probably was nothing else

like it in the world. So many lamps of different colours. So many shop windows, all brightly lit. A theatre was just letting out its customers. There was a giant mirror above the door and I was almost blinded by the white rays of light which streamed out from it into the street. Everywhere there were cheerful voices and laughter. The restaurants and cafés were full of customers eating the finest foods. You couldn't think that in Ireland people were eating grass and dying. A pale-faced girl was selling hot corn on the steps of a bank. I had seen her before, but now I noticed a small boy beside her too. Suddenly a man came out of the building and shooed them away. I could hear him shouting, 'Clear out, you dirty brats. Don't come on these steps again, or I will throw your corn in the gutter.'

Horace shook his head and drove on.

We passed some grand houses. Through the windows I could see happy faces in lamplit parlours with beautiful wallpaper and paintings. I couldn't imagine that I might ever live like that. I ran my hands over the smooth surface of the leather seats, and leaned back, listening to the sound of Romeo and Juliet's hoofs across the streets. It was late and I was so tired after all the excitement that I had almost drifted off by the time we arrived back at the Old Brewery.

It was only as we were about to go inside that I remembered I still hadn't found my brother.

CHAPTER TWENTY-FOUR

My new friend Horace was the best thing that ever happened to us. He came down into the cellar and saw how we were living, but he never said a bad word about it. My family had been so worried about me, and there was still no news of Henry. I realized once again I had failed and become distracted. I was clearly not to be trusted in New York. Jack had been a long way looking for him, but with no luck. We should have been upset, but Horace had a way of making everyone feel much better. He cooed at the baby, treated Bea and Mrs Kavanagh as if they were the finest of ladies, and admired Toby's pig so much that I thought my little brother would burst with pride.

'That's a clever-looking creature,' he said,

petting Hamlet. 'I bet you could teach it to do tricks.'

Toby beamed, and I'm not even sure Hamlet didn't look rather pleased with himself.

So far Da had said nothing but Horace moved to stand in front of him. He bowed slightly and said, 'Mr Hannigan? My name is Horace. I had the honour of escorting your daughter Slim home this evening after her excitement of shooting a lion on your behalf.'

Da's eyes flickered and Bea laughed. 'A lion? Whatever have you been up to, Slim?'

Horace, not seeming to mind the terrible old mattress, sat down next to Da and insisted that I tell the whole story. I was a little shy at first, but soon I was telling them all about the German people and the stalls and how the fellow had let me have a go with the gun for nothing.

'A lion? A real lion?' asked Toby, his eyes out on stalks.

'It looked real,' I said. 'With a great big mouth and rows of teeth.'

'And you shot it right in the mouth?' laughed Bea with delight.

'I did,' I said, feeling as proud as I had ever felt in my life. I felt happier than I had in ages and . . . I don't know . . . taller somehow.

I told them everything but I did not mention Kyle. I don't know why but something stopped me.

Horace clapped his hands. 'You've left out the best bit!' he said excitedly. 'The prize! Wait till you see this, Mr Hannigan.'

Slowly I pulled the precious penknife out of my pocket. I stood in front of Da and carefully opened the bag it came in. Both Bea and Mrs Kavanagh gave a sound of appreciation and looked at each other.

'It's not just a knife, Da,' I explained. 'There's hooks and a saw and everything. It's for you because I . . . because I ruined everything . . . because I made you go away when I knocked your knife into the water and . . .'

I couldn't go on. I put the knife in Da's lap and

was going to turn away when I heard him say, 'It's beautiful, Slim.' It was the first thing he had said in ages.

'Oh, Da,' sighed Bea, overwhelmed.

For the first time since Ma left us, Da looked right at me. Then he took the knife and turned it over in his hand. 'It's beautiful,' he repeated, and soon we were all hopeless with tears running down our faces. I started sobbing because I felt I had finally done something right. Mrs Kavanagh put her arms around me as I wept and wept with happiness.

Horace took it all in, looking around the room.

'We haven't been able to get him to speak,' explained Mrs Kavanagh. 'Not since his lovely wife . . .'

Mrs Kavanagh had been very fond of Ma and she couldn't finish the sentence. Horace reached out to pat me on my shoulder as if to say that it was going to be all right now. I knew then he was my friend. I was so pleased I could hardly contain myself. I dried my eyes and pulled away from Mrs

Kavanagh. I felt I'd behaved like a silly girl so I went to put my hands in my pockets. That was when I remembered our dinner.

'Chicken!' I cried. 'I've got chicken.' I began pulling the meat out of my pocket. 'And some potato!' It had all become a little squashed with all my running around but it was still better than anything we had seen in a long time.

'Is this what you eat?' asked Horace as we shared it out.

'We're not usually this lucky,' explained Bea, tucking into a chicken wing and smiling.

'Have some!' offered Toby.

Horace put up his hand. 'No! You have so little.'

'Where we come from in Ballysmaragaid,' my little brother said solemnly, 'we share what we have.'

Horace went home, but the next day he returned and fixed the door of our stove. He brought bread and milk. I heard him speak in a low voice to Da. I don't know what he said, but he persuaded Da for the first time up into the street to meet Romeo and Juliet. Da still wasn't talking much but the fact that he was willing to go out was a huge step forward.

After that Horace would come by every morning to take Da out for a drive. Bea was bolder now that she had Mrs Kavanagh with her, and the two of them would dare to go out with the baby for a stroll when the weather was fine. Jack followed along behind, making sure no one bothered them.

One day Horace discovered that Mrs Kavanagh couldn't read and mentioned it to Da. 'She needs to become an abecedarian,' he exclaimed.

Da smiled at that – it was so good to see him smile.

'An abecedarian,' repeated Horace. 'It's a marvellous word. It means a person who is learning the alphabet.'

Da had never heard that word and liked it very much.

'Words are my life, Mr Hannigan,' Horace explained solemnly.

I watched Da play with the word in his mouth. 'Abecedarian,' he repeated, and you could almost see him trying to think how he might use such a word in a story.

'I don't think Jack can read either,' I said. Jack looked embarrassed. 'It's all right, Jack,' I soothed, 'you'll learn in no time and then you can help with the printing press.'

Soon Da was doing what he did best, spending a little time every day teaching. He made his own little school with Elsie and Mrs Liu, Mrs Kavanagh and Jack as they all learned to read. They would sit for hours, drawing the alphabet over and over again, and I think it was good for all of them. Jack had scavenged some pencils, and on days when it was too much for Da, Bea taught them all how to draw. She would do pictures of fine ladies while Jack liked to invent magic flying machines. Da was watching his little class scribbling away when he said to me

'Thank you, Slim. Thank you for looking after everyone. Your ma would be proud of you.'

He pulled me into a great hug and kissed the top of my head. I nodded and then had to leave the room in case I started doing silly crying again.

Still there was no sign of Henry. I think we were all more disappointed in him than worried.

'I thought he'd learned his lesson,' said Bea.

'We should still look for him,' insisted Toby. 'Maybe he needs us.'

Maybe he did, but I was too scared to go looking in case I bumped into Kyle again. Even with Horace's help I knew that we couldn't live in this dreadful place for ever. I knew we needed to do something but I couldn't think what. It was Jack who came up with a plan. One morning, perhaps a month later, I was sitting with him and Mrs Kavanagh and baby Hero on the steps of the Old Brewery. The weather had warmed a little and we were enjoying a little sun. Mrs Kavanagh had just fed the baby and was patting my little sister on the back. She had started smiling and it was making us laugh.

Suddenly Jack said, 'How long before Oregon?'

I looked at his kind face and realized he hated being here as much as I did.

'We need money, Jack, and we need to find Henry,' I replied. 'New York is so big and we don't know where to look for him.'

Jack nodded, and then he came up with the most brilliant plan. 'Make your newspaper,' he said.

'Our newspaper?'

He nodded again. 'It's why you came. You told me. Make your newspaper and look for Henry.'

Mrs Kavanagh looked at him and declared, 'That's brilliant!'

I still wasn't sure what he meant, and Mrs Kavanagh had to explain. 'Print your newspaper, Slim, the one you talked about on the ship,' she said. 'Use your machine to print a newspaper and write about looking for your brother. This is a big city. There must be others who have arrived and can't find their families. You could sell a paper that helps them as well as helping us.'

It was a splendid idea but I knew I would need help. That evening, when Horace returned from taking Da for a drive, I took him to the old shop on Mulberry Bend where Liam, Jack and Henry had left the printing press. He seemed even more interested and impressed than I had hoped.

'Have you printed things before?' he asked.

'I haven't,' I said honestly. 'But Henry printed leaflets in Ireland so I know it works and I know *how* it works. I just need paper and ink and I don't know where to get them.'

'Where did your brother get it in Ireland?'

'From some people at a paper in Dublin called *The Nation*,' I replied. 'He said they were happy to help. Do you know anyone?'

Horace smiled and said, 'I believe I do.'

He turned and left while I covered the precious machine back up. I was just leaving the shop when a great gang of young men came round the corner.

'Hey, you!' called one of them – and I saw that it was Kyle. He was quick and had grabbed me before I had a minute to think. 'Where's my knife?' he demanded.

'Let me go!' I yelled, but I couldn't get away. There must have been six or seven lads with him and I saw that one of them was Liam Byrne. He was staring at me and I thought he looked embarrassed, as if he wanted to help me but didn't know how.

Liam pushed his way to the front of the crowd. 'Never mind some bloody knife,' he said gruffly to Kyle. 'Where's your brother, Henry? That's who we want. Snivelling little so and so.'

'What do you want with him?' I demanded.

Kyle squeezed my arm. 'Never you mind. Bad enough he put that Parker Crossingham after me in Ireland – now he's trying to cheat us. We will find him. You tell him that!'

'Let her go,' suggested Liam, 'and we'll follow her home to find the rotten Hannigan.'

What was wrong with Liam? I thought he was

our friend. Kyle let me go and I knew enough to run in the opposite direction to the Old Brewery. I ran and ran, with the gang of boys running and yelling behind me. I reached a wide avenue and saw an omnibus barrelling towards me. I waited till it was nearly beside me and then raced in front of it. I just made it, but the omnibus stopped quickly and blocked the way for the gang of boys to get past. I ducked down an alleyway and hid for ages before daring to go home.

Later, I told Bea and Da what had happened. Bea looked confused. 'But Liam knows where we live,' she said. 'If he wanted to, he could just come here with the gang.'

It was true and it didn't make sense. Why had he said they would follow me to find out where we lived when he knew all along?

'Perhaps he isn't so bad after all,' said Da. 'He seemed a good lad when we were on board together. He likes you, Bea. I can't think he would want to hurt you or your family.'

That was true but even so I felt anxious. The only good thing was being able to talk things over with Da again and not feel as if I had to be in charge. If we could just find Henry things might even get back to normal.

The next morning Horace called for me and took me for a walk down a narrow street known as Nassau. It ran parallel with Broadway, but unlike that great thoroughfare this place was much narrower. The road was hardly big enough for two carts to pass each other, and the small pavement gave the sense that no one was ever expecting a crowd. The houses on either side were so tall that the street could never be in anything but shadow. It wasn't a cheerful place.

Horace strode ahead. 'It may look like nothing, this thoroughfare, young Slim, yet this is the pulsing heart of the city for there is money here. Such money as you and I cannot imagine.' He waved his hands at the buildings we were passing. 'Why, from cellar to attic these rooms are jammed full of busy, scheming men. Some of the best known and most trusted banking houses of this great city are here dealing with millions of dollars every day. There are real-estate men selling houses for as much as a thousand dollars apiece. Why, behind these doors you can buy diamonds of the purest water—'

Horace leaned down to whisper – 'And others that had better be kept out of water.'

He waved his arm in the air again as if to gather in all that was so valuable around us. 'The most priceless of watches may be obtained here, and advice so expensive you will wish you had never asked.'

In no other part of New York had I seen so many signs. The fronts of the houses were covered with them. They were in nearly every window. The walls of the halls of the buildings, and even the steps themselves were covered with them. There were counsellors at law, publishers, artists, jewellers, engravers on wood and steel, printers, stockbrokers, gold beaters, restaurant keepers, translators of foreign languages, fruit sellers, boarding-house brokers, matrimonial agents and, in almost every cellar, a bookseller.

'We must bring Da here!' I exclaimed.

'Indeed we must,' agreed Horace.

No one in Nassau Street was lounging about. Everyone was on their way somewhere, and usually at great speed. Even in the restaurants people seemed to bolt their food and gulp their drinks before darting out as if their lives depended on it. Several people bumped into us; a couple of times only Horace's steady arm saved me from landing in the street.

'Where are we going?' I asked.

'You, my dear Slim,' he replied smiling, 'are going to see a man who' – we came out into a wide square where three large office buildings all faced each other – 'owns that place.' He pointed to one of the buildings, above which the words *New York Tribune* were written. 'This, Slim, is Printing House Square. Here you will find the greatest newspapers in the

world – *The Times*, *The World* and *The Tribune*.'
He carried on walking towards the *Tribune* building.
'The man who owns the *Tribune* came to New York
with nothing but a plan to start a newspaper. You need
a friend in the newspaper business to help you.'

'Will he see me?' I asked, astonished.

Horace stopped and looked most serious. 'I don't
doubt it for a moment.' We stopped at the front
door. 'Let me go in first. You wait a few minutes,
then come in and ask for the editor.'

'But I'm nobody,' I protested.

Horace looked quite severe. 'My dear friend.
This is America. We are all somebody.' Horace
wiped a little dust from my shoulders.

'What shall I say?'

'That you are also in the newspaper business and
you would appreciate his help.' And with that
Horace opened the door and went inside.

I waited and nearly lost my nerve as I stood there,
until at last I gave a great sigh and pushed open the
large door to the newspaper offices.

Just beyond the main door there was a counter where a very thin man was reading the paper. He didn't look up for ages, until at last I spoke. Then everything I had to say came out in a great rush: 'I want to see the editor because . . . because I am also in the newspaper business and I need his help . . . and it's America.'

He put down his paper very slowly and stood up to look down at me. 'Indeed,' he said. 'I believe he is expecting you.'

I was amazed by this. Horace was a marvel. 'He is?' I managed.

The man now led the way through a little gate in the counter, turned left through an open doorway and then climbed a short, narrow flight of stairs until we found ourselves in a small room with a green carpet. I saw an open bookshelf filled with old almanacs and beside it, a bed, a writing desk, three armchairs, a small low table and a marble sink. The desk was covered in paper, as well as an old straw hat, an open pot of glue, a half-broken box of wafers, a small box of sand and a great mass of newspaper clippings. Half-opened letters still married to their envelopes covered the small table, while balls of paper littered the floor. On the wall was a certificate of life membership to something, as well as maps of the world, New York and New Jersey.

A man was seated with his back to us at the desk.

'Mr Greeley, your guest,' announced my guide, and then turned away and left.

The man at the desk had been writing but he stopped and slowly swivelled round in his chair. He held a beautiful fountain pen in his hand. It was Horace.

'Horace!' I exclaimed.

He nodded and smiled at me. 'Indeed, Horace Greeley.'

I was so astonished I sat down on the floor with a bump. 'You own a newspaper?' I managed at last.

'That I do.' He smiled again, and then tried to look serious. 'Now let's get down to business. How old are you, Slim?'

'Twelve,' I replied.

He thought about that for a moment and then declared, 'Perfect age to be in the newspaper business. What kind of newspaper do you want to make?'

'I want to find Henry, but there must be others having the same trouble – looking for people off the boats,' I said. 'Who's arrived and from where – that sort of thing . . . People want to know what's happening to their own kind.' Horace didn't answer so I carried on, 'And stories maybe. Everyone likes a good story.'

He didn't say anything but instead put his pen in his teeth as he looked at me. It made me lose confidence.

'Do you think I can't do it because I'm a girl?'

Horace shook his head. 'Goodness me, no,' he replied. 'I have the most wonderful woman who writes for me. She's called Margaret Fuller and she's my literary editor. She would shoot me if I said you couldn't do it. No, I was thinking of a proposition for you. I want you to write about your family, about the Hannigans. The life you came from and the life you have found here in New York. If you help me to do that then in return I will give you the paper and ink you need. Would you want anything else?'

I shook my head. 'No, thank you. I have my own printing press.'

He smiled and sat back. 'Indeed you do. So do I. Would you like to see it?'

'When will I get the paper and ink?' I asked.

He gave a short laugh and declared, 'Soon as you like. Come and see.' He got up and led me to a large room on the ground floor.

I could hear the noise of the printing long before Horace opened the door. In a room the size of a warehouse a giant machine was busy churning out newspapers. Men were working on three levels, which had been built around the massive press. In the centre a colossal wheel turned, while workers were kept busy feeding giant sheets of individual blank paper into the press and carrying away printed ones.

'Where are the letters?' I shouted.

'The letters?' Horace frowned and then said, 'Oh, the type. That's what's on the central cylinder.' He turned and put his hand on my shoulder. 'You're right to start a newspaper, Slim. Information is the backbone of democracy and there was never a more exciting time for it.'

I couldn't take my eyes off the great steam press, which was churning out paper so fast I could hardly believe it.

'Do you know how many papers there are in New York?'

I shook my head.

'No indeed. There's one started practically every day. I'd guess at any one time there are about twenty-five, but they come and go so make sure yours has something special that people want to part with two pennies for. Now come down here,' he said.

We left the monster machine and walked towards another room. It was quieter than the printing room but just as big. Here a small army of men in shirt-sleeves were busy folding the papers by hand, ready to sell.

'Ten thousand papers a day come out of here. As soon as they're ready, they'll go out onto the streets for the newsboys to sell.'

Horace walked back to the Old Brewery with me, helping me to carry the great pile of paper and pail of ink I had been given in the vast printing room. He carried an umbrella, and I remember the steady tapping noise it made on the cobbled streets as we walked. I realized he was striding along as though he owned the place, and I tried to swagger beside him. I was tired of feeling afraid.

'I'll pay you back,' I said.

Horace smiled at me. 'When I first walked up

these streets, Slim, I had everything I owned in the world tied up in one handkerchief. I didn't have any friends or any money. I know what it's like, so let's not worry about how you can pay me back just yet.'

Horace put his head up and smiled as if to embrace the whole city. 'If ever there was a place to turn your dreams into gold, this is it. You and I, Slim, we need to tell the stories of this city. Why, it's the greatest gathering of people on earth. There's a story on every corner. Take Bayard Street – you go up there and you'll find the North American Hotel. Look up on the roof and you'll see a wooden statue of the owner, Jimmy Reynolds. You might think that guy must be pretty rich, but here's the real story. Before the hotel was built there used to be a large tree in that street. One day a young man about your age helped a stranger carry a trunk to the wharf and the traveller gave him a few pennies to say thank you. Instead of spending the money, the young man bought some apples which he sold under that tree.

From those profits he set up a fruit stand, and eventually he had enough money to build the hotel on the very same street. The tree meant so much to him and his success that he had the statue carved from it.'

I loved that story and thought how anyone getting off a boat here would want to hear such a thing. How they might imagine having such a statue of themselves one day.

That night we were all very excited at the thought of printing our newspaper and finding Henry. Even Da seemed ready to help.

'We need something Irish in the title and we ought to get down to the docks to get news from back home that is as fresh as possible. What a wonder this is going to be, Slim.'

Da seemed almost his old self and how we all loved those chats with Horace. He came round most evenings and would write notes in his little journal as he asked questions. He also met Mrs Liu and heard her sad tale. She wasn't used to visitors and was shy and nervous, but when Horace said he might be able to find news of her brother, she smiled and smiled. He stood in her room, tapping the floor with his umbrella as he asked about her life. The point of the umbrella was tipped with a thin sheet of brass, and as he listened to her story he poked it into the wall behind the stove. The wall was so soft and damp that when he drew the point of the umbrella out again it left a deep round mark, as if the whole building were made of rotten cheese. He took his small notebook and a pencil out of his pocket and wrote these things down.

Da watched and said quietly, 'Take an interest in life, Slim, and you'll never need to look for a single story.'

Jack knew that I was scared of Kyle's gang so when we took the paper and ink up to the shop in Mulberry Bend he stood guard. Da came with us, and Horace took time to be impressed.

'And you made this?' he asked Da, and my father almost managed a smile.

'And my brother Aedan,' he added quietly.

'But he's still in Ireland,' I added, 'and we never even said goodbye.'

Horace looked at us both and said, 'Then you need to send him your newspaper when it is ready so he can see what great work has been produced.'

I looked at Horace and asked, 'Will you help us?'

He turned away from the press and put out his hand. 'I most certainly will.'

We shook hands, and with that I, Slim Hannigan, went into the newspaper business.

CHAPTER TWENTY-FIVE

The best thing that happened about then was that Da came back to us more and more every day. I don't know what helped the most. Maybe it was Horace and his Shakespearean horses taking him out and about in New York, maybe it was little Hero, maybe it was Mrs Kavanagh, or maybe it was the knife I had got him but something made him wake from his long sad sleep. I introduced him to our neighbours and he was shocked by what had happened to Mrs Liu just because someone hated the Irish.

'What a terrible thing to do to a woman,' he kept muttering.

One night he returned from his drive with Horace with a determined look in his eye. Bea and Mrs

Kavanagh were chatting by the stove while little baby Hero slept on the mattress. Jack and I were looking through a copy of the *Tribune* someone had left in the street the day before.

'See how they have one main story on the front page to make people want to buy it but they also have advertisements to help pay for everything,' I was pointing out.

'We've some supper,' said Bea when she saw Da arrive with Horace.

'I can't,' he replied. 'Horace and I have been talking and I've a story for Mrs Liu that can't wait.'

He headed down the corridor, where Toby was teaching Hamlet to stand on his hind legs in exchange for a piece of bread. We hadn't seen Da excited like this for so long, and everyone got up and followed him; Toby and the pig tagged along too.

Mrs Liu was sitting in her chair as usual while Elsie slept on the floor.

Da went in and crouched down beside her while the rest of us stood in the doorway. 'Come outside with me, Mrs Liu,' he began but she shook her head.

'I can't,' she whispered.

Da thought for a moment and then began a story the way I had heard him start a tale a thousand times before.

'Here's the thing, Mrs Liu: tonight the stars are especially beautiful, and as I was making my way home it made me think of you. Many years ago there was a man called Tycho Brahe. Funny sort of name, isn't it? Anyway, Tycho was a brilliant fellow. There was nothing he didn't know about the stars and about mathematics, and he was passionate about both subjects. One day he was arguing with a man about mathematics and the two of them got so cross that they had a fight. They fought with swords, and poor old Tycho got his nose cut off.'

Mrs Liu looked at Da. 'Is that true?' she asked.

Da put his hand on his heart. 'As true as I'm an Irishman in New York. If I could get you to the library you could read all about it. So poor Tycho had no nose, but do you know what he did? Did he hide away? No. He had a new nose made of copper which he wore every day, and a silver one for parties. It was so shiny no one could help but notice it, but he didn't mind because he said it reminded him of the stars. And he carried on studying, and what he learned about the stars is still some of the most important information about the heavens that we have. He was a Danish man, but I think there might have been a bit of Irish in him because he liked a laugh, did Tycho.'

He turned to Toby. 'You'd have got on with him, Toby. He had a pet elk, which is a kind of deer the size of a cow with great big antlers. He kept it in the house and they used to drink beer together.'

'Can an elk drink beer?' asked Toby, wide-eyed.

Da grinned. 'Well, they shouldn't. One day the elk had too much and, very sad, he fell down the stairs and died.' He paused to think about that.

Horace had been listening quietly. Now he

nodded. 'There's a lesson in there, Patrick, but I have no idea what it might be,' he commented.

Then Da turned back to Mrs Liu. 'Someone took Tycho Brahe's nose from him but he wouldn't let them take his self-confidence. He knew he was still worthwhile and so are you, Mrs Liu. It isn't how we look in this world that matters but how we behave. So tonight, with the stars being so beautiful, I thought about Tycho and how hard he worked to help us understand the lights in heaven and I wanted you to come with me to see them.'

He stood up and held his hand out to Mrs Liu. She looked at him for ages and then put her hand in his and stood up. Slowly he led her out the door, down the corridor and up the stairs, while the rest of us, Jack, Bea, Toby, Hamlet, Mrs Kavanagh, Horace and me, all followed. Mrs Liu had not been outside the house for almost a year, but that night she stood in the street and looked at the stars. Da was right. They were especially beautiful.

'I used to look at the stars at home in Ireland,' said Mrs Liu.

'Well, they're the same ones you can see here,' replied Da.

'Do you think Ma is up there?' asked Toby. Bea gave him a sharp look. No one had dared mention Ma, and now Da was getting better she didn't want him to spoil things.

But Da nodded, put his arm round Toby and carried on looking up. 'I'm sure she's watching over us. It doesn't matter where we go, Dublin or New York, we can still see the stars so she will be able to see us. The heavens cover us just the same wherever we are.'

Mrs Kavanagh, who was usually quite quiet, suddenly said, 'There was no Mr Kavanagh. Not ever. I left Ireland because I had a baby and now I don't even have that.'

Da smiled. 'But now you have us, Mrs Kavanagh.'

'Kate,' she said. 'My name is Kate.'

* * *

That night Horace fetched some special bread which he said was good for us, some fruit and a large bottle of lemonade. Mrs Liu woke Elsie, to join in. She was so excited to see her mother out of the room that she almost ran down the corridor and when Mr Liu popped in he was amazed to see his wife with other people. He beamed and said a lot of things very fast in Chinese, which none of us understood. When he finished, he kept bowing and saying, 'Thank you. Thank you,' in English over and over.

Mr Liu was always surprising me by appearing out of nowhere. He never came down the corridor from the stairs like the rest of us, but would just either be there or not. I never ever saw him come and go from his room next door. One minute he would be there fussing over his wife and child; the next he would be out in the street selling his second-hand clothes.

Now he went to his room and came back with a pot of some medicine. It smelled strong and he got

Mrs Liu to put some on the scar on Da's face. It had never really healed.

'Can you not use that for your nose?' Toby asked Mrs Liu while she gently rubbed the stuff on Da's face.

'Nothing will fix me, I'm afraid,' she said quietly.

'We all bear scars,' said Horace. 'Some are just more visible than others.'

'We could make a copper nose,' I suggested.

'Maybe we could,' agreed Horace.

'I go now,' said Mr Liu. 'I hear news of a shipment of yellow fever patients' clothing arriving.'

He was just about to leave when he spotted Jack's wooden brick lying on the mattress. He picked it up and examined it. 'You have magic box,' he said, carefully running his fingers along the edges.

'It's not a box, it's just a piece of wood,' explained Toby.

Mr Liu disagreed. 'No. This box definitely magic. You need to be patient and it will open.'

Then Mr Liu excused himself and raced towards the docks for a chance to buy the infected rags, which he said he could 'sell at a hundred per cent profit'.

For the rest of us, well, it was almost a party as we ate our dinner.

Da had been silent since his story about the stars but now he said quietly, 'We need to find Henry. He's been gone at least a month.'

'And my brother,' added Mrs Liu.

'Indeed,' agreed Horace, 'there must be many missing in this vast city.'

'Then you and Jack had better get going with your newspaper,' concluded Da.

Da was better, and I couldn't stop grinning. After that, even though we were poor, often hungry and Henry was missing, we still managed to laugh sometimes like we used to.

One night Horace had managed to get free tickets to a theatre and taken Da with him.

'Tell them about the show,' urged Horace when they returned, and Da laughed. It was a wonderful sound.

'We have been to see the most marvellous production of *Othello*,' he exclaimed. 'Horace and I share a great love for Shakespeare but this was truly terrible. The king lisped and stuttered through the whole thing, and then he danced while Desdemona played the banjo. This annoyed Iago, who was as Irish as you and me, and he decided to end their fun with a fire hose. The audience couldn't get enough. They were cheering and yelling. They applauded almost every line, and then some fellow got very agitated and shouted at Iago, "You lying scoundrel, I would like to get hold of you after the show and wring your infernal neck." Can you imagine such a thing? It was thrilling.'

'Oh, Da, how wonderful.' I sighed, so happy to see him almost like his old self.

Da smiled back and added, 'Apparently they did *Romeo and Juliet* last week and the audience enjoyed it so much that they got Romeo to drink poison twice.'

Kate laughed and clapped her hands at this. I had not seen her happy since we had left Ireland. Perhaps she felt relieved that she had told us about herself. She picked up Hero and, as she had done every night since she arrived, she put the baby in Da's arms. Hero was growing, and that night she put out her chubby little hands and brushed them against Da's lips. He looked down at her and smiled. It made us all want to cry we were so happy.

After our meal Toby put on Da's old hat and made the sound of a trumpet.

'Ta-da!' he exclaimed and then declared, 'Ladies and gentlemen, please be seated for a great show in which this pig will perform astonishing tricks!'

Well, we were all amazed. Toby had done exactly what Horace suggested and taught Hamlet tricks. The pig could sit up and beg; then Toby balanced a piece of food on his nose, and when he clapped Hamlet threw his snout up in the air, the food flew up and he opened his mouth to catch it. How we all laughed and clapped. There were five or six tricks: my favourite was the pig lying on the floor with all four feet in the air, playing dead.

'You could make money with that!' declared Horace, wiping tears of laughter from his eyes.

Poor as we were, and in that terrible room, we were happy that night.

CHAPTER TWENTY-SIX

Jack, Da and I started work on the paper. Every day we would go down to the docks, where Jack knew who to talk to on the ships. He would climb aboard and make friends in a moment. We got news of Ireland, learned the names of who had arrived and heard stories which we thought others might like to hear.

'Be clear what you are offering,' advised Horace, so we called the paper *Éire Nuacht*, which meant *Irish News*.

Everyone got involved. We knew we wanted our first headline simply to be the word MISSING! with Da writing about how many people who were new to America could not find loved ones who had already arrived. Kate went and spoke to Mr Brennan at his shop and arranged to have a notice board put up outside. That meant that when Da wrote about wanting news of people like Henry and Mrs Liu's brother, he was able to suggest a system of notices at Brennan's as a way of people getting in touch with each other.

'Good!' praised Horace. 'Find a problem and present a solution.'

Da came to Mulberry Bend and helped Jack put the metal letters into the press. The day Jack pulled the lever and our first paper appeared was one of the most exciting of my life. Horace came to watch, and held up the piece of paper with the ink still wet. He stood looking at it for ages, with none of us daring to speak, until at last he said, 'Brilliant. Absolutely brilliant.'

How we all clapped and danced about with delight.

Toby used his loud voice to sell the papers, and then sometimes got a few extra pennies by having Hamlet do a trick or two in the street. We started to get into a routine. We published once a week on a Friday and spent the rest of the week gathering our information. Notices started going up at Brennan's and people would sometimes stop us in the street to thank us for helping them find someone who had been missing. Probably the best day of all was when a man left word about Mrs Liu's brother. He was well and would be home soon. It made her so happy that soon she was even going outside in the daylight to take walks with Bea and Kate. Elsie would skip ahead while the women walked with baby Hero and it was lovely to see. It was wonderful – except that there was still no word about Henry.

Horace spent so much time with us that he decided to write not just about us but about life in general at the Old Brewery in his big newspaper. He was a good man and angry that so many people in New York were living in such a terrible state of despair. I read his words aloud to Jack. He wrote beautifully:

The gorgeous rainbow that spans the whirling
torrent of metropolitan life rests its base on
such dark depths of misery and crime as
makes one shudder to think of.

'Imagine being able to use words like that?' I wondered.

And so people began to learn how the poor lived right beside the rich. Horace saw some of Bea's drawings and asked her to sketch a few things for the paper. She did wonderful pictures of the life around us and he published a few in his *Tribune*. Bea got a little money and I thought she would burst with pride. Even Jack took a turn at writing. He had learnt such a lot from Da and now he used Uncle Niall's letter and map to write about Oregon and how we were all planning to go there one day. He was shy when he showed it to us but Da couldn't stop grinning.

'You're a Hannigan now, Jack, and no mistake!' he declared, slapping him on the back with delight.

Jack beamed and after that there was no stopping him writing all manner of things. It was wonderful to see.

Every day I watched out for Kyle and the gang of boys but reports in the *Tribune* showed that they seemed to be causing trouble elsewhere. Horace wrote about gangs. There were lots of them. Some had names like the Dead Rabbits who hated the Irish gangs and fought them whenever they could. It seemed as though we couldn't all just get on.

Slowly Jack and I were making money. Not a lot, but enough to make sure we had food with a little put by for the future. We still owed Liam Byrne five dollars but I hadn't seen him in weeks. I certainly had no intention of looking for him after the way he had behaved the last time. Bea kept charge of all the money, and at night would sit doing the sums, working out what we needed. We even began to talk about maybe getting a place with two rooms and even a window in the new year.

It began to turn cold and Mr Liu got us all shoes.

They were old, but how grand we felt! It took me ages to get used to them, and at first I kept tripping over. What little we had we shared, and we always made Mrs Liu and her little Elsie come in to eat with us. Our life was busy every day and I stopped thinking about Oregon. I was getting used to New York. It was hard, but it was better than where we had come from.

Horace taught me to love the city. There was nothing he didn't know. When he finished work he would sometimes take me for a walk up grand avenues like Wall Street.

'Before we all came to New York the red people, the Indians, lived here. Then the Dutch came, and one day the red people left Manhattan Island and crossed to the mainland. There they made a treaty with the Dutch, and they named the place the Pipe of Peace, which in their language is *Hoboken*. The Dutch then called Manhattan New Amsterdam. But the Dutch man in charge, a fellow called Kieft, was not good. He sent his men out there one night and killed all the Indians. You can imagine this made the other Indians who lived nearby very cross indeed and they wanted to attack the Dutch. The people of New Amsterdam became frightened and they built two great walls to protect themselves. The space between those walls is now called Wall Street.'

As we walked he pointed out the Custom House on Wall Street, where George Washington had once been sworn in as the first President of the United States, and he made me feel part of it all. That I was an American who could do whatever I wanted. That one day I might even meet an Indian and be nice to them to make up for what happened.

I wrote about that, and about all the other things I saw. I wrote about Christmas. Watching New York get ready for Christmas Day was wonderful. Charles Brown, the butcher, had flocks of dead birds hanging up outside his place ready for a feast. There were pictures of angels and St Nicholas in the shop windows. Some German people were getting ready to have a tree in their house but most New Yorkers didn't think that was good idea. I loved to see all the shoppers rushing to get home from the cold, carrying their brown paper parcels tied up with string. Bea and Kate arranged a little party on Christmas Eve. They invited Horace and asked if he had a wife he wanted to bring. I realised I had never asked him but he said, 'She isn't very well but thank you.' It had never occurred to me that he had a family.

Mrs Liu lent us her table. On it Bea and Kate laid the bread filled with caraway seed and raisins that you have to have for an Irish Christmas, as well as a large pitcher of milk. We had no one called 'Mary' in the family to light a candle, but Elsie was youngest after baby Hero, so she did it and everyone said how beautiful it was. Toby had somehow got new handkerchiefs for everyone, and Horace brought a cake. Mr Liu had asked me for some paper. He had cut it up into squares for each of us with our names written in bright Chinese letters. Then, as the greatest gift of all, Mrs Liu's brother turned up and soon everyone was crying with happiness. We sang hymns while Hamlet tossed pieces of bread in the air from his nose and caught them.

It was a terrible room, that place in the Old Brewery, but the night of Christmas 1847 in the light of a single candle, it was almost beautiful. It was home.

Afterwards Horace drove us up and down Broadway looking at the lights and listening to the bells he had put around Romeo and Juliet's necks. A group of ladies and gentlemen were singing songs on the corner of Forty-Second Street, their voices rang out in the cold air. It was perfect and I never thought I would leave.

'I love it here,' said Bea. 'It's so beautiful.'

'You never wanted to come,' I teased.

Bea agreed. 'I didn't know it could be like this,' she admitted.

Da held Hero tight to keep her warm.

Suddenly Jack laughed and pointed at a man on the pavement. 'Our paper!' he cried, and we were all thrilled to see that the man had our *Irish News* tucked under his arm.

'You've done a wonderful thing, Slim,' said Da, his voice choking with pride. 'Maybe we should just stay here now.'

'What about Oregon?' asked Toby.

'And Uncle Niall,' I added.

Da looked out at the beautiful snowy streets. 'We can't be going anywhere till we find Henry.'

And that was the truth of it. However much trouble Henry had caused us, he was a Hannigan and we weren't going anywhere without him.

The new year came and the newspaper carried on doing well. A few people started to ask for it ahead of time. 'Regular customers', Da called them.

We decided that in another month we would definitely move somewhere better, although by now we all were quite settled in our new home. Jack had found two more mattresses and Mr Liu had come home with a little table and chair. Everyone was busy. When she wasn't drawing, Bea liked nothing better than to go down to Broadway for the afternoon and look in the shop windows with Kate and the baby. She would come back all wide eyed about the dresses she had seen and how one day she would walk down Madison Avenue looking fine. If I saw a picture of a lady's gown or a hat or some gloves in an old paper I always saved it for her. She pinned them all up on the wall in our room and would sit looking at them for hours.

One Friday we had done the printing and I had just finished putting away all the letters while Jack cleaned the printing press. As I stepped out of the shop I realized that the sky was blue and the sun was shining. It was a beautiful winter's day. It was a new year – 1848 – and I decided I'd done enough work for the day.

As I walked along, Toby came running down the street. 'Finished, Slim!' he called. 'Sold all my papers!'

'Well done!' I said, pleased, as he handed over his coins. There was quite a lot.

'Fifty cents!' he said, proud of his new ability

with adding up, which Bea had been teaching him.

Fifty cents, I thought. That was enough for both of us to go and see the mermaid at the American Museum. I knew we were supposed to be saving for Oregon but I had wanted to go to the museum since the day we'd arrived in New York. Perhaps Toby and I could go and I could write about it, I told myself – as if that made spending the money all right. It shows you how well we were doing that I even had such a thought. I mean, fifty cents may not sound a lot now, but when you think the place where we were living was seventy-five cents a week then it will give you some idea!

'Shall we go to the museum?' I suggested to Toby and he whooped with excitement. We left Hamlet with Jack and headed off. Toby was so happy that he skipped along the road. As we walked, a few of my 'regular' newspaper customers called out, 'Hello!' and I felt as though I belonged, as though I was part of this great place.

Just before we got to the museum there was a

booth set up selling medicines. Behind the counter was a very tall man with crazy hair who said his name was Dr D'eath. I didn't know much about doctors, but apparently he was the sort who could cure anything. How I wish we had had him with us on the *Pegasus*. The doctor had awful pictures of people with terrible diseases, and then pictures of them looking well and happy after he had cured them. He was selling bottles of something which could 'sort most things'.

'Be restored to health!' he shouted as people queued up.

I was going to walk past but Toby pulled on my hand. 'Look!' He pointed at the doctor's pictures. 'He could fix Mrs Liu,' he said. 'She and Mr Liu had medicine for Da, now we could help her.'

I looked down at my little brother and thought about Mrs Liu with her poor missing nose.

'Could you fix a nose?' I asked the medicine man.

He bent right down to me. 'A nose?' he repeated.

427

'Yes,' I said.

'What's wrong with this nose?'

I couldn't think how to describe it.

'It's missing,' said Toby clearly.

'Yes,' I agreed.

I thought for a minute he was going to say it couldn't be done, but he suddenly stood up and grabbed one of his bottles.

'Fifty cents like everyone else! A panacea for a proboscis, I'll be bound.'

I didn't know what that meant but Toby squeezed my hand. 'It's magic,' he whispered.

I looked down into his big green eyes and knew whatever else we did that afternoon, we would not be seeing a mermaid. I remembered not getting the Holloway's Pills for Ma in Dublin and I didn't ever want to make that mistake again.

I handed over my money. The doctor wrapped the bottle in brown paper and gave it to me. 'You live in New York, child?' he asked.

I thought about the question and tried to answer

honestly. 'I suppose we do, but we're supposed to be just passing through. We're supposed to be going to Oregon to see Uncle Niall.'

It seemed odd when I said it because we had practically stopped mentioning Oregon.

Dr D'eath thought about Oregon for a moment. 'That's west, isn't it?' he said. 'Would you like a pill to protect against earthquakes?'

I had no more money so couldn't buy anything else. Toby and I took the bottle home. I don't suppose the medicine did any good but I know Mr Liu was so happy that we had tried.

Da beamed at Toby when I told him what had happened. 'You're a good boy,' he said. 'If only my other son was not such a disappointment.'

And so life continued. We were still worried about Henry, but Jack and I were busy with the newspaper and Da was getting better every day. Bea and Kate had become inseparable friends and most nights I would see Mr and Mrs Liu standing in the street looking up at the stars. Toby was a wonderful newsboy and Hamlet was very popular with all our customers. Before I knew it, spring had arrived. There was blossom on the trees and even the dreadful streets where we lived seemed more cheerful. Hero took her first steps and we all cheered. It was hard to believe, but we had been in New York for almost a year.

Things were going well. We had friends and we were beginning to make a little money. I think we might have just stayed in that great city for ever, but one morning I was coming back from fetching some more ink when I saw two lads fighting outside the Old Brewery. I had got good at staying away from trouble, but this was right by our front door. As I got closer I saw that one of the boys was Jack.

'Stop it!' I yelled as he picked the other fellow up by the collar and shook him. 'Jack!' I called again.

I had never seen him fight anyone. Even though he was big Jack had never been anything but gentle. He heard me shout, and with a grunt dropped the unfortunate man on the stone steps. I was startled to see it was Liam Byrne.

He was very pale and his once fancy clothing was filthy and torn. He had a huge black eye and there was blood in his wild hair. He could hardly speak. 'Slim . . .' He coughed and tried to stand up. He was clearly hurt and clutched his stomach as he moved to greet me.

Jack moved to stand between us. 'You leave her alone!' he said sharply.

I was appalled by what I could see. 'Jack! Did you do this?'

Liam put his hand up. 'It wasn't Jack. It wasn't him. He was just trying to keep me out of your house. Someone else did the rest.'

'Who?' I asked.

Liam shook his head. 'It doesn't matter. You have to leave. I came to warn you that you have to leave.'

I was completely bewildered. 'Leave where?'

I thought Liam was going to cry. 'I don't know – this house, the city maybe.'

He started coughing and there was blood on his lips. Something was very wrong, but he had been kind to us when we arrived and I wasn't going to leave him on the street.

'Jack,' I decided, 'help him downstairs.'

Jack had to half carry Liam to our room. Bea and Kate were there with Hero but there was no sign of Da or Toby.

'What's happened?' cried my sister as we helped Liam lie on the mattress. Kate went to get some water to clean his mouth.

Slowly Liam came back to life. 'You have to leave,' he repeated.

'What's happened?' said Kate calmly. 'You have to tell us.'

Liam's shoulders shook. 'I've been such a fool. I thought I could make money. Lots of money.'

'But you had money,' said Bea, 'from your brothers. For the farm.'

'I thought I could make more,' he explained. 'I met some fellows and they had all sorts of schemes about winning at cards, but they're a bad lot and soon I couldn't get away. All my money's gone . . . but that's not the worst of it . . . Henry, Henry . . .'

'What about Henry?' I demanded.

'Henry owes them and he can't pay and . . . I think they might come here looking for their money,' explained Liam. 'I don't want anything to happen to you.' He looked straight at Bea, pleading with her to understand but she wasn't happy at all.

She stood right in front of him and poked him in the chest. 'You shouldn't have come here. Now they'll know where we live. They'll follow.' She was clearly very angry with Liam.

'I was careful – please believe me.' He tipped his head back and moaned, 'What have I done?'

'Have you really spent all that money for the farm?' I asked, amazed that it could all be gone.

Liam hung his head in shame. 'I thought it would last for ever. It seemed like such a lot.'

I was confused. 'What's this got to do with Henry?'

'It's my fault,' he whispered. 'I met this man from back home . . .'

I began to think I knew where this was heading. 'A fellow called Kyle?' I asked.

Bea looked astonished. 'Kyle? That dreadful boy from Ballysmaragaid? Is he here?'

I nodded.

'How do you know that, Slim?' Kate asked.

'I've seen him.'

Bea threw her hands up in despair. 'Did he not cause enough trouble when we were at home?'

'The police caught him but he put the blame on Henry,' Liam went on.

'So where is Henry now?' I asked.

'He's been arrested,' said Liam. 'I don't think you can help him. The best thing you can do is leave. Henry owes a lot of money and Kyle will find you if Henry can't pay.'

'What's he been arrested for?' asked Kate, trying to be practical and get the facts.

'Pickpocketing,' explained Liam. 'Taking things

straight from other people's pockets. There's a skill in it, I will say that, and Henry is very good. Lots of people do it. I know a woman who goes by the name of Anonyma. She has two rooms in a very nice part of town with watercolours on the wall and a piano which she plays beautifully. She can steal a whole card of lace from a shop quicker and better than anyone.'

'Never mind all that!' exploded Bea.

'Bea!' Liam tried to sit up and move towards her, but Jack pushed him back down on the mattress.

'He didn't want to do it but he had no way of paying them back,' he continued.

'Be quiet, Liam,' yelled my sister. 'We don't need to know all that. All we need from you is to tell us where Henry is now.'

Liam looked at the floor and whispered, 'He's at a terrible place they call The Tombs.'

CHAPTER TWENTY-SEVEN

'The Tombs' were really the 'Halls of Justice', but for some reason the place had been built to look like a giant Egyptian tomb, which is how it got the nickname. It took up a whole block of the city, sitting in the middle of Centre, Franklin, Elm and Leonard Streets. It wasn't far from where we were living but I had never had any reason to go there. It was a dreadful, damp place full of criminals.

We needed help, and the only grown-up I could rely on was Horace. I knew I had to see him and fast, but it was late and the newspaper offices would be closed by now. Da knew where he was.

'Horace wrote about it in the *Tribune* today. He's a guest of Dagger John tonight,' he said. 'Up at Astor House.'

'Dagger John? Is that a bad man?' I asked.

Da shrugged. 'I expect he doesn't think so. He's the Catholic Archbishop of New York but they call him Dagger John for the way he puts a cross by his name when he signs it. He has his own church newspaper.'

Da and I left Jack keeping guard on everyone at home and ran to catch the omnibus up Broadway. Da pulled the leather strap which told the driver to drop us outside a fancy hotel called 'Astor House'. It stood opposite the City Hall Park where I had once so admired the fountain and it was quite a sight. I've never been to a great palace but I can't imagine a king or a queen living in a finer place than Astor House. Made of pale grey stone, it was five-storeys high and took up four square blocks of city street.

Da looked up at the magnificent building. 'I never thought I'd step foot in such a place,' he said with a sense of wonder. '309 hotel rooms. Not a place like it in the world. Gas light and bathing facilities on every floor. You'd like it, Slim, they have a printing press in the basement to print their menus fresh every day.' Da shook his head as if he could not believe it. 'Just think. Perhaps 600 people might sleep in there on the same night and it wouldn't be crowded. A whole village in one building.'

I took Da's hand. I was afraid but I still pulled him towards the door.

'Da! We need to find Horace.'

All around us carriages and omnibuses were dropping off fine ladies and gentlemen. Four giant white pillars marked the grand front door. A carpet had been laid from the curb stone to the front door. I had never seen a carpet in a street. I'd never really seen much carpet of any kind and I wasn't alone in marvelling at it. Everyone who was going in was magnificently dressed and many of the women had a maid with them who was busy fussing and adjusting their dresses as they descended from their carriages.

At the door I suddenly noticed quite how ragged

my father and I looked. Da too seemed as though he had lost his nerve.

'Come on, Da,' I said. 'This is America. We can all go where we like. No one can stop us.' And in we marched.

Da was right. It was just like a village or even a whole town. There was everything you could think a person might need all in the one building – a barber's, a hairdresser's, a drugstore, a tailor's and boot makers, a room to get oysters, one for smoking and even one just for reading. At a door to a dining room for GENTLEMEN ONLY there was a long list of food available most of which I had never even heard of.

At first no one even seemed to notice that we was there. We wandered down several corridors not at all sure how to find Horace. At last we came to the most magnificent giant room. Four pillars, just like the ones at the front door, white and as tall as trees, held up the entrance way. Brilliant chandeliers hung the length of the room and lit the stunning scene.

There were hundreds of guests and everywhere you looked servants were busily serving, dressed in black swallow-tail coats and trousers with immaculate waistcoats vests, cravats and gloves.

Perhaps the party had already eaten because now they were dancing. At one end of the room a whole orchestra was placed. Ladies and gentlemen were standing in groups of four, bowing to each other and then taking a few steps before bowing a bit more. The men wore beautiful black suits and had to mind they didn't trip over the long trains of the ladies' dresses. A large banner hung between two of the pillars bearing the words THE SOCIETY OF ST. VINCENT DE PAUL. Beneath it, at last, I saw Horace standing chatting to a woman. She was about the same age as Horace but she looked rather stern and tired. She wore a beautiful dress. It was long with a rich blue satin skirt. A white shawl covered her shoulders and she carried a fan which had the most exquisite painting of the fountain at City Hall. How Bea would have loved to see such a splendid sight.

I was just about to speak when a waiter grabbed my arm.

'Hey, you can't be in here, you little thief.'

He pinched hard on my arm and it hurt so I cried out.

Horace looked over at the commotion and asked 'What's all this fuss about?'

'Horace!' I yelled as the waiter tried to drag me away.

He put his hand up and called, 'Stop! Let her go!'

The waiter was not at all pleased but he delivered me into Horace's care and went off grumbling.

Horace looked at me and Da and gave a slight bow. 'Miss Hannigan, Mr Hannigan,' he said as if we were guests like anyone else. 'May I introduce my wife, Mrs Greeley?'

So this was Horace's wife.

'This is the girl I told you about,' said Horace to her, 'the one who has started a newspaper.'

'Heavens, yes.' Mrs Greeley looked at me and

gave a slight smile. 'Whatever next? The vote?' For some reason what she said made me feel a bit cross.

'It's a very good newspaper.' I said. 'I can run it same as any man. They say a woman might one day even be a doctor.'

She looked at me and could see I was serious. 'Do they now?' she said quietly.

Horace smiled.

Da had gone back into one of his silences and just stood staring at everything. I knew it was now up to me to get the help we needed.

'Horace,' I said. 'We found Henry but he's been arrested and you have to help him.'

'Who's Henry?' asked Horace's wife.

She seemed quite nice and I thought perhaps I could get her on my side but it all came out in a great jumble.

'He's my big brother. He didn't mean any trouble. I know he didn't,' I explained. 'He's only fourteen but I think he thought he had to be the man of the family. My ma died on the boat out having my baby sister and Da hasn't been able to work because he's been so sad and we're all doing our best but Toby's only eight and he thinks the pig he found is the one from home even though it looks nothing like it. He's a dreamer, a bit like my sister Bea who means well but I don't think she could get a job really especially as no one wants the Irish. And then we had to take Mrs Kavanagh in because that man cheated her and now she can't even get to her sister in California and the Chinaman, Mr Liu says—'

'Where is Henry now?' interrupted Horace.

'In the Tombs,' I said.

Mrs Greeley looked at her husband. 'It seems to me Horace that you have no choice. I mean, this party was held so we could raise money for the poor you're always writing about. Surely we should help her?'

We left and Horace and his wife came with us.

* * *

The Tombs felt like a place where the sun never shined. It was damp where we lived at the Old Brewery but nothing like as bad as the prison. They had built the jail on top of an old pond and you could almost feel the building sinking back into the water. Inside there was a large courtyard, in the centre of which stood a second prison where all the men were kept. It was connected with the outer building by a bridge.

'They call that the Bridge of Sighs,' said Horace.

'Why?' I asked.

'Because if you do something so bad that a judge says you have to die then you must walk across that bridge to get to the place where they hang you.'

I was terrified. 'Will they hang Henry?'

'Not if I can help it,' answered my friend.

We rushed to the court room where the noise was terrible. The large room was full of people waiting to have their case heard by the judge. Policemen were busy bringing and taking away those who had been accused of a crime, while dozens of men and women sat waiting to be heard. The judge was a small man with a funny triangular face. He sat at a high desk and I thought he looked a good judge because he made decisions very quickly. No sooner was someone brought before him, the case explained, than the judge had decided what should happen to them – prison, a fine or let them go. It was as though he knew someone was guilty or not the moment he laid eyes on them. Every kind of case was put to him – people who had had too much to drink, women complaining about their husbands, men complaining about their wives, thieves and others caught for fighting. I thought I even saw Dr D'eath who had sold me that medicine sitting waiting his turn but I was soon distracted by the sight of Henry.

He no longer looked the man of the family. It was as though he had shrunk inside his new clothes. Horace put me, Mrs Greeley and Da on one of the long benches to wait while he spoke to one of the officers. Mrs Greeley sat calmly waving her fan as if nothing unusual was happening.

'You!' I heard a voice hiss as someone grabbed my arm from behind. 'I know you,' he said. 'You're one of the Hannigans.'

I looked down and saw a hand with a terrible burn mark on it. I jumped because I thought it was Kyle again, but when I turned round I saw that it was Mr Hughes from the boat. He looked quite changed. His clothes were filthy and he had a wild look in his eye, but it was definitely him. Mr Hughes whose wife had died and left him with the two small girls. Mr Hughes who had cheated dear Kate Kavanagh of all her money with those false tickets to California.

'You have to help me,' he whispered urgently. 'They're trying to say I'm a thief.'

'But you are,' I whispered back. 'You stole from Mrs Kavanagh. You sold her those tickets that were no good. She couldn't go anywhere.'

Mr Hughes shook his head. 'I was trying to help my girls. You have to understand.'

He told me what had happened. A man had come on board and offered him a gold watch if he would help sell tickets. It had been a lovely watch and real gold as well. Mr Hughes had taken it thinking he could sell it and get his girls home, back to Ireland.

'I don't want to be here,' he moaned. 'I want to go home.'

He had helped the stranger sell tickets telling everyone, including Mrs Kavanagh, that he knew the man, that he could vouch for him. All the time he had the gold watch in his pocket and he felt rich but as soon as he had gone ashore the ticket seller had called the police and told them Mr Hughes had stolen his gold watch. He had been in the Tombs ever since.

'Tell them what happened,' he pleaded. 'Tell them I'm a good person.'

The judge looked over at us and I lowered my voice to a whisper.

'But you're not,' I said. 'Mrs Kavanagh lost everything. She can't go and see her sister now.'

A policeman called for quiet and I turned away from Mr Hughes. The judge was just finishing a case in which two men called Big-Mouth Scotty and Billy Clews were charged with pickpocketing at a funeral.

'What have you to say, Scotty?' asked the judge.

'Oh, well,' replied Big-Mouth, 'I don't think I've got much to say, only to ask your Honour to deal mercifully with us.'

The judge sent them to prison. Henry was next but as the judge turned to him he noticed Horace.

'Mr Greeley,' the judge said with a smile, 'surely the *Tribune* takes no interest in our ordinary affairs?'

Horace bowed his head and replied, 'The *Tribune* is interested in all matters, your honour.'

'How can I help you today?'

'I'm here to vouch for this young man.' He pointed at Henry and the judge signalled for my brother to stand up. 'It is a first offence, your honour, but I can vouch for his character. I would beg the court to release him into my custody and I shall see that he causes no more trouble.'

Just then Mr Hughes got to his feet.

'And me, vouch for me!' he called.

Horace looked at me. 'Do you know this man too?' he asked.

I thought about Kate Kavanagh and what had happened to her.

'No,' I said looking straight at Mr Hughes. Da looked at Mr Hughes for the first time and started to say something but I interrupted before he could get a word in. 'I've never seen him before in my life,' I declared.

Mr Hughes was furious. He rose up in his seat as if he were going to come after me but a policeman pushed him back down.

'I'll get you for this, Hannigan,' he called. 'I'll get you!'

The judge was very clear. Henry was to cause no more trouble and Horace was to make sure of it.

Henry could hardly look at us as he was released.

'Da . . .' he began, but Da shook his head.

'Not now,' he said.

We went back to the Old Brewery with Henry, Horace and his wife. We left Mr Hughes at the Tombs. It was a mistake. A mistake that I would live to regret.

CHAPTER TWENTY-EIGHT

Horace drove us back to the Old Brewery in his carriage. Mr Liu was waiting outside. He was very agitated.

'Quick, quick,' he called. 'You come quick.' He hurried us inside and down the stairs.

Horace was trying to find out what was wrong. 'What is it, Mr Liu?' he asked.

Mr Liu was very upset. 'The Dead Rabbit come here. Soon. Someone tell me. Dead Rabbit come here soon.'

I couldn't think how a dead rabbit could come to the Old Brewery.

'The Dead Rabbit gang?' asked Horace. 'Why?'

Henry looked pale. 'It's me. I owe them money.'

The Dead Rabbit was the name of a gang who lived up on the Bowery.

Horace looked confused. 'What were you doing with them?' he asked. 'They hate the Irish.'

'I lied to them. Said I wasn't Irish. Liam said it was best. They're the ones with most power here and I was trying to—'

Suddenly Da exploded with rage and standing on the steps he turned on Henry. 'What is wrong with you, Henry? Do you never learn? How is it that you cause us nothing but trouble?'

'I was trying to do the right thing. Where were you, Da, when we needed you? I was trying to make us some money because you were no use to anyone. I was trying to be the man of the family because our actual father wasn't up to it. I made a mistake, and then I didn't come back because I knew Kyle would cause trouble for you all. Don't you think I wanted to be with you? Don't you think I'd rather have been here?'

I suddenly realized that Henry was now as tall as

Da. They stood squared up to each other and I thought Da was going to hit him, but instead he reached out and pulled Henry into a great hug.

'I'm sorry, Da, I'm sorry,' Henry kept repeating.

'No time. No time,' said Mr Liu, looking around nervously. 'Jack, you watch,' and leaving Jack standing guard, he hurried us inside. We went downstairs but could see straight away that our room was empty.

'Where is everyone?' I called.

'This way, this way.' Mr Liu herded us along to his room where he revealed the rest of the family sitting in the shadows. They looked afraid, but soon there was much hugging. Whatever Henry had done, we were glad to have him back. Even Hamlet seemed pleased.

Bea explained why they weren't in our own room.

'Kyle came to the house with a handful of men. Jack heard them coming and got us in here while he pretended not to know anything. He was very brave.'

'Mr Liu kept us safe,' said Kate, 'but they are coming back.'

'They want money,' said Mr Liu.

'How much do you owe them?' demanded Da.

'A lot,' admitted Henry.

'It was my fault,' mumbled Liam. 'I bet everything I had, and then I couldn't seem to stop. They gave me credit – said I could pay any time – but I can't and I'm late with the money. Henry tried to help me.'

Da could not believe it. 'You bet all the money your brothers raised for a farm?'

Liam nodded and looked away, ashamed.

Da was appalled. 'That was your future, you idiot boy. What will you do now?'

Liam didn't answer.

Mrs Greeley had been standing silently but now she spoke up. 'If this gang is as bad as they say, then we had better get all of you, including Liam, out of here,' she said quietly.

'They'll kill you if they catch you and you don't

pay them,' said Horace, looking very serious indeed. 'I've done a lot of unhappy stories about the gangs over the last few years and they never end well.'

'Can't you protect us, Horace?' I asked.

'I could try but . . .' He shrugged, and for the first time since we'd met he looked helpless.

'You need go. Go now,' insisted Mr Liu.

'Go where?' asked Da. 'They'll recognize us.'

I was standing where I always did in Mrs Liu's room beside the screen of colourful Chinese pictures when suddenly I had an idea.

'What if we were Chinese?' I asked.

'What do you mean?' asked Kate.

'If we were Chinese no one would think it was us. Everybody knows the Hannigans are Irish.'

'Chinese clothes!' declared Da. 'That's brilliant! Do you have any, Mr Liu?'

'Of course, of course.' Mr Liu clapped his hands and he and his wife began rummaging in a large trunk in the corner. Soon they were hurrying forward with a pile of silky and colourful clothes.

'Put these on,' ordered Mrs Liu, handing us tops and trousers in different sizes. 'Now you won't look Irish at all.' The clothes were made of silk. They were all Chinese just like Mr Liu's. We even had little black hats with silk bobbles on.

Bea shook her head. 'No! I don't want to. I don't want to go anywhere. I like it here. We're happy. I do my drawings and . . .'

Da looked so sad. 'We've no choice, Beatrice. Henry's in trouble. We're a family and we stick together.'

'What about me?' said Kate in a small voice. 'I'm not your family.' She was holding baby Hero and looking frightened. Hero, however, was fine. She was not quite speaking but starting to gurgle at everything. She put her little baby hands on Kate's face and smiled at Da, saying his name in her own baby talk.

Da put his finger in Hero's hand and smiled back. 'Well, don't you tell Hero that because she would be most surprised. Put the clothes on, Kate. What would we do without you?'

'I can't do without you, Kate,' added Bea, and Kate smiled, tears starting to run down her face.

'And me?' asked Liam. He was very pale and looked as frightened as a little boy. Liam looked at me and I remembered how he had helped us when we first arrived. I remembered about his brothers dying and how he had cried on the boat.

Even though I knew Bea wouldn't be pleased, I said with determination, 'We can't leave him here.'

Mrs Liu had had enough. 'Oh, for goodness' sake! Will you all just get dressed? You can have this great discussion when there isn't someone trying to kill you.'

In just a few minutes Bea, Kate, Henry, Liam, Toby, Da, me and even little Hero were all transformed into a Chinese family.

'I don't think it's going to work,' said Henry once we were all changed. 'They'll see us leave. They'll suspect something.'

Da was the last to get dressed. He had been so clear about what we needed to do, but now he looked dazed again as if it had all been too much for him. I was worried he might be slipping back into being unwell again.

'I wish your ma was here to help,' he kept repeating – and I know it sounds strange, but suddenly it was as if she really was. As he took off his greatcoat to get changed, he dropped it on the floor and we all heard something thud.

'What was that?' asked Bea. She picked the coat up off the floor and Toby held up the hem, feeling along it with his fingers.

'There's a great lump of something in the lining,' he declared.

'Da, where's your knife?' I asked, and he took out the penknife I had won for him and cut the lining. He put his hand inside and pulled out a velvet bag.

'Ma's money bag!' exclaimed Bea with wonder.

'It must have fallen through a hole in my pocket,' said Da. 'No wonder we hadn't been able to find it all that time.'

'Is it all there?' asked Henry.

Da opened the bag and looked inside. 'Every penny,' he said.

We could hardly believe it.

'I think your wife heard you,' said Horace quietly. 'I think she is helping you.'

'Now we could pay them back,' said Toby. 'The bad people.'

Horace looked at Da. 'You could, but I don't think that's a good idea. I don't think it matters how much you give them – you will never be free. Weren't you always planning to go west? To Oregon? Go now. Use the money for that. Make a fresh start. Here is your chance.'

Da looked at the money bag and turned to me. 'I think you'd best take charge of this, Slim. I'm not really to be trusted, but we all know we can rely on you.'

I nodded, feeling overwhelmed at Da's trust in me, and took it.

Mrs Liu had found an old carpet bag and put

some food in. We quickly added what few precious items we had – Jack's magic box, our names written in Chinese letters, the handkerchief with the piece of Irish turf which Da had cut all that time ago and a few cloths for the baby. I remembered my box with Uncle Niall's letter and map, and was pleased to see my new Chinese trousers, which I loved, had a pocket for it to go in. Mrs Liu grabbed a small brass candleholder with half a candle in it, lit it and handed it to her husband.

Henry and Liam were both very anxious but there was no time to calm anyone for just then we heard footsteps in the hall.

'They're coming, they're coming,' cried Toby, terrified, and Hamlet began grunting in sympathy.

Jack appeared in the room completely out of breath. 'They're on their way. I couldn't stop them. I'm sorry. I'm sorry.'

'Mr Liu,' said Horace, 'is there another way out?'

I saw him look at Horace as if he were trying to

decide whether or not he could trust him. It only lasted a second and then Mr Liu went over to the wooden screen by the stove which was covered in the colourful drawings. I now knew that the pictures were Chinese letters, but Mr Liu was not interested in the writing. He grabbed the side of the screen and pushed it to one side. We were all amazed to see an open door behind it. We had no idea where it led to, but we could see that there was no light.

'This tunnel. We come out by Mulberry Bend,' said Mr Liu to Horace. 'You get horse, wait there.'

'Right!' Horace turned to Mrs Greeley. 'Mary, go and hail another carriage. We'll take Jack with us. Let me have some clothes for him.'

Mrs Liu found the largest clothes she could and gave them to Horace.

As they raced off, Mr Liu quietly said, 'This way.'

'It's so dark,' wailed Toby. Footsteps were running towards us now. We heard them stop and say something to Horace but there was no time to hope he had persuaded them to go away. Without another

461

word Mr Liu hurriedly turned away and went through into the darkness. I could hear the footsteps start up again. They were getting closer. There was no time to waste. Mrs Liu hugged me and pushed me towards the dark entrance. I was the last one in, and heard her put the wooden screen back just as the sound of angry men filled the room. I disappeared into a dark and narrow tunnel. Ahead I could see the faint light from Mr Liu's candle as he led the family away. So this was how he had come and gone each day without ever using the front door. Hamlet grunted by Toby's side.

We must have walked for ten minutes or so in the tunnel before at last we came to a winding staircase leading up to the street. We emerged beside a small shop in Mulberry Bend, and there was Horace waiting with Romeo and Juliet, along with Mrs Greeley and another carriage. We scrambled into the two carriages, only to find Jack appearing with the printing press on Uncle Aedan's old hand cart.

'Jack!' I called. 'There isn't time.'

Jack shook his head. 'I can do this. I can push.'

'Pier Number Two, Jack,' instructed Horace. Jack set off and I called out, 'Thank you, Jack.'

Da shook Mr Liu by the hand. 'I can never thank you enough,' said Da to our lovely neighbour.

Mr Liu bowed. 'You help my wife. Now we look at the stars. It is I who thank you.'

'We must hurry,' urged Horace as he flicked the reins to push Romeo and Juliet on. I sat beside him, feeling bewildered by how fast everything was happening.

'Where are we going?' I asked, waving a final farewell to our kind Chinese friend.

'I made some enquiries,' explained Horace. 'You need to go south first, before you can head west. You need to take the ferry.'

It was late, and there was hardly anyone about as Horace and the other driver hurried their horses down to Broadway, turned right to Battery Place and out to the docks.

463

'Pier Number Two!' he called out as we pulled up by the water. 'You'll get the ferry here to South Amboy and then you can catch the train south. I'm not quite sure after that. You'll have to ask.'

The ferry terminal was deserted. The last ferry had already left, so we waited in Horace's carriage. There were dock buildings all around. A long low shed ran alongside the slip. Its doorways were dark, but I could hear the sound of some work going on inside. Both Liam and Henry were afraid of every noise and jumped when we heard the sound of someone approaching but it was Jack, safely arrived with the cart. We stayed quiet until dawn. No one slept except Toby, who lay against Hamlet in the bottom of Horace's carriage, and baby Hero, who slept in Kate's arms while she whispered to Bea and Mrs Greeley.

As soon as there was the tiniest bit of silver light from the rising sun we began to hear the crunch of oyster shells underfoot as people began to arrive. Huge wooden barrels and great crates of goods were loaded and unloaded from carts pulled by exhausted-looking horses. Small stands opened up with men in aprons and neat moustaches selling oysters and throwing the shells on the street. Horace bought us some and we stood eating as the first ferry arrived.

'See that stand on the end?' Horace pointed to the last of the wooden oyster shacks, which had a low counter for people to eat at. 'There's a copy of your paper sitting on the counter.'

Jack and I looked and smiled.

Bea thought Mrs Greeley's clothes were marvellous and I heard her whisper, 'I can't believe how beautiful your dress is. Do you think it would be too much to hope that one day I might have a dress as lovely as yours?'

Mrs Greeley smiled. Her gorgeous fan with its incredible painting hung from a ribbon on her wrist. She took it off and gave it to Bea. 'Here,' she said. 'When you get that dress you will have a fan to go with it.'

It was while we were enjoying ourselves that

Liam suddenly shouted, 'Over there!' and pointed to the corner of the shed along the dock. Out of the gloom appeared a small group of Bowery boys. They were clearly looking for something or someone. They stared in our direction.

'Bow!' whispered Da.

'What?' asked Toby, who was getting Hamlet to lie on his back and play dead.

'Put your hands together and bow your heads,' said Da.

We did as he said, and if those boys really were the Dead Rabbit gang, then all they would have seen was a line of Chinese people in varying sizes standing completely still with a society couple and a pig who didn't look at all well. Hamlet lay with all four feet in the air, his head tipped back and his eyes closed. After a minute we heard the boys move away. Hamlet opened one eye to look, grunted and got to his feet.

'Time to get on the boat,' said Da.

For three cents each we could leave the city and

head out across the bay. The deck of the wooden ferryboat was very wide. It hung over the hull at the sides and there were three separate gangways leading up to it – two outer ones for foot passengers and a middle one for vehicles, which Jack used to slowly push the cart holding our precious printing press.

Horace was guiding me to the boat when he stopped, bent down and held me by the shoulders. 'Oregon or bust, kid,' he said. 'If anyone can do it, you can. Be part of the manifest destiny that will make this country great.'

'I owe you money,' I said.

He shook his head. 'Not at all. Everything I gave you was a down payment.'

'On what?' I asked.

'On the letters that you are going to write and I am going to publish about your great journey.' He smiled at my sister. 'And drawings, Beatrice. I shall want drawings.'

I didn't want to say goodbye to Horace. He had been my friend and I couldn't bear not to see him again. I hugged and hugged him and didn't want to let go, but a bell was sounding from the pilot house where the captain steered on a covered deck above our heads.

'It's all right, Slim,' soothed Horace, but I knew it wasn't. Great tears ran down his sweet face as he helped me onto the boat. He stood watching from the dock.

'Let's go. Let's go!' muttered my father as the crew fussed about helping a man get his cart of pickled fish aboard. Da kept looking to make sure that no one was after us, and I knew he wouldn't be happy until we were off across the bay.

At last steam billowed from the tall iron chimney at the centre of the boat. A great metal shaft above our heads began to rock back and forth as it cranked into work action and pushed the two vast paddle-wheels, one at either side, through the water. The captain gave the order, the ropes were let and go and the ferry moved off from the narrow slip lined with timber. We were underway. It was the second time we had escaped by boat. We stood on the deck in our silk clothes and waved to Horace and his wife. I could just see the oyster stand with our newspaper still sitting on the counter. As I watched, a gust of wind blew up and caught it, throwing it in the air. It danced in front of the city. I thought it looked beautiful but I did not know then the trail we were leaving behind for others to find us.

We waved till we could see the Greeleys no more and New York, that great city, disappeared from our view for ever.

'I don't want to leave,' wept Bea, but we had no choice. That gang Henry had got involved with were not going to give up easily. Once more someone was after us and the only way forward lay west, across the prairies and the mountains, two and a half thousand miles to Oregon.

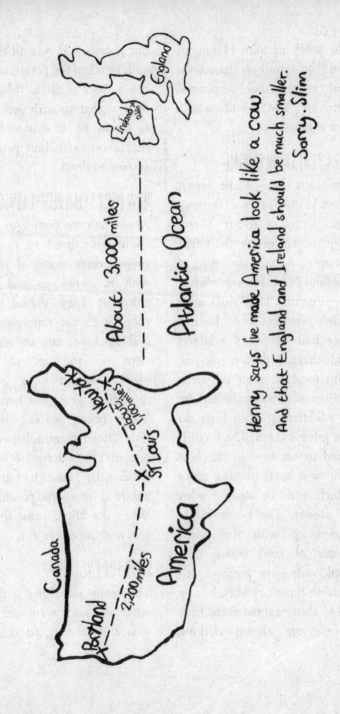

England

Ireland
Slim

About 3,000 miles

Atlantic Ocean

Henry says I've made America look like a cow.
And that England and Ireland should be much smaller.
Sorry, Slim

Canada

New York
X

about
1,100 miles

St Louis
X

2,200 miles

Portland
X

America

The story of Slim Hannigan and her family is based on real events that happened between 1845 and 1852. It was known as . . .

THE GREAT IRISH FAMINE

This was one of the worst times in the history of Ireland. The Irish called it Gorta Mór, which means 'the Great Hunger'. At the time most of the land in Ireland was owned by English landlords who didn't even live there. Instead they had houses in England and charged rent to anyone who lived on their property. The money was collected by a 'middleman', hired to do the job for them. The English liked to eat beef so the best land was used to raise cows which could be sold for a lot of money. The poor people ended up with the worst pieces of land where they could only grow potatoes. It's hard to imagine today, but by 1845 about a third of the Irish people ate almost nothing but potatoes. It was all they had, so when the potato crop got a disease called 'blight' many ended up with nothing to eat at all. It was so bad that about a million people starved to death.

HOW POOR IRISH PEOPLE LIVED

About half the people in the countryside lived in single-room cabins made of mud with no windows and no chimney. They shared the cabin with the family's pig and chickens, and everyone slept on the ground. A blanket would have been thought of as a great luxury. Most poor people could only afford to rent between one and five acres of land which wasn't enough to grow anything on except potatoes. When the blight came there was nothing else to eat.

FOOD FOR ENGLAND

The really sad thing is that while the poor were getting sick and starving to death,

Ireland actually had lots of food. There was plenty of Irish beef, peas, beans, onions, rabbits, salmon, oysters, herring, honey and butter – but it was all sent to England. The tragedy is that there was enough food to feed everyone but it was not being given to the Irish. Some people became very angry and wanted to fight.

EVICTION

For many people there was no food and no work and they couldn't pay their rent. Because the landlords didn't live there they didn't really understand how bad things were. This was a long time before television or radio and people in England didn't believe the stories they heard about the starving Irish. Landlords started telling the middlemen to get rid of their tenants. In the beginning no one counted how many people were thrown out of their mud cabins, but between 1849 and 1854 about half a million lost their homes. The landlords often knocked the mud cabins down so that they could rent the land for more money to someone else.

LEAVING IRELAND

Often the people who were suffering thought about leaving Ireland for a better life somewhere else. A million Irish people emigrated to other countries, including England, Scotland, Australia, Canada and lots to America which was said to be the 'land of plenty'.

THE COFFIN SHIPS

In those days anyone who wanted to travel overseas had to go by wooden sailing ships. Some landlords paid for their tenants to leave because it was a cheap way of getting rid of them. Other people asked relatives already living abroad to help pay their way. No one had very much money so they couldn't afford to go on nice ships. They had to sail on terrible vessels, most of which had not been properly looked after. The captains wanted to make as much money as possible so they let far too many passengers pay to sail with them. The ships were very overcrowded and people soon became sick. In fact, so many became ill and died on them that the ships earned the nickname 'Coffin Ships'.

AMERICA

Almost a million people left Ireland and went to America which meant that by 1850 the populations of Boston, New York City, Philadelphia and Baltimore were twenty-five per cent Irish. Far from being a 'land of plenty' however, life in America was tough. Not everyone was pleased to see the newly arrived immigrants and it was hard for them to find work or even somewhere to live. The average Irish person died within six years of arriving in their new home.

Today, however, there are still a large number of Americans who trace their heritage back to Ireland.

THE OREGON TRAIL

There were no real roads heading to the west coast of America in the 1840s. People who wanted to go to Oregon just followed in the tracks of those who had gone before them. The Oregon Trail was a rough path which went from St Louis, Missouri, to Portland, Oregon. It was 2,200 miles long and took many weeks to travel. Most people had to walk, with their things in covered wagons pulled by oxen.